On the Surface

NIKKI ASH

Dedication

To the readers who see under the surface, through the fakeness, beyond the shattered, and love the broken characters. This book is for you.

We are all broken. That's how the light gets in.
—Ernest Hemingway

CELESTE

"Two weeks until I'm finally Mrs. Shaw," Olivia squeals loud enough that the patrons sitting at the table next to us look over. Her hands clasp together in excitement as her eyes run along everyone at the table and land on her fiancé, Nicholas Shaw, who is known to most as the newly retired quarterback from the New York Brewers. To me, though, he's my childhood best friend. Despite our four-year age difference, I've spent the last two decades following Nick around while he's chased his dream of playing pro ball, and I've chased mine of becoming a model. There was even a short span of time when we almost got married—a stupid decision on both our parts, stemmed from a teenage pact in a moment of weakness.

Of course, that was all before he met Olivia, who swooped in with her sweet and adorable self and stole his heart—while simultaneously winning me over and becoming one of the few people I call a friend. She and Nick are expecting their second baby in September. Their son, Reed, is eighteen months old, and at home with his grandparents tonight.

In response to what Olivia says, Nick snakes his arm around her shoulders in a protective manner, pulling her into his side with a wide grin. His lips press against hers softly in a loving gesture, and I'm almost positive they've just given me a cavity from all the sweetness that's radiating off them.

"Which means a bachelorette party is in order!" Olivia's best friend, Giselle, states. She's also pregnant—due in November—and someone I consider a friend. Her husband, Killian Blake—who is a receiver for the Brewers—also wraps his arm around his wife and pulls her in for a kiss. Only theirs is more intense, more passionate. I can't help but watch as things between them become heated. It's one of those kisses where you want to look away to give them their privacy, but you can't stop watching. *Yep! I've definitely got a cavity, maybe two.* It isn't until Nick clears his throat that they come up for air. Giselle's face is bright red—not sure if it's out of embarrassment over their public display of affection, or if she's turned on—either way, she's completely captivated by her husband.

"Oh, I don't know." Olivia's nose scrunches up, and she shakes her head. "I'm half-baked." She points to her protruding belly. "And you're pregnant too." She eyes Giselle. "The only person who'll actually get to party is Celeste!" She laughs, shooting me a soft smile.

My gaze goes to my—and I use the term loosely—

boyfriend, Chad Vacanti. Chad is forty-five years old and the VP for the investment banking firm he's a partner in. We met at a function we were both attending and hit it off. Shortly after, I left for the UK to promote my new clothing line that went international. Apparently, he had some business over there as well and reached out. We spent several weeks together—when we weren't both working eighteen-hour days—and decided to keep things going when we returned. It's worked out well for both of us—giving us someone to attend functions with and get lost in after long days of work. He's a lot like me and knows the score, so there aren't any hurt feelings. Chad's nearly twenty years my senior, which is the way I prefer it. Older men tend to have their shit together and are far more mature than the guys my age.

"And it will stay that way," I say with conviction in response to Olivia's comment. Chad looks up from his phone as I finish saying the words, completely focused on work and having no clue what the conversation is about.

"What will stay what way?" he questions—apparently he's somewhat good at multitasking—good to know he at least hears me when I speak.

"My getting pregnant." His eyes go wide in fear, completely misunderstanding. "That I *won't* be getting pregnant anytime soon," I clarify, and he lets out a harsh sigh of relief, like having a baby with me would be the absolute worst thing in the world. It's not as if I would want to have kids with him—or with anyone for that matter—but Jesus, does he have to look so relieved?

Taking a bite of my shrimp salad, I try to ignore the four

pairs of eyes staring at me—not including Chad's as his are already back on his phone. It's no secret I'm the odd one out in our group of friends. Unlike Olivia and Giselle, who are both happily doing their part to add to the ever-growing human race, I have no desire to ever procreate. I have one goal in this life. To make something of myself. Which I happen to think I'm doing a damn good job at. I've learned over the years that independence is the key to a woman's success. While Chad is decent in bed and someone I can talk business with, he'll never be anything more than that. I don't need him or any man for that matter. I push back the thoughts of the one guy I allowed myself to need and how that turned out...*with my heart broken and my future nearly destroyed.*

"I still say we need to throw a party!" Giselle insists. "We can do a combined bachelor and bachelorette party at an upscale club." She stops talking, so I look up, and she's giving Olivia the stink-eye. "And not at a strip club."

A loud laugh escapes me as I remember not too long ago, when Olivia convinced Nick to take her to Assets, a high-end strip club. I thought he was going to kill me when I surprised her with a lap dance. The poor guy wasn't sure whether to be turned-on or upset that his fiancée was thoroughly enjoying another woman grinding on her.

"No, not at a strip club," Olivia agrees. "But it would be fun for all of us to go out and have a good time before we get married." She looks to Nick, who of course nods in agreement. She could tell him she wants him to participate in a shit-eating contest and the guy would nod in agreement if it meant making her happy.

"Mind if I invite Jase?" Killian asks, and it doesn't go unnoticed that his gaze quickly meets mine before he looks away. The hairs on the back of my neck stand at the mention of that name. Jase Crawford. The one who… I shake myself out of my thoughts, refusing to even finish that sentence. He doesn't deserve a place in my thoughts, in my head, in my… Nope, not going there. He's nothing more than a mistake from my past. A lesson learned the hard way.

"I saw him yesterday," Killian says, "while getting some work done. The guy seems like he doesn't get out much."

"Of course!" Olivia speaks for Nick. "He's actually invited to the wedding." Her hand comes up and rests on top of Nick's. "After we ran into him on Giselle's birthday, he and Nick have been keeping in touch again. Jax and Quinn are both invited as well." Jax and Quinn are Jase's brother and sister. They own a tattoo shop here in New York called Forbidden Ink. We went there the night of Giselle's birthday so she and Olivia could get their first tattoo. Olivia chickened out, but Giselle ended up getting a beautiful quote along her upper back just below her nape.

"How many people are coming?" I ask, trying to remain calm, even though the reality of having to see Jase at the wedding has me feeling anything but calm. "I thought you were keeping it small and intimate." Nick doesn't speak to his parents, which only leaves Olivia's family and their friends. She didn't want something huge, which could easily happen since Nick's a four-time Super Bowl champion, and Olivia's dad is an NFL coach, and her mom—who is no longer alive—was a huge international model.

"Only about a hundred and fifty people. We're still

keeping it small." She gives me a questioning look. "Jase isn't in the wedding party if that's what you're worried about."

"I'm not," I say far too quickly. Everyone's gaze swings to me—except Chad, who's still typing away on his phone. "I'm not," I repeat in a tone that makes it clear to drop whatever they're all thinking. It makes sense that Jase and his siblings are invited since Nick has been friends with them since high school.

"I like your new hair color," Olivia says, changing the subject. "It makes you look less…harsh."

"Less like an evil witch?" I wink, and she laughs. When Olivia and I first met, Nick referred to me as the evil witch in their story, and I've yet to live the nickname down. So I figure, if I can't beat them, I might as well join them. But she's right, the black hair gave me an edgier look, which is what the modeling agency I used to be signed with was going for. Since I'm no longer signed with anyone, and I'm free to do as I want with my hair, I dyed it back to my original color—a brownish shade with hints of auburn mixed in.

"Yes! I mean you can totally pull off any color, obviously, but this auburn is really pretty."

"Thanks," I tell her.

"Hey Chad," Giselle calls out from across the table. He looks up to see who said his name. "What do you think about Celeste's hair?"

Chad looks over to me in confusion. "It looks nice," he says with a shrug.

"What does?" she presses.

"Uhh…the length?" he says, but it comes out more like a question. "Did you get it cut or something?" he asks.

"Actually, it's a different color," Giselle points out—with a big fake smile—before I can answer. It's no secret my friends aren't a fan of Chad's. Olivia is too sweet to say anything mean, but Giselle has no problem calling him out.

"Really?" he asks.

"Yep," I say, taking a bite of my food.

The rest of the meal is spent with everyone hammering out the details for the party, but my mind can't get off the fact that Jase and Nick are hanging out again. He's going to be invited to the party. And he's going to come to the wedding. I try to think of a reason to get out of going to either one, but I know I can't do that. Nick has been there for me my entire life. I'm not just going to ditch one of the biggest days of his life because of who will be in attendance. I refuse to be affected by this. He will just be another guest attending the wedding. Of course, since I'm in the wedding party as Olivia's bridesmaid, I'm going to have to walk down the aisle in front of everybody, including Jase. I've walked down a million runways at fashion shows—sometimes more than half-naked, been on dozens of billboards...I've been in more commercials than I can count. Yet the thought of having to walk down the aisle, knowing Jase will be there—most likely with a date—has me feeling sick to my stomach. He shouldn't make me feel like this. Not after all this time. Not after the way things ended.

When the bill is paid, everyone makes their way outside to say their goodbyes. Chad's driver comes around and we slide into the back of his town car. Since it's Saturday night, I'd usually go back to his place, but tonight I tell him I'm going home instead. He simply nods, not even questioning why I'm canceling our evening plans. He doesn't ask me if anything is wrong. The entire drive he's on his phone. His arm never snakes around my shoulders like Nick's did to Olivia. His hand never touches mine like Olivia's did to Nick. And when his driver drops me off in front of my building, he doesn't kiss me the way Killian kissed Giselle.

After showering and changing into silky pajamas, I pour myself a glass of white wine to help calm my nerves before bed. Usually, this is when I go through my emails. I confirm my meetings and engagements with Margie, my assistant, for the upcoming week, since she doesn't work Sundays. I check my company's financials to make sure we're where we need to be. But tonight, I do none of that. Instead, I head outside onto my balcony, which overlooks Central Park. With my condo being on the tenth floor, I'm able to just barely make out the people bustling about. Some are walking their dogs, others are strolling hand-in-hand. It's dark out, and just after ten o'clock, but this is the city that never sleeps.

I take in a deep breath, then bring my lips up to my glass, swallowing a taste of the fruity wine. This is what I wanted. A sky-rise condo in Lennox Hills overlooking Central Park. And I finally got it. The day I signed the papers on this condo, I felt like I'd finally made it. I purchased it on my own, with my own credit and my own money. Yet, as I look out at the luscious trees that fill the park, it feels like every goal and dream I've ever made wasn't enough. I should feel complete, fulfilled. I should feel accomplished. But I don't. I feel empty.

After I finish my wine, I rinse the glass out, and then climb into bed. I lay here for several minutes, trying to figure out what's wrong with me. I barely even touched my cell phone tonight. *That's because you were too busy watching the sickeningly-sweet couples at the table.* Usually I don't pay attention to how the couples around me act with each other. I don't care whether Chad pays attention to me, or if he kisses me goodbye.

I snuggle into my blankets, trying my hardest not to remember a time when I wanted nothing more than to be one-half to a sickeningly-sweet couple. When my world, for just a brief moment, was filled with hand-holding and kissing and sweet words whispered to one another. I close my eyes, refusing to let the tears come, only my heart—and tear ducts—seem to have a mind of their own, and when the memories of him surface, the tears fall of their own accord.

Two

CELESTE

The Past

"Tell me everything!" I bounce up and down on Nick's bed, in his old room in his parents' house. He's home for my graduation, and I'm beyond excited to have my best friend back—even if it's only for a short time. He may only live a hundred miles away, and in the same state, but without me having my own vehicle, it might as well be a million miles away. This past year without Nick has been excruciatingly difficult. I've lost my best friend, the person I talk to and hang out with. He's now an uber-famous professional football player, and I'm just a high school senior.

"You know everything." He laughs. "We talk every day." He strips out of his sweatpants and shirt he wore for his drive over and into a pair of distressed jeans and a collared shirt.

"It's not the same," I whine. "You're living this amazing life, and I'm stuck here in Piermont without you." I pout. Up until this last year, Nick and I have always lived close enough that I could walk or take the bus to visit him. He even went to school locally at North Carolina University. Now, though, things have changed.

"I need details," I beg. "Tell me about the traveling, the money, the fame. I saw you on TMZ at a charity function in New York with Alessandra Starr!" I sigh. Alessandra Starr is an up-and-coming model. She was a lot like me—a nobody from a small town—trying to make a name for herself. She was at the right place at the right time, and boom! Now she's the face of several different companies, including MAC and Lancôme.

"She's not really my type," Nick admits, like I care about who his type is. I want to know what it's like, not who he's in love with this week.

"Nicholas Shaw!" I shriek. "I don't care who you like or don't like. I want to know about New York... about the event! Did you meet a lot of famous people? When you travel, do you get to order room service? Did you go to any popular clubs? What's it like to see your name and picture plastered all over the magazines?"

Nick rolls his eyes and sits next to me on his bed. "You know I don't care about any of that. I'm doing what I love. Playing ball." It's my turn to roll my eyes. I shouldn't have expected Nick to understand. He was raised with money. To him, this is all just another day in the life of Nicholas Shaw. He might be my best friend—and our moms might be best friends—and we might've only grown up less than two miles apart—on opposite sides of the train tracks—but we may as well be from two different planets.

"But," he continues, "I have a surprise for you." He grins wide and stands, walking over to his luggage. He pulls an envelope from it and hands it to me. Just as my fingers are about to grasp the paper, he pulls it back and laughs.

"Nick!" I growl, "give it to me."

Chuckling, he hands the envelope to me, this time letting me take it from him.

I open it and read over the document once, twice, a third time. This can't be real. "Nick," I whisper, "what did you do?" Tears form in my eyes. The paper falls from my hands, and my arms wrap around his neck. "Is this for real?"

"It is." He laughs. "I had to do a photoshoot with Elite for Movado, and while I was there, I ended up having brunch with Alessandra and Brenna Myers.

I gasp. "Brenna Myers? The VP of Elite?" Elite is one of the top modeling agencies in the world.

"Yep. I mentioned I have a friend who would give her left arm to get her foot in the door..."

"Please tell me you didn't make me sound desperate, Nick," I chide.

He laughs. "Give me some credit," he says. "Anyway, Elite has a summer internship program, and after showing her your photos, she opened up a spot for you."

"Eeeeeek!!!" I squeal. "I can't believe it. This is really happening." I hug Nick again. "Thank you so much!" I grab the paper from the floor, where it fell, and read it again and again. This is actually happening. Next week I'm going to graduate and get out of this hellhole. I'm going to New York.

"Wait," I say, thinking about the details. "Where am I going to live?" This is New York we're talking about. I doubt I can even afford a cardboard box there.

"While you're in the summer program, you'll be living in an apartment with the other girls. It'll all be paid for by Elite. Once it ends, if I need to help you, I will. Don't worry about that now, though," he says, assuring me. "Just focus on your dreams."

I don't even realize I'm still crying, until Nick swipes a falling tear with his thumb. "Celeste, I know this is what you want, but trust me when I say, being famous isn't all it's cracked up to be. Everybody is so damn fake." His voice is soft, non-judgmental. He's simply being honest—as honest as he can be as a man who's grown up with money, while I've grown up in a trailer park. "I thought once I was away from my parents it would be different," he adds. "The women are all fake. Alessandra…she's fake." Nick frowns in disappointment.

"I told you once, and I'll tell you again," I say, "the world revolves around money and status, and until you accept that, you're going to keep getting your heart broken." While Nick is looking for love—some non-existent soulmate to give his sappy heart to—I'm looking for a future.

"And I'll tell you once again, we'll have to agree to disagree." He pulls me into a side-hug and kisses my temple. "One day you're going to meet a guy who's going to knock you right off your feet, and you're going to finally understand that no amount of money can buy love."

"That sounds like it would hurt," I joke. "I'll leave the falling to you…on the football field." I shoot him a playful

19

wink. "So, what's going on tonight?" I nod toward his outfit. He's obviously dressed up for a reason. Unless Nick is going somewhere, he's always in basketball shorts and a t-shirt.

"Party tonight. Some friends from high school are getting together for a reunion of sorts." He pulls on his shoes. "Wanna go?"

"Hmm, let's see here…" I tap my lower lip with my index finger as I pretend to contemplate whether I want to go. This is the first time I'll get to meet Nick's high school friends. Because of our age difference, he'd never let me tag along to any of the parties he attended while he was in high school or college. "Rich, hot, older guys all in one place, or another night spent with my drunken mother…What do you think?"

Nick frowns. "How is Beatrice?"

"Same as she's been my entire life. Drunk and waiting on the love of her life to mend her broken heart."

His frown deepens. "You could be a little more understanding…"

"Seriously?" I scoff. "Some biker guy knocks up my mother and takes off, promising to return, only to disappear. My mom chooses to pine after him for the next eighteen years, forcing me to live in a rusted metal can in a damn trailer park, barely working enough to pay our electric bill and rent, and I'm supposed to be understanding?"

My blood is now boiling, and my skin is heating up. My mother could've gotten us out of our shitty situation. She's best friends with Victoria, Nick's mom. She's been introduced to dozens of wealthy men. But instead she refuses to leave our seven hundred square foot trailer, and continues to work at the same hole-in-the-wall diner in hope that one day he'll come back like he promised. I've tried to look him up a couple times at the public library, but the only thing I know is that his last name is Leblanc—same as mine. Apparently, he once referred to me as baby Leblanc, and when my mom asked, he confirmed that was his last name.

According to my mom, he was a member of some biker gang and went by the name of Snake—really classy, huh? He met my mom while passing through town. They fell in love and spent the next few months planning their life together. My mom got pregnant, and supposedly Snake was just as excited as she was. He said he had some affairs to get in order and promised to return soon, only he never did—making my mother a single mom at the ripe age of eighteen. And yes, in case you're wondering, Snake is actually written on my birth certificate. Who in their right mind falls in love with a man but never takes the time to learn his real name? My mother, that's who!

"I get it," Nick says, "but you've never been in love, so you don't understand."

"And you have?" I snort in disbelief.

"No, but I'm at least capable of it," Nick volleys back. "If I met the love of my life and she promised to return, I would wait for her. Your mom is heartbroken. She can't imagine loving anyone else but him. It's kind of romantic."

"Yeah, well, if that's how love works, you can have it," I hiss. "Her love for my father destroyed her, and I refuse to ever be destroyed by a man."

"No, you'd rather do the destroying," Nick smarts.

"What's that supposed to mean?" I snap. It's not often

Nick and I argue, but when we do, it's usually over this very subject. We don't see eye-to-eye on love and never will.

"Never mind." Nick sighs. "Just try not to destroy any of my friends' hearts tonight. I prefer to keep them as friends."

"I can't help if they fall for me and get hurt." I turn on my heel, done with this conversation. "I need to run home and change my outfit. Drive me?"

"Sure."

We pull up to my place, and Nick parks his Audi along the road since my mom's piece of shit clunker is parked in the tiny driveway. She's sitting outside with a beer in one hand and a joint in the other, and our neighbor, Dale—the nasty drug dealer I know she fucks on occasion when she's feeling extra lonely—is sitting next to her with his hand resting on her thigh.

"Want me to go in with you?" Nick offers. Anyone else and I wouldn't have even let him bring me here, but Nick has seen my home more times than I can count, so it's pointless to hide it from him. I'm not sure why our moms have remained friends over the years, but it's the one thing I'm grateful for. Their friendship was the only good part of my life growing up. Nick's mom has always treated me like I'm her own daughter—always including me in their trips and holidays.

"No." I shake my head. "I'll be quick. Plus, we might come out and find your car to be missing." I laugh humorlessly, and Nick rolls his eyes.

I jump out of the passenger seat and head up the sidewalk. My mom notices me and gives me a small smile.

"Hey, pretty girl," she coos. I bend at the waist and give her a kiss on her forehead. I want to hate her for this life—and many days it feels like I do—but then she smiles and calls me pretty girl and my heart breaks for her. She fell in love and had her heart broken. If you want to know what a broken heart is capable of, spend a day with my mom. It looks just like this—a once beautiful, vibrant woman who was full of life, burnt into ash. With wrinkles around her lips from smoking, and dark circles under her eyes from never feeling rested or content. She's nothing more than the rubble left in the wake after the fire has gone out.

"What are you and Nick up to?" she asks, taking a hit of her joint and then passing it to Dale.

"Going to a party."

"That was nice of him to come in for your graduation. Victoria said she's going to host a gathering at her place for you afterward."

"Sounds good, Mom. I'm going to go change."

Stepping into the trailer, beads of sweat instantly surface on my skin. I check the thermostat and it shows eighty-nine degrees. I try the light switch to see if the AC is broken or if the electric is out. The light doesn't come on. Damn it, Mom! She didn't pay the electric bill. I try the water and no such luck. She didn't pay that either. Looks like I'm going to have to dip into my savings to pay it. I have no clue what she's going to do once I leave for New York, but my hope is that once I hit it big, I'll be able to convince her to move with me, or at the very least, buy her a better place to live in. Although, if I'm honest, I know she won't allow either option to happen. That would mean moving out of this piece-of-shit place, and if she hasn't moved yet, I doubt it will ever happen.

After changing into a cute yet sexy burgundy tank dress that Nick's mom bought me for my eighteenth birthday last month, and sliding on a pair of cute wedges, I use a bottle of water to quickly brush my teeth, then head out.

When I step outside, the cool air sends goosebumps running up my arms. I give my mom a knowing look as I dab my forehead with a paper towel.

"Sorry," she whispers, her face filled with apology. She's said the word so many times over the years, it's been desensitized.

Once I'm back in Nick's car, he takes off to his friend Jared's house, which is in the same gated community Nick's parents live in. Apparently Jared's parents are on a cruise and he has the house to himself. Most of Nick's friends are still in college. The only reason he's not is because he was drafted into the NFL at the end of his junior year. When we pull up, the street is already packed with expensive cars, which line both sides of the road.

"How long do you give it until someone calls the cops?" I joke.

"Maybe another hour." Nick laughs. We get out and head up to the front door. Nick doesn't bother knocking since the music is thumping so loud no one would hear it anyway. It's only nine o'clock, but it's clear this party's been going on for some time.

When we enter, it's a typical rich kid party. Tons of expensive liquor everywhere. Guys dressed in Lacoste, and girls donning Louis Vuitton and Burberry. Nick might've gone all big brother on me over the years, but that didn't stop me from finding my way into parties elsewhere, especially once he left last year for the NFL and couldn't keep tabs on me. I follow Nick over to the large dining room table where several guys are playing poker. Chips are stacked high and hundred-dollar bills are being thrown around like they're singles at a strip club.

When one of the guys spots Nick, he yells out his name, and everyone at the table stands to give Nick attention. I mentally roll my eyes. Nick is right about one thing. Rich people are fake. But you know what else they are? Rich! I'll gladly take a fake, wealthy man over a heartfelt, poor one. Love doesn't pay the bills. Love doesn't have connections. These guys…they are the future of America. They'll graduate from college and follow in their rich daddy's footsteps, going on to work at Fortune 500 companies all over the world, and I'm going to snag one of them. Nick might've gotten me in the door with Elite, but that will only get me so far. Everyone knows money talks. My last name means nothing to anybody. But some of these guys…one mention of their name and I'll be heading straight to the top.

"How's it going?" Nick asks, greeting each of his friends, who are probably already thinking of how they can use their friendship with a famous quarterback to their advantage. Nick went into the NFL as a first round draft pick as a backup quarterback. Due to an injury of the starting QB, he got a chance to show everyone what he's made of, and soared. He took Carolina straight to the Super Bowl and won. Something that almost never happens with a first year rookie.

"Jase!" Nick fist bumps his friend. "It's been too long, man."

His friend nods in agreement, but his eyes aren't on Nick—they're on me. And now, mine are on him. I take in his gelled ink-black hair, short enough not to be messy, but long enough I could run my fingers through it. His eyes, just as dark. Hard. Unforgiving. He's wearing a button-down white shirt with the sleeves rolled up to his elbows. I immediately spot several tattoos donning his muscular forearms. All shades of black and grey, no color. It's obvious, whoever this guy is, he isn't one of Nick's typical friends. He doesn't even try to suck up to Nick like the others do. My eyes continue their perusal down his front. He's lean, and if judging by the veins running down his forearms, he works out, but he's not a gym rat. He's wearing jeans that fit him just right and a pair of Nike's. Football player, maybe? The business majors usually wear Tom Ford or Brooks Brothers.

"And who's this?" Jase asks Nick with a knowing smirk. He's caught me checking him out.

"Just a friend of mine," Nick says dryly. When Jase clears his throat, indicating, not so subtly, he wants Nick to introduce us more thoroughly, Nick groans. "Celeste, this is Jase. We played ball together at Piermont Academy and at NCU. He was two years ahead of me." Hmm…so, he is a football player, and a rich kid.

"Jase Crawford," Jase says, extending his hand. I give it willingly. "I'm pretty sure I've seen you on campus, but we've never formally met."

"Celeste is—" Nick begins, but I cut him off.

"…busy with school," I say, finishing Nick's sentence

for him as I shake Jase's hand. There's no reason for Jase to know the school I'm busy with contains grades nine through twelve. I'm eighteen. That's all that matters.

I hear Nick groan again, and I quickly shoot him a look that says if he groans one more damn time I'll kill him.

"Nice." Jase grins, still holding my hand in his. "I graduated a couple years ago. Definitely don't miss the school work." Wealthy, educated, in shape, and hot as hell. I'm pretty sure I've just hit the jackpot.

"It's nice to meet you. How about you take a break from playing poker and get me a drink?" I bat my lashes, and Jase throws his head back with a laugh—one that has my insides melting like a pile of goo. What is wrong with me? I don't melt. I'm not that girl.

"All right." He grins. "What would you like?"

"Something fruity would be great." My gaze stays glued to his mesmerizing smile.

"Got it." He lets go of my hand, and I miss it immediately. Jesus! Get a grip. He's just a guy. A rich guy who's hot and educated, but just a guy all the same. He went to Piermont Academy like Nick. He comes from an influential family, and my goal is to see if he's someone I can use as a stepping stone to get me to where I want to go. Stick to the plan, Celeste!

When he walks away, Nick turns toward me. "Listen, Celeste, I know what you're thinking, but…"

"Nick, don't you dare cock-block me! I will beat your ass," I hiss lowly, so no one can hear me.

Nick laughs. "One, you don't have a cock…"

"Fine! Vagina-block me," I cut in. "You know what I

27

mean!"

"Celeste, listen to me. Jase…"

"Jase!" I say, a tad too loudly as I spot him walking back toward us. "That was quick." I take the drink he's holding out for me and take a sip. It's mostly liquor with a splash of…sprite? I choke down the burning sensation in my throat as I swallow. That…whatever it is…is definitely not fruity.

"Sorry." He cringes. "You took a sip before I could warn you. There wasn't anything fruity. The only thing close I could find was vodka and Sprite."

I let out a deep breath. "That's okay." I smile. "I love vodka." Nick laughs under his breath, knowing I'm lying through my teeth. I'm more of a rum girl…mixed into a fruity daiquiri.

"Celeste, can I talk to you for a minute?" Nick asks. My eyes swing over to him. I know he's protective of his friends, but he's never tried to block me like this, and I've gone on dates with a few of his college friends.

"Later, Nick," I say, trying to make it clear he needs to mind his own business.

He opens his mouth to speak again then closes it. Then he smiles wide and says, "All right." He nods and laughs softly. "I'm going to play poker. You two enjoy yourselves." I'm not sure what made him suddenly change his disposition toward me going after Jase, but I'm not about to question it. Before Jase or I can say anything, one of the guys yells over to him to get his ass back to the poker table.

"Join me?" he asks. "You can be my good luck charm."

"Sure." I dramatically roll my eyes. "But you are aware every guy has at some point used that same line, right?"

Jase laughs. "I like you." Before he sits down in his seat, he grabs another chair and pulls it next to his.

"All right, now that Nick is here, we can play a real game," some guy says, throwing some more cash onto the table.

Nick chuckles. "Shut up, Ross. I'm on a damn rookie contract! Your allowance from your mommy and daddy probably pays more." The guys all laugh.

"Just deal," Jase says dryly. His hand lands on my thigh, and he leans into me. "All good luck charms have to do something to create the good luck." Before I can ask him what he's referring to, his lips meet mine. The kiss is soft and sweet, only lasting a brief moment. Yet in that short time, my entire body shivers in pleasure, my heart picks up speed, and if I wasn't sitting, my legs would've probably given out on me.

Jase pulls back and grants me a boyish grin. "Even if I lose, I'm considering that kiss getting lucky." I release a giggle I didn't know I had in me at his cheesy flirting.

"Real smooth!" I joke. My hand smacks his shoulder playfully, and he grabs it, entwining our fingers together and bringing it up to his lips for a quick kiss before settling our hands in his lap. Nick eyes me warily, but I ignore him as I try to push away the butterflies which are currently fluttering in my belly. Nick might be worried about me destroying Jase, but right now, I'm more concerned about being the one destroyed.

I sip on my drink as the guys play. I've watched Nick play poker a few times with his friends when he lived on campus, but I don't know enough about the game to know who's winning. Several guys say they're out. Then the ones remaining lay their cards down flat for everybody to see.

"Hell yeah!" Jase cheers. He swipes all the chips toward him then turns in his chair to face me. "It's official, you're my good luck charm." He grins wide then slants his mouth over mine. This kiss is harder, more possessive, as if he's claiming me right here in front of everyone with this one kiss. Those fluttering butterflies are now attacking me as Jase's tongue pushes through my lips. He tastes of vodka and sprite, and it feels like I could get drunk from this kiss alone. I can't help the small moan of pleasure that releases as his hand lands on my thigh and squeezes. But just like the last kiss, this one also ends much too quickly, leaving me breathless and turned on, wanting, for the first time, more from a guy.

One of the guys says he's done and another guy takes his place, and then the cards are dealt. Everyone places their bets. Jase's hand finds my thigh, once again, and he gives it a soft squeeze. My eyes find Nick's and he smirks. It's almost as if he knows I'm losing all my control to Jase. I don't know anything about him: does he have a trust fund? Where does his father work? What's his ten-year plan? But for some crazy reason I don't seem to care about anything other than when his lips will find mine again.

Once again I have no clue who's winning or losing, but it wouldn't matter, because I can't focus. As Jase plays his hand of cards, his fingers run up and down my flesh, leaving a burning sensation in their wake. As his hand travels farther up, I clench my thighs together. He isn't going to do what I think he is…

He glances my way, asking for permission, and I open my legs for him—Jesus, when did I become so easy? His fingers find my panties, but he doesn't move them to the side. Instead, he teases me from the outside. His one finger trails up and down my slit through the thin material. I squirm in my seat. I know I'm wet, probably drenched. There's no way anybody can know what he's doing, or see my reaction, yet I feel like all eyes are on us. I can't believe I'm letting him do this. I don't even know this guy. For all I know, he does this with every girl he meets. I'm well aware everyone our age hooks up at parties, but that's never been who I am. Feeling like things are moving too quickly, I reach down and take his hand in mine. If he's annoyed I stopped him, he doesn't show it. He just continues to play poker one-handed like that's completely normal.

Jase wins for the third time, and the guys all groan. He leans over and presses his lips to mine. "One more hand and then I'm done," he murmurs against my mouth.

Less than ten minutes later, Jase wins. "I'm out," he announces as we stand. My eyes move to the front door, where I spot Killian Blake walking in. He glares my way, and I roll my eyes. Killian is Nick's other best friend. They met their freshman year of college. He's in his senior year at NCU and was recently drafted to the New York Brewers in the first round. To say we can't stand each other is a gross understatement. It's a good thing Jase is done playing poker and guiding me away from where Killian is walking toward. Had we stayed, I know, without a doubt, Killian would've made it a point to talk shit about me to Jase.

"So, you mentioned you recently graduated," I say to

Jase, trying to get to know him as he pulls me toward the kitchen. Both of our cups are empty, so I'm assuming he's going to refill them.

"Yeah, I received my business degree." He takes my empty cup from me and sets it on the counter next to his. He drops a few ice cubes into both cups then pours some alcohol into them. Then he tops them off with a new can of sprite. "Cheers," he says, handing me my cup and taking a large drink from his own.

"Cheers," I say back. My sip is far smaller. Unlike Jase, who must be a good six feet tall, almost two hundred pounds, and clearly a seasoned drinker, my tiny one hundred and ten pound body can only handle so much alcohol before I'm drunk.

"Jase! Get your ass over here!" someone yells. "Drinking game!"

Jase laughs but shakes his head. "Nah, next time!"

"Now, bro," the guy demands. Jase gives me a look, silently asking if I mind. Not wanting to be the girl who takes him away from his friends, who he obviously came here tonight to see, I nod my okay.

"Fine, what game?" Jase yells over the music.

"Never have I ever!" a bleach-blonde girl shouts. I've seen her around NCU a few times, and I pray she doesn't ask me if I go there. "You in?" she asks me, not giving a shit about where I'm from.

"Sure." I hold up my drink.

Everyone goes around the room calling out things they've never done, and those who've done them have to drink:

Gotten wasted—most drink

Stolen their parent's car—a few drink

Went skinny-dipping—most drink

Smoked weed—almost everyone drinks

Had a three-some—only a couple drink

And then some girl yells through a fit of drunken laughter, "Had sex." I watch as everyone around me drinks and laughs at her because she's just announced she's still a virgin. Until she joins in with everyone else and downs her drink. "Whoops! My bad!" She laughs harder.

Jase's eyes go to mine, and I realize I haven't taken a drink. I tip my cup back and take a large gulp. He smiles and raises his cup in a 'cheers' motion, so I do the same.

The questions continue for a little while longer, but when Jase notices that I've run out of alcohol, he excuses us from the game. We head out the back door and onto the patio. There are people out here, but not as many. With the door closed, the music is now muffled, allowing us to hear each other better. We walk down the dock and find an empty spot on the beach. In contrast to the warm weather we've been having lately, it's a bit chilly tonight, but luckily there's hardly any breeze. In an attempt to look good, I didn't think to bring a jacket.

Jase, the gentleman he is, shrugs out of his jacket and drapes it across my shoulders. "Thank you." I smile over at him. "I was clearly going for sexy and not practical." My words are a tad slurred from the drinking I've been doing, and we both laugh.

"Well, you did sexy to perfection," he says as he sits down on the damp sand. I eye it, afraid my dress will get ruined or my butt will end up frozen. But before I can make the decision whether to sit, Jase pulls me into his lap. My dress rises, and I'm thankful we're in the dark because my panties are definitely on display. I'm straddling his thighs, my legs wrapped around him, so the only part of me touching the sand are the tips of my wedges. Alarm bells should be going off in my head. This is all happening too fast. But all I can focus on is the way his strong hands grip my hips. The feel of his lips as they work their way down the side of my neck and over to my throat. My fingers run through his hair as he trails soft kisses down my throat. I relish in the delicious friction our bodies are creating as my butt grinds against his pelvis.

And then the sound of police sirens ring through the air. Jase's eyes lock with mine. "I've drank too much to drive," he says. "Let me call my brother." With me still sitting on his lap, he pulls his phone out of his pocket and dials a number. "Jax, it's me. I need you to come get me from Jerad's. The cops have been called." There's a pause. "I've been drinking." Another pause. "Thanks, bro. I'll meet you down by the south pier." He hangs up, and lifting me off him like I weigh nothing, stands me on my feet.

"I came with Nick," I point out. "He wouldn't leave without me."

"Call him and let him know that I'm dropping you off," Jase says, walking us down the beach toward the pier. I do as he says and call Nick. He answers on the first ring. When I tell him Jase is going to drop me off, he points out he's been drinking and insists on finding me. But when I tell him his brother is coming to get us, Nick concedes and makes me promise to text him as soon as I'm home.

When Jase's brother shows up, Jase opens the door for me to get into the front seat. Once I'm in, he climbs into the back. "Quinn grabbed your car," Jax says. "She's meeting us back at home."

"Thanks, bro."

"I'm Jax," Jase's brother says, introducing himself.

"I'm Celeste. Thank you for getting us."

"No worries. Where am I taking you?"

I feel Jase's hand land on my shoulder, squeezing it softly. Then I feel his cool breath at my ear. "Come home with me," he whispers. My body thrums at the thought of spending more time with Jase, of our night not coming to an end just yet. I've never spent the night with a guy before, and while it makes me somewhat nervous, I remember that Nick is friends with him, and he wouldn't have introduced us, or let Jase and his brother take me home if he was worried something would happen to me. For a few seconds I weigh my options, but ultimately my need to spend more time with Jase wins out.

I nod once. "Okay."

"Just take us back to our place," Jase tells his brother.

We arrive at their apartment, and just as I suspected, it's in a nicer part of town. The apartment itself isn't huge, but it's clean and decorated beautifully. When we walk inside, a gorgeous woman is standing against the island, drinking a bottle of water. She's wearing a cute grey hoodie and matching tiny shorts that show off her thick, toned legs. At a second glance, I spot a few colorful tattoos peeking out from under her shorts. Her black hair is down in waves, and her face is free of all makeup. She throws a set of keys at Jase. "You're welcome."

Jase gives her a simple chin lift. "Thanks." He puts his arm around my shoulders and pulls me into his side. "Celeste, this is my baby sister, Quinn."

"Baby?" She scoffs. "I'm a whole five years younger." She rolls her eyes.

"You're nineteen. A baby," Jase volleys back, and I stiffen. If she's a baby in his eyes, he would throw my ass out if he knew that I'm only eighteen. Sure, I'm legal, but I'm a good six years younger than him.

"And yet, I'm the one playing the parent by picking up your vehicle because you're out partying." She snorts.

"Yeah, yeah, we're going to bed," Jase calls over his shoulder as he walks us away from the kitchen and down the hall. When we get to the last door on the right, he opens the door so I can walk through first, then closes it behind him.

Suddenly I'm nervous. I never imagined I would end up here with Jase—or any guy for that matter. I attend parties for the sole purpose of finding myself a wealthy guy to take me to dinner, to use as a contact. Men have never been anything more than a potential stepping stone to me. Until now. I knew what I was agreeing to when I said okay to coming back here. I know what the kids our age do when they go back to each other's places, but it didn't hit me until this very moment that, for the first time, I've agreed to go back to a guy's place. And surprisingly, while I am nervous, I'm not scared, and I don't regret saying okay. "I better text Nick to let him know I'm here," I tell him.

"Okay." He shrugs. "I'm going to change." He pulls a

shirt and boxers from his drawer and hands them to me. "So you're more comfortable."

"Thank you."

I pull my phone out of my bra where I keep it since I have no pockets. I'm about to text Nick and tell him where I am, but something stops me. It's not like Jase is going to murder me here. He lives with his brother and sister. He played high school and college ball with Nick. If I text Nick where I am, I'll never hear the end of it. So, instead, I text him I made it home safe, and he texts back that he'll see me tomorrow.

I change out of my dress and peel off my wedges. Then I throw on Jase's shirt and boxers, the masculine, fresh scent of him hitting my senses. Not having a hair tie on me, but wanting to get my hair off my neck, I pull my hair up into a makeshift bun and tie it using my hair. While I wait for him to come out from his attached bathroom, I take a slow stroll around his room. It's guy's room. Simple for the most part. Plain wood dresser, matching nightstands. A large king size bed with a simple black comforter. But the walls are another story. Each one is filled with beautiful hand-drawn art. Some are shades of black, white, and grey, and others are vivid colors that pop out like the images are coming to life. One of his walls looks like it's been graffitied, but it's too pretty to call it that.

Jase comes back into the room as I'm staring at one of the pictures on his walls. It's a wolf that looks to be morphing into some kind of scary looking skeleton. "This is…amazing," I tell him. "Did you draw all these?"

When he doesn't answer, I look over at him. He's

leaning against the dresser, his hands in the pockets of his sweatpants, staring at me like he wants to devour me. "You look sexy as hell in my clothes," he says, his eyes dragging down my body. I swallow thickly at his statement. I'm so far out of my comfort zone here. With him now in a short sleeved T-shirt, more of his tattoos are on display. They cover most of the skin on his arms. I wonder if he has any on his chest or back. I bet he does.

Without saying another word, he stalks toward me and pushes me against the wall. His hands find mine, and he pushes them over my head, my wrists making a thumping sound as they hit the wall. My mind goes foggy with lust as I get lost in this man's touch. His knee parts my thighs and grinds against my core, forcing a shudder of pleasure from me. Then Jase's hands release mine, and he grips my hips, lifting me. My legs wrap around his waist as he carries me to the bed, dropping me onto the middle of the mattress. He climbs on top of me, his lips immediately finding mine. We kiss hard as his hand cups and massages my breast. I squirm under his touch. I've never felt like this before. This turned on. This reckless. All of my man-goals have flown out the window.

Without breaking our kiss, Jase pushes the boxers I'm wearing down my thighs along with my panties. Alarms of warning sound off, but they're too faint to pay attention to. My brain is too hazy. My judgement is too clouded. I want him. Bad. Jase's hand pushes my thighs apart and his fingers enter me. "Fuck, you're wet," he murmurs against my lips. I can't speak. I can't respond. All I can do is moan in pleasure as he fingers me. His thumb finds my clit and massages slow circles over the tight, swollen nub.

Ending our kiss, he dips his head down, and with his nose, pushes my shirt up, trailing kisses up my stomach. My bra is still on, so he places kisses to my nipples through the material. I pull his shirt over my head and throw it to the side. His teeth clamp down on my nipple, and that's all it takes for my orgasm to rip through my body.

Before I can catch my breath, Jase is pushing his sweatpants down, gripping his thick shaft in his hand, and then he's entering me. I could've stopped him. But I didn't. The pain rips through me. Not wanting to scream, my mouth finds his shoulder, and I bite down. The act spurs him on, and he thrusts deeper into me, pushing through the barrier of my virginity. Then he stills as if he felt it.

"Celeste," he murmurs softly. He's about to pull out. I can feel it. But before he does, I lock my ankles around his ass.

"Keep going," I whisper. His head lifts, and his eyes meet mine. They're dark and filled with regret. "Please," I plead. His eyes squeeze shut as he wars with himself. It's too late now. He's already taken my virginity. "Please," I repeat. My hands come up to his head, and I tug on his hair, pulling his face toward mine. My lips fuse against his. Without opening his eyes, he kisses me back and thrusts into me again. This time, though, it's slower, more gentle. He knows. One of his hands cradles the side of my head while the other comes down between us, landing on my clit.

Jase continues to fuck me, but I'm not sure if what he's doing can even be called fucking. It's more like he's making love to me, only it can't be called making love either. We barely know each other. You can't love someone you barely know. He works me up once again, and before I know it, I'm climaxing for a second time with Jase following right behind.

We both still as we catch our breath. Jase's head falls onto my chest, and I feel his thick eyelashes flutter against my over-sensitive flesh. He lets out a groan and shakes his head. I'm afraid to say anything. I should've told him I was a virgin. That's on me. He lifts off me as he pulls out, taking his warmth with him. His eyes go wide as he looks down. My gaze follows his, and that's when I see it. Blood covering his still semi-hard length, proving what he was probably hoping wasn't true.

He stands, and without saying a word, heads into his bathroom. I'm stuck, frozen in place, unsure what I should do now. I need to clean up. And that's when it hits me. We didn't use protection. I'm on birth control, but that's beside the point. I consider joining him in the bathroom, but wonder if that would be too intimate. Should I wait for him to get out and then haul my ass inside? Before I can figure out what to do, Jase exits the bathroom carrying a washcloth. He spreads my legs and wipes down my center. The cream-colored material turns crimson.

He tosses it into his hamper, and then picks the shirt I was wearing up off the floor. He hands it to me, and I shrug it on. I think he's going to hand me back my panties or his boxers, but he doesn't. Instead, he lifts his shirt off his body, exposing all of the tattoos he has on his chest, and crawls into bed next to me. He pulls me into his body and pushes my hair out of my face.

"You should've told me," he murmurs.

"I'm sorry," I whisper back, feeling completely embarrassed.

"I should've used a condom. I know it's going to sound cliché as fuck, but I always use one. I don't know what the hell got into me." I flinch at his words, but try to hide it. I'd rather not think about all the other women he's been with.

"I'm on birth control," I admit softly.

We lay together in silence for a few minutes, and then Jase murmurs, "I've never felt anything like this. I've been with my fair share of women, but I've never felt this connection. I know we've only just met, but tell me you feel it too."

I nod in agreement. It's crazy to feel the way I do. To let this guy I barely know take my virginity. There's a good chance I'm going to regret it tomorrow, but right now, it feels right.

"Tell me something about you," he says, his lips curling into a beautiful, lazy smile. "But first, what's your last name?"

I laugh. We're obviously doing this all backwards. "My last name is Leblanc."

"And…"

"And I want to be a model," I admit. It's the only thing I can think of that won't scare him away. My age, where I go to school, where I live…it's all off limits.

Jase smirks. "You're definitely beautiful enough. What kind of model?" He takes my fingers in his hand and brings them to his lips for a kiss. "A hand model? Because you have seriously sexy fingers." He sucks my middle finger into his mouth erotically, and a soft moan escapes my lips. How can something as simple as him sucking on my finger turn me on?

"No," I croak, then clear my throat before I continue. "A real model." I gently pull my finger out from between his lips. "My dream is to be on billboards across New York. I want to walk the runways for high fashion designers during the New York, Paris, and Milan Fashion Weeks. I want to get a deal with Victoria's Secret or Tommy Hilfiger, or maybe Donna Karen or Chanel." I can't help the excitement I feel when I talk about my goals and dreams. Growing up, I used to toy with the idea of wanting to become a model. I would play dress up with Nick's mom's clothes when she wasn't home, and force Nick to watch me put on fashion shows.

When I got older, I would watch the various fashion shows on television when Mom remembered to pay the bill. But it was confirmed the first time Nick's mom brought Nick and me along with her for Fashion Week when I was twelve year's old. Nick's nanny got sick and canceled last minute, and his dad was out of town on business. Like always, my mom was in a drunken stupor, so Victoria ended up taking us with her to New York. She was able to find a replacement nanny for the rest of the week, but that first night we went with her, and it was that one night that changed my life. Up until that day, my dreams were puffs of clouds in the sky— beautiful to look up at, but unreachable. But as I watched the fashion show from the third row, it was as if I was floating in the air. I could taste it, smell it, feel it. For the first time, my dreams were within reach, and I knew I would do everything in my power to grab ahold of them.

"But I don't want to stop there," I continue when I see Jase's eyes are on me, that he's actually listening and waiting for me to explain. I can't remember the last time someone just listened to me. "It's common knowledge that a modeling career peaks by twenty-two and is over by twenty-seven, thirty, if the model is lucky. Modeling is my dream, my foot in the door, but I don't want that to be it. I want to start my own jewelry and makeup lines. Maybe even a clothing line. I love fashion," I exclaim.

"Why?" he asks thoughtfully.

"I love the way an outfit can give a woman confidence. The way makeup can make her feel beautiful. I love how a single necklace or bracelet can make her feel…more." I don't know how to explain it without telling him I was raised in a shitty trailer park, in an ugly, tiny trailer. I grew up being made fun of for wearing the Walmart clothes my mom would buy me secondhand from the thrift stores. The no-name brand shoes that she would pick up from the local consignment shop. Kids were mean, and I always felt so ugly.

That was until Nick's mom, Victoria, bought me a beautiful Marc Jacobs gown for the function we were attending. She took me to get my hair and makeup and nails done. Then she lent me a pair of pearl earrings and a matching necklace. That night, not only did nobody make fun of me, but I was complimented on several occasions on how beautiful I looked. I watched the models strut up and down the runway as everybody oohed and ahhed, and it was in that moment I knew I would do whatever it took to become a model. I want to travel the world, wear gorgeous, expensive clothes, get paid to put on makeup. I want to live in a penthouse that overlooks Central Park. I want a husband who's rich and takes care of me and thinks I'm beautiful.

Jase eyes me curiously and then says, "You don't need to do anything to make you beautiful. You already are." We've only just met, yet it's as if he has the ability to read the words I'm not saying. Say the things I long for someone to say. Tears sting my eyes, and I force them away.

"What about you?" I ask, my throat clogged with emotion. "What do you want to be?"

"I want to open my own tattoo shop." His answer should be the equivalent of ice being thrown onto my overheated body. A tattoo shop. That's hardly a fortune 500 company. He's nothing like the wealthy husband I envisioned for myself. But for some reason, I don't care. Instead, his answer makes me smile. I can totally see it. The drawings all over his walls, the gorgeous ink covering his body. The dark aura that surrounds him. It all fits.

"Is that why you majored in business?" I ask him.

He nods. "Yeah, Jax and I both have our licenses to tattoo, but he wasn't able to go to college. We didn't have the money." He frowns, appearing to be embarrassed. "I got a football scholarship to attend NCU and figured it would do us good for me to learn how to run a business." He grants me a soft smile. "Now we just have to save up."

"Didn't you go to Piermont Academy with Nick?" I ask, confused. He's clearly not from a family with money and that school is over fifty thousand a year alone just for the tuition.

"Yeah, another scholarship." He shrugs one shoulder. "My brother went to Piermont Public."

"Your sister?" She's only a year ahead of me, but I've never seen her at school.

"Piermont Academy on an academic scholarship. She's

now attending The Art Institute. Between her financial aid, and Jax and I helping her, we're handling it okay." He flinches at his own words, telling me there's more to it than him and his brother handling it. Is it possible he comes from a home like mine? One where your parent doesn't handle shit? I want to open up to him, but if I do, he'll find out I'm not in college and that I'm younger than I led him to believe, and there's no way he won't push me away.

"Does she want to do tattoos like you and your brother?" Absentmindedly, my hand finds its way to Jase's scalp, and I thread my fingers through his thick hair. It's like I need to touch him in some way at all times. He must feel the same, because as we talk, his hand, the one that isn't trapped under me and gripping my hip, roams over my body.

"No, she's more about the traditional type of art. She loves photography, graphic design, sculpting." The way he speaks about his sister, it's obvious he's proud of her.

Jase's gaze drops to my mouth, and he dips his head down to snag my lower lip, pulling it roughly and sucking on my flesh. "We should get some sleep. I'm on the verge of wanting to take you again, and I imagine you're sore." Before I can respond, his lips find mine, deliciously contradicting his words. This kiss is soft and sweet, and when it ends, I sigh in need. Jase chuckles under his breath before rolling onto his back and pulling me into his side. No words are spoken. No promises of tomorrow. Instead, we remain in the present, falling asleep in each other's arms.

Three

CELESTE

The Past

I wake up to the feeling of…well, I'm not quite sure what it is. Something is tickling my back. My eyes open, and it only takes a second to remember where I am. At Jase's place in his bed. I'm lying on my belly, only Jase is no longer my human pillow—albeit a firm one. The light glaring in through the blind slats have my eyes closing. My hand reaches out blindly for Jase, but his side of the bed is empty. That's when I feel it again. The tickling on my back. *Oh, God, please don't let it be a bug or an animal…* I'm about to turn over to see what it is, but a strong hand weighing down on my butt prevents me from moving.

"Don't move," Jase's husky voice says. "I'm almost done." Twisting my head without moving the rest of my body, I peek behind me and see the tickling is Jase drawing on my skin.

"Are you drawing on me?" I ask.

"I couldn't help it. Your body is flawless. It's like a blank canvas." I feel the hand that was on my butt cup my cheek and then slide down the back of my thigh. "You were sleeping so soundly, and when I woke up to take a piss I noticed my shirt had risen, exposing this sexy ass"—he gives my backside a playful slap—"and these perfect dimples." My head falls forward onto the pillow. I feel his cool lips graze my lower back as he gives the two dimples located just above my ass a kiss.

"I had to mark you," he adds. My eyes flit over to him again. He's still drawing on me while he talks. "You know, I've done quite a few dimple piercings. Do you have any piercings anywhere?"

"No." I shake my head.

"Tattoos?"

"Nope. Piercings and tattoos are a no-no when you're trying to become a model. Most high-class agencies frown upon that sort of thing."

Jase grunts his displeasure, continuing to draw on my body. "Nobody would know if you got one here," he states. His fingers trail down to just above the crack of my ass. "Or here." He continues his descent along the center of my ass. Then he spreads my legs open and pushes a single finger into my pussy. "Nobody should ever see these parts of your body. They're mine," he growls lowly. "This body, and this pussy, is mine." He pulls his finger out of me, and I immediately miss his touch.

"It's a little soon to be claiming me, don't you think?" I

sass.

"Nope, you made it mine the moment you let me take your virginity," he says matter-of-factly, and my cheeks flush at his words.

"Don't move," he demands. He pushes off the bed, and a second later, I hear the sound of a camera clicking. "Perfect."

I try to flip over, but his hands prevent me from doing so. Jase spreads my thighs wider and pushes his fingers back inside me, my body accepting the intrusion all too willingly.

"Jesus, woman, you're so wet," he groans. While he fingers me with one hand, his other comes around and lifts my lower half slightly off the bed, so I'm on my knees. He palms my breast and plants sweet kisses down my spine until his lips are back where he was drawing. He blows softly on my skin, sending chills up my spine. Then his lips once again kiss each of my dimples. He makes his way downward, and when his teeth sink into my butt cheek, I let out a girly screech.

He laughs softly. "Sorry, I needed a taste," he admits, and I can't help the grin that makes its way across my face in response.

He continues to fingerfuck me, and then his tongue hits my clit. He sucks it into his mouth and then licks up my center, causing my entire body to shudder in pleasure. With his tongue, and lips, and fingers, Jase works me up until I'm calling out his name as I orgasm around him.

Then he flips me over onto my back and crawls up my body. My legs wrap around his waist as his hands cage me in. His lips angle against mine as he pushes into me. I'm still a tad sore, but those thoughts are overpowered by our kiss.

This kiss. It ignites something deep within me, heating my frozen walls and melting the ice away until there's nothing left to protect my heart and soul. They're visible and vulnerable, leaving Jase with full access to every exposed part of me. Our kiss becomes more heated. Like a wildfire that can't be contained. I've always been so careful—never to let anyone in. Yet, here I am, handing myself over to this man, knowing if I'm not careful I'm going to get burned. The heat between us is all-consuming. I'm lost in everything that is Jase.

My hands hold on to his shoulders, my nails digging into his skin, as his thrusts turn frantic. His pelvis grinds against mine, rubbing my clit just right. We're both chasing our release. My climax builds, and builds, and builds, until I'm so high, I have nowhere to go but down. But with Jase in charge, I'm not afraid to fall. In fact, I welcome it. And with one last thrust, he pushes me off the edge, taking himself with me. Our lips find each other, swallowing our moans as we both lose ourselves in one another.

Once we've reached the bottom safely, Jase breaks our kiss and nuzzles his face into the crook of my neck. We stay like this for a long moment as we calm our beating hearts and labored breaths. When he lifts slightly, pulling out, I wince at the tenderness I feel between my legs, hoping I never stop feeling it so I always remember the times Jase and I became one.

"Shit, I didn't use protection *again*," he admits, looking down. It's then I feel the liquid between my thighs *again*. I should be bothered that Jase and I have yet to use protection.

I know this is a one-night stand. But for some crazy reason, being with Jase feels like so much more.

"It's okay," I blurt out, "I trust you."

Jase pulls my face into his for a hard kiss. "What are you doing to me?" he murmurs against my lips. "All my sanity flies out the window with you."

"Because you forgot to use a condom?" I ask, confused.

"I never bring women back here. Not to my apartment, not to meet my family, and definitely not into my bed." I can't help the grin that splays across my face at his admission.

"I should get cleaned up," I tell him shyly. He backs up so I can climb off the bed. Following me into his bathroom, he insists we shower together. The entire time he's touching me in some way. Whether it's soaping me up, or massaging the shampoo into my scalp, Jase's hands are on me.

When we get out, he tells me he'll be right back. He returns with a pair of sweats and a hoodie. They're pink and similar to the outfit Quinn was wearing.

"Thank you. I'll wash them and then get them back to her." I pull my hair up into a messy bun then get dressed. I put my bra back on but go commando, not wanting to wear my day-old panties. I gather up my clothes from last night and fold them into a neat pile while Jase gets dressed. My heart tightens in my chest when I hear the clinking of his keys. This is it. Our night together is over. He's going to take me home, and then he'll continue his life while I continue mine. Tears prick my eyes, and I quickly lift my finger to wipe them away. I don't cry. Why am I crying now? Grow up, Celeste! This is what people our age do. We have one-night stands. We hook up and then go our separate ways. Don't act like an immature weirdo.

"I almost forgot to show you," Jase says, breaking me out of my crazy silent monologue. I take a deep breath and turn to face him. He's dressed in a plain white T-shirt that stretches across his broad chest and shoulders, and a loose pair of jeans. His one arm comes up so his fingers can run through his damp hair, and I spot a hint of his thick happy trail leading down to the Promised Land. I should've spent more time getting to know his body while I had him. I didn't even have a chance to taste him yet.

Jase clears his throat, and it's then I notice he's facing his phone toward me and sporting a knowing smirk. He totally caught me checking him out. I simply shrug. No point in denying it. I step closer to see what's on his screen and immediately recognize the one dimple on my lower back. And then my focus turns to the most beautiful artwork I've ever seen. A black and grey dandelion that looks like it's blowing in the wind comes up my hip with stray petals dancing in the wind. A smaller one next to it. Along the stem of the larger dandelion is a quote: *And from the chaos of her soul flowed beauty*

"Jase," I whisper. How could he possibly write something that hits so close to home without even knowing me?

"My mom used to wish on dandelions," Jase says, his voice thick with emotion. "We would take walks in our neighborhood when we were little, and she would find every one she could, blowing on them as she made wish upon wish."

"What did she wish for?"

51

"I don't know." He shrugs a shoulder. "But my guess is success. She wanted to be an actress." He smiles warmly. "She was beautiful. At least from what I can remember." The corners of his mouth turn down slightly. "She was actually in a couple small shows, but then she met my dad. She fell in love and found herself pregnant with my brother. A year later came me." I notice he doesn't mention Quinn. "She didn't know it at the time, but my dad was already married. His wife couldn't have kids...or so they thought. A few years later, Quinn was born. My dad juggled his two families for a while, but eventually he got caught. When his wife found out about us, he proved my mom to be an unfit parent and got custody of us. My mom couldn't handle it—losing my dad and us. She ended up committing suicide."

"Oh, Jase!" My arms wrap around his neck for a hug. "I'm so sorry."

"You remind me of her," Jase murmurs into my ear. "I saw that quote captioned under an image at an art gallery I visited once with my sister. I can't remember who said it, but the words always stuck with me. I don't doubt one day you will conquer the world, Dimples." He backs up and shoots me a playful wink to lighten the mood, but my heart is still with Jase's mom and her chaotic, beautiful soul.

"Where's your dad now?" I ask. He obviously accepted Quinn as his sister even though she has a different mom.

"He died of a heart attack when I was thirteen." Jase doesn't sound the least bit sad when he tells me this. "Quinn's mom thought she would get his life insurance, but it came out that he wasn't really married to her either. He was married to another woman, Tricia, and had two other kids with her. He had left her several years back but never got a divorce. She got everything in his will, leaving Quinn's mom broke. She lost it, and the minute Jax turned eighteen, he got a job and moved out. He petitioned the court and got custody of Quinn and me."

"Wow," I say in awe of how well they handled everything.

"Yeah, talk about some crazy 60 Minutes meets Jerry Springer shit." Jase laughs humorlessly. "My dad was a fucking liar, and his lies destroyed not one but two women who loved him." He shakes his head with disgust. "I hope he's rotting in hell." His words hit me like a brick to a glass house. Jase's hard limit is lying, and I've lied to him several times since we met. No, I didn't actually say the words, but I might as well have. I should tell him the truth now. What do I have to lose? But if I walk away with things the way they are now, he won't think of me the way he thinks about his father. As a liar.

My eyes dart to his phone, the screen is still showing the fake tattoo he drew on me. "Can you send me that picture?" I ask. It's the only thing I will have left of our night together once I walk away.

"Sure." He grins. I give him my email address since my phone is one of those crappy prepaid ones, and he sends it over.

We walk out of his room and find Jax cooking in the kitchen with Quinn sitting on a stool watching him. "Morning," Jase announces. Jax and Quinn both glance our way. Quinn grants me a soft smile, and Jax waves the spatula in the air.

"Morning," they both say in unison.

"You hungry?" Jax asks.

"Starving!" I admit before I can stop myself. Jase is probably ready to send me packing, and I'm over here practically begging to stay and eat.

"Well, have a seat." Jax points to the empty stools.

"Oh, umm…I think Jase was about to take me home." I avoid looking at anyone in the room, instead choosing to focus on the pancake batter that's bubbling in the pan. It's embarrassing enough having to do the walk of shame…

The contrast between the coolness of Jase's lips on my ear, and his warm body pressed up against mine, sends a visible shiver straight down my spine. He must notice because he chuckles softly before he says, "You aren't going anywhere, Dimples. Sit." I do as he says, while trying to school my excitement over his somewhat public display of affection and sweet yet commanding words, but a grin stretches across my lips anyway.

Quinn laughs. "Such a gentleman," she jokes.

"Hush your mouth," Jase volleys back.

Jax serves us each a stack of delicious-smelling pancakes and eggs then has a seat as well.

"What's everyone up to today?" Quinn asks.

"I have a guy coming into the shop to get more of his sleeve done," Jax says.

"What about you guys?" Quinn turns her attention to Jase and me.

"Not sure yet," Jase answers her. The hand he's not using to eat squeezes my thigh. I assumed Jase was going to bring me home, yet he told me I'm not going anywhere. Did he just mean to stay for breakfast? We haven't discussed what happened between us last night, and for all I know this was just a one-night thing to him. At least that's what I keep telling myself when I justify why I haven't told him the truth about my age and where I go to school. Maybe he just plans to fill my belly with food before he sends me on my way…

"I'm heading to the beach to take pictures," Quinn says. "I have my final photography project due next week."

Jase swallows a mouthful of food, then turns to me. "Want to go?" The look he gives me is so hopeful. Before I can think about the ramifications of my answer, I'm nodding my head yes. He smiles an adorable lopsided grin. "Cool. We can go by your house to get your suit on the way."

Shit! This is exactly why I should've given this more thought before saying yes. I need to tell him the truth. He needs to know I'm only eighteen and in high school. That I live in a trailer park with my drunken mother, and my only way out is the summer internship in New York Nick surprised me with. Jase would understand. He comes from a broken home. And I am of legal age…

I open my mouth to tell Jase I need to talk to him, when Quinn says, "I have a spare." She shrugs. "It'll save time."

"You good with that?" Jase asks, taking another bite of his food.

"Yeah," I mutter with a plastered-on smile. *Later…I'll tell him later.*

Once we're done eating, and we've worked together to get the dishes done and the kitchen cleaned, we head out in Jase's Dodge Charger to the beach. It's such a man's car. Black on black with smooth leather interior. It's not flashy or expensive, but it's damn sexy. And it totally fits him.

When we arrive at the beach, Quinn takes off on her photography mission, and Jase and I head toward the ocean to find an empty spot to lay a blanket down near the water. It's a cool day in North Carolina, so actually swimming isn't ideal, but it's warm enough to lay out and enjoy the sun.

After stripping off Quinn's shirt and shorts, leaving me in only her bikini—which fits a tad loose on my body since she has more curves than I do—I turn my attention to Jase. He reaches back and pulls his shirt over his head, exposing his delicious tattoos, along with his firm chest and ripped abs. I never imagined falling for a guy like Jase. I always pictured a wealthy, put together businessman, dressed to the nines in a designer suit. Nowhere in my fantasies did it include a tattoo artist bad-boy. The term causes my heart to skip a beat. My mom fell for the tattooed bad-boy. She's not only brokenhearted but *broken*. It's not the same, I tell myself. Jase isn't really a bad-boy. He just looks like one. He's educated. He has a college degree, and he wants to open his own business.

Does it really even matter when this time next week I'll be in New York?

My heart sinks at the thought of leaving Jase. Can I do it? Can I walk away from him?

You don't have a choice, my inner self argues. It doesn't matter how fast and hard I'm falling for him. New York is my future. I can't give that up for a *man*. There will be plenty more men in New York.

"You okay?" Jase asks, forcing me out of my thoughts.

"Yeah," I say, and then quickly add, "tell me about your

tattoos," in hope of distracting myself from my own thoughts. My mind and heart are warring with one another, and it's not a battle I am ready to enter yet.

Jase looks down and runs a hand along the planes of his abs. "Which ones?" he asks. "I kind of have a lot." He laughs, and the melodic sound calms my nerves. No, he's not a bad-boy. He's a good guy wrapped in a bad-boy body.

He drops onto the blanket and lays next to me. His leg entangles with mine as he explains each one. They all mean something to him in some way. We spend the next several hours laughing and talking and kissing, completely lost in our own little world. We watch people come and go, and eat the lunch we packed. Eventually Quinn makes her way back over to us, ready to go home. I have no clue how the entire day passed so quickly, but what I do know is I'm not ready to say goodbye to Jase yet.

So when he murmurs, "Come home with me" against my lips, I agree without thought. On our drive back, Nick texts, asking where I am. I text him back that I have a couple things I need to do before graduation, and immediately feel guilty for lying. But I'm not ready for him to know about Jase yet. Next week everything changes. Nick got me an internship. It's pointless for him to know about a man I can't have a future with. It's not like I'm going to stay. I lied to Jase…about school, my age. Sure, it was a lie by omission, but a lie is still a lie. He doesn't even know I'm planning to leave soon.

Jase's hand squeezes mine, and my heart feels like it's going to thump right out of my chest. How did this happen? How did I manage to fall in love with someone in less than twelve hours? This isn't who I am. I want to be mad at myself for being so stupid, but I can't muster up the negative energy. My heart feels too full...too happy. And suddenly I can almost empathize with my mom. Imagining how I'm going to feel when I leave next week nearly has my heart crumbling into pieces.

Grabbing our stuff, we head upstairs to their apartment. Jase unlocks the door and opens it wide for Quinn and me to walk through. I stop in my place when I see a woman sitting on the couch, fiddling with her cell phone. I glance around and don't see Jax anywhere. Does she live here as well?

She looks up, and it's as if she doesn't even notice Quinn or me in the room as she smiles at Jase. She's naturally beautiful with fiery red hair and emerald green eyes, but she looks exhausted. Like she has the weight of the world sitting on her shoulders. Her eyes then dart to me, and she glares daggers my way. When her gaze goes back to Jase, her smile comes back. *Interesting...*

"Jase!" She jumps off the couch and flies into his arms. His eyes meet mine, and he shoots me, what looks like, a silent apology. The woman is dressed in black jeans that are clearly too tight on her, and a tiny blue tank top. A large tattoo peeks out from under her shirt on her lower back, disappearing under the top of her jeans. And a twinge of jealousy surfaces as I wonder if Jase was the one to give it to her.

"Amaya," he says, pulling away from her. "How are you?" His gaze trails down her body, not like he's checking her out, but more like he's making sure she's okay.

"I'm fine," she says a bit too upbeat. It reminds me of the way my mom speaks to Victoria to hide how drunk she is, or when she doesn't want her to know we're without electricity or water. "Are you going to introduce me to your friend?" She nods my way. "Or is she Quinn's friend?" she adds, hope evident in her voice.

"She's with Jase," Quinn says matter-of-factly to the woman, and I stifle a smile. Quinn just got major points for that in my book.

"This is Celeste," Jase says, then turns toward me. "This is my friend, Amaya."

"Best friend," Amaya corrects with a bit of snark in her tone.

"Nice to meet you," I say politely. "I'm going to shower the sand off me." I give Jase a soft smile so he knows I'm trying to be nice and leave them to talk. She's obviously here for a reason.

"Bye!" Amaya waves at me like she's five years old.

Jase shoots her a cool glare, then mouths a *thank you* to me.

I let out a soft sigh as the hot water rains down and massages my scalp. My eyes are closed so the shampoo doesn't burn them as the water rinses the suds and salt from my hair. I'm completely lost in myself, in my thoughts, so I don't hear Jase come in. When the shower door opens, and the cool air pricks my heated flesh, I let out a loud shriek. Jase laughs, but when his eyes land on my now pebbled nipples, his laughter stops, and the smile he was just sporting turns into pure hunger.

"Get in or get out! It's cold out there!" I yell, trying to sound mad. A laugh breaks through, though, giving me away.

Jase steps in and closes the door behind him, and that's when I notice he's naked—which makes sense since he's getting in the shower with me. His dick is semi-hard, and it bobs heavy between his thighs as he steps toward me. The shower is a decent size, but not huge, so he doesn't have far to go. Wordlessly, Jase picks me up and pushes me against the wall. The water continues to fall around us, but it doesn't deter him in the slightest. My legs wrap around his waist, and my fingers grip his shoulders. His mouth finds mine, and he devours me. His tongue pushes through my lips, and I taste everything that is Jase. His cock pokes against my ass, and I let out a moan, needing him to be inside me. The air around us grows thick with lust. Our bodies go from zero to one hundred in a split second, with a single touch. And a million thoughts hit me at once, like how is it so easy to get lost in this man? Is it like this for everyone in the beginning? Will it always feel this way with Jase? This explosive? Is this how it was for my mom?

My heart constricts as Jase pushes up into me, filling me completely. Our kiss turns rougher, more demanding. I can feel him everywhere. His fingers digging into my ass, his mouth devouring mine. His dick thrusting in and out of me. Every part of him is touching me. It's as if he's become an extension of me. He's gotten under my skin, and there's no getting him out.

The thought of leaving him has my throat tightening. Tears of devastation leak from my eyes. My arms wrap tightly around Jase's neck, needing to mold myself to him— to feel him even closer. I want to burrow myself just as deeply in him as he's done to me. My tears fall as Jase makes love to me against the shower wall. As reality hits that I can't leave this man. I need to lay my cards down, put it all on the line— tell him the truth and see where it takes us. Maybe I can convince him to join me in New York. He could work at a shop there and eventually open up his own place. Of course that would mean his brother and sister would have to move too...

"Celeste," Jase moans, "stay with me, baby." How is it that he already knows me so well? I push all my thoughts aside and focus on Jase. On how good he feels inside me. His face nuzzles into the crook of my neck, and he bites down on my flesh as he comes deep inside me. Once he catches his breath, he lifts his head, pulls out of me, then sets me down on my feet.

"You didn't come," he says with a frown. It's not a question, he knows I didn't. We've only had sex a couple times, but every time he's made sure I find my release before him.

"I'm sorry," I whisper in embarrassment. I was so lost in myself, in him, I didn't even notice.

"What's going on?" Jase asks. He runs two fingers down the side of my cheek.

"Nothing." I shake my head. "Was everything okay with your friend?"

Jase's brows furrow. "Is that what's wrong? You have nothing to worry about. Amaya is only a friend."

"I know." I nod emphatically. I wait for Jase to further explain himself, but he doesn't.

"Hurry up and finish rinsing off," Jase says, "I owe you an orgasm." He shoots me an adorable wink before stepping out of the shower.

Four

CELESTE

The Past

My skin is overly warm, and it feels like there's a two hundred pound weight on top of me. When I try to roll over but can't move, I tilt my head to the side and see Jase's body is wrapped around mine. His legs are entwined with mine, and his free hand is holding my breast. We fell asleep naked last night, after devouring a pizza while we attempted to watch a movie on Netflix, which only ended in us making out and eventually making love.

"Morning," Jase murmurs against my ear. His dick presses against my ass, and I let out a groan, which has him chuckling darkly. He pulls away from me, only to flip me over so he can hover above me. "What's on the agenda for today?" he asks. I love that he's assuming we're going to hang out.

"I don't know." I shrug my shoulders. "Do you have to work?"

"Nope." He shakes his head then dips it down to grab one of my nipples between his teeth. He tugs on it playfully, then looks up, releasing it. "I was thinking I would quit my job and spend the rest of my life with you in this bed." He waggles his eyebrows, and I giggle, rolling my eyes. "I'm just kidding," he says. "It's Sunday, so I have off, which means…if you don't have anything going on, I was thinking we could hang out." He smiles shyly, his cockiness and confidence waning a couple notches.

"That sounds good to me," I tell him as I run my fingers through his hair and pull him to me. We kiss for several minutes before we finally get out of bed to get ready for the day. Jase surprises me with my clothes, as well as the outfit I borrowed from Quinn, neatly stacked. Apparently, when he left the room to get our pizza from the delivery guy, he threw a load of laundry in the wash, and then Quinn threw them in the dryer. I throw on my undergarments and then my dress. Grabbing my wedges from next to the door, I slip them on then head into the bathroom. Using Jase's toiletries, I brush my teeth and put on deodorant. When I come out, Jase is ready to go as well.

"Where are we going?" I ask as we head toward his car.

"I was thinking we could go downtown, check out the farmer's market, maybe go see a movie." His eyes seek mine for approval.

"That sounds perfect."

Jase opens my door for me, and once I'm in, closes it, but not before ducking his head in and giving me a swoon-worthy kiss.

The drive to downtown is filled with comfortable silence with the music playing in the background. My phone buzzes in my hand, and when I check it, I see it's almost dead and there's a text from Nick asking what we're up to today. I feel like the worst friend in the world when I text him back that I have more stuff I need to take care of, with the promise we will hang out soon.

"Everything okay?" Jase asks, eyeing my phone.

"Yeah, it's almost dead. I'm turning it off."

He nods. "Quinn has exams this week. I can't remember…Does NCU too?" His gaze bounces from the road to me.

"I'm done with my exams," I tell him. Technically, I'm telling him the truth. I finished my exams last week. Seniors get out a couple weeks earlier than everyone else as a senior privilege. The day before graduation, I have to attend the rehearsal, but other than that, I'm completely done with school. A few of my friends headed over to White Oak to spend the week camping and going water rafting, but that's not really my thing, so I didn't join them.

"Cool."

Jase pulls into the parking garage and finds a spot. Before I can open my door to get out, he jogs around and opens it for me. "A girl could seriously get used to this kind of treatment, Mr. Crawford," I joke.

"Good." He leans down for a kiss, then taking my hand in his, walks us over to the Farmer's Market. We spend the next couple hours checking out all of the homemade goods. We stop at one stand where there's an older couple who are selling fresh baked treats from their bakery. Jase buys us a giant cinnamon bun for us to share. We also stop at a couple fresh grocers and buy some delicious looking strawberries and blackberries to munch on while we walk around.

When we stop at a cute homemade jewelry booth, I spot the most beautiful dandelion necklace. It reminds me of the fake tattoo Jase drew on me yesterday morning and the story he told me about his mom. The necklace is silver and dangling from it, in a clear, thin, circular glass, is a real dandelion. With its petals flailing out every which way, it looks as if it's been frozen in time. And hanging from the charm is a tiny plaque that reads **wish** on one side, and **dream** on the other.

"This is beautiful," I tell the woman.

"Thank you. I find them and make them myself." She smiles softly. When I see the price, and know I can't afford it, I set it down and walk over to another area of the tent to check out her other pieces. When I look around to see where Jase is, I spot him talking to the woman.

"Thank you," he says to her.

"You're very welcome." She grins.

Once we're out of her tent, I ask him what he was thanking her for.

"This," he says, pulling a small bag out of his front pocket. "Turn around."

I do as he says, and a second later, I feel something cool touch my chest. When I glance down, I see the dandelion charm is there.

"Jase." I twirl around to face him.

"I saw you eyeing it." He shrugs nonchalantly. "You

said yesterday that a necklace has the capabilities of making a woman feel more." His gaze lands on the necklace before he locks eyes with me. "It looks beautiful on you."

"Thank you." I wrap my arms around his neck and give him a hug. Tears threaten to fill my eyes, and emotion clogs my throat, but I will them both away, not wanting to scare Jase. It's not his fault that the girl he brought home has fallen for him this hard and fast.

I'm about to pull away when Jase grips my hips, holding me close to him, and says, "Never stop wishing and dreaming, Celeste." Then he kisses me softly. The kiss doesn't last long since we're standing in the middle of the sidewalk, but it's one of those moments, one of those kisses, that I know I will remember for the rest of my life.

With our fingers entwined, we continue to walk until we reach the end of the farmer's market and the beginning of the promenade. The area contains a movie theater, a couple restaurants, some upscale stores, and a coffee shop.

We stop in front of the lit screen that displays the movies and show times. "You pick," he says. I decide on a romantic comedy—I've clearly lost my mind and have decided to just embrace it. After getting a large soda and popcorn for us to split, we head inside the theater. The movie either must suck or be on its way out because aside from one other couple who are sitting all the way in the front, the theater is completely empty.

We head straight to the top of the theater and sit in the corner. A few minutes later, the lights go out and the previews begin. Jase raises the armrest between us and tucks me into his side, his arm curling around the back of my neck.

I have to stifle my giggle at how couple-y we must look. I've been on plenty of dates, but with the type of guys I usually give my time to, a date generally consists of an expensive dinner or charity event. This is my first time at the movies with a guy.

The previews end and the movie begins, but I can't focus on it because Jase is running his fingers up and down my arm. Goosebumps pebble my skin, and when I look up at him, he glances in my direction, granting me the sexiest smile. I don't know what comes over me but suddenly I have an insatiable need to be close to this man. Closer than is allowed in the middle of a public movie theater.

Pulling his face down to mine, I kiss Jase hard. My tongue pushes through his lips, and the kiss deepens. But it's not enough. I need more. As our kiss continues, I run my hand along the top of Jase's jeans. The bulge in his pants is prominent and spurs me on. Undoing his button and zipper, I pull his dick out. Jase groans against my lips, and his hand, which has been massaging circles into my thigh, tries to stop me.

"Uh-uh," he whispers against my lips, noncommittedly.

"Yes," I murmur back. And then breaking the kiss, I look around real quick just to make sure nobody is watching, before I bend at the waist and take Jase's entire shaft into my mouth.

"Fuck, Celeste," he moans quietly. His fingers run through my hair, but he doesn't make any move to push my head down. Instead, when I glance up, I notice his head is tilted back, his eyes closed. I bob up and down over his entire length. Licking and sucking on his plump head. I feel his dick begin to swell and know he's about to come. I've never even given head, let alone swallowed a man's cum, but we're in the middle of a theater, and there's no way I'm spitting it out on the floor, so I squeeze my eyes closed as Jase moans out his orgasm, the hot seed spurting into the back of my throat. I do my best not to gag and choke, but it's hard. It's salty and warm and thick.

Once I'm sure he's finished, I lick him clean and then sit back up. Jase's eyes meet mine. They're glossed over and, even in the dark, I can see the lust and awe in them. He shakes his head and leans in to whisper into my ear, "My turn." My eyes go wide as he spreads my thighs to reciprocate.

For the third morning in a row, I wake up in Jase's bed to the sunlight seeping in through the blinds. *I'm going to need to purchase some curtains* is my first thought. My second is that I'm going to be graduating this week, and once I leave, I'll never sleep in this bed again, so there's no need to purchase curtains. My stomach tightens at that horrible thought. I roll over to find Jase's side of the bed empty. *Jase's side of the bed…* Three nights with him and I'm already assigning us sides of the bed. I spot a piece of paper and pick it up to read it.

Dimples,

I had an early appointment. Feel free to stay as long as you want. If no one is home just lock the door if you leave. There's a key under the mat in case you need it. I realized we never exchanged numbers. Here's mine. Text me yours.

Xo Jase

Directly under his name is his phone number. Grabbing my cell phone from atop the nightstand, I program it into my phone. I'm about to send Jase a text to give him mine, when a text comes in from Nick: **Where are you?**

Still not ready for him to know about Jase, I text him back that I'm getting things situated before graduation since I'll be leaving shortly after. I hate lying to Nick, but I'm afraid to tell him the truth, like if I tell him about Jase, it will make what we have that much more real, and with it will come the reality that I'm supposed to be leaving soon.

Another text comes through from Nick, telling me he wants to take me shopping for luggage and anything else I might need for my trip to New York. I want to tell him I can't make it. For one, shopping for luggage means I'm leaving, and right now, leaving is the last thing I want to think about. And two, the only thing I want to be doing is spending time with Jase. But I know Nick, and if I tell him I can't make it, when I've been so excited about New York, it will send up a huge red flag. So, I send him a reply thanking him and agree to meet up with him later, then get out of bed. My body feels relaxed and well-rested, despite having been up most of the night with Jase. *It must be from all those orgasms he gave me.*

I stretch my arms over my head, and my stomach rumbles. We were too caught up in each other last night and completely forgot to eat dinner. And then an idea forms. Heading out into the living room to see if anyone is home, I find Quinn sitting on the couch working on her computer.

"Morning," I say.

She looks up from whatever she's working on. "Hey, morning."

"I was…umm…thinking about surprising Jase at work. Maybe bring him some breakfast. Do you think he would be okay with that?"

"I think he would." Quinn grins. "Need to borrow another outfit?" She nods toward me. I'm in another one of Jase's shirts and my panties.

"That would be great," I tell her. "Thank you."

After showering and getting dressed, Quinn gives me a ride to pick up some food. I also run into the store to grab a charger before my phone goes completely dead. When we arrive at the shop, I ask her if she's coming in, but she tells me she's around them enough and needs to get her project done for class so she can officially be done with the semester.

The sign above the door reads Get Inked. I've seen it many times in passing but never gave it a second glance. When I open the door, a bell jingles indicating someone has entered. The guy standing behind the counter looks up and smiles. With inky black hair formed into a high mohawk, tattoos covering every inch of his visible skin, gages in his earlobes, and a hoop jutting out of his bottom lip, he reminds me of Travis Barker from Blink-182.

"Good morning," he rasps, "how can I help you?"

"I'm here to see Jase," I explain.

"Aren't they all?" He laughs with a quick roll of his eyes. It's meant as a joke, but my stomach plummets at his words. Jase is a beautiful man on the inside and out, so it doesn't surprise me that women are lined up to get their body's permanently altered by him.

"He's booked up today." He pages through the calendar. "He has an opening for Monday, next week." My throat clogs with emotion. Monday, next week, I'll be in New York, and Jase will be here. Will he have already moved on? Will I have been nothing more than a blip in his radar? My nose tingles and my eyes blur at the thought.

There's a throat clearing, and it's then I realize I'm just standing here, mourning the loss of Jase and me before we've even happened. I look up and see Jase standing next to the other guy.

"Dimples." Jase grins wide, and I shake my head at his nickname for me. "To what do I owe this pleasure?"

I lift the bag of food. "I brought you breakfast." I shrug, suddenly feeling stupid for showing up at his place of work. He's booked all day—probably with beautiful women, who will let him mark their skin, and afterward, they will give him their number, because they aren't going anywhere. They aren't planning to move over five hundred miles away.

"I'm starved," Jase says. "Come back with me. I just finished my appointment, and I have a few minutes before my next one." He saunters around the counter and takes my hand in his, leading me down a narrow hallway and into a small room. There's a burley guy standing in front of the mirror, checking out his newly tattooed shoulder.

When he sees us come in, he nods once. "Looks great, man," he says to Jase. Not wanting to be in the way, I sit on the stool that's situated in the corner of the room.

Jase smiles at the guy. "Damn right it does." He grabs some thin plastic, and after covering the art with some gooey looking stuff, lays the plastic over it, securing it with tape. "You know the drill. Keep it covered for a few hours. Once you remove the bandage, wash it with soap and apply more ointment. Pete will make your next appointment up front."

"Thanks." The guy fist bumps Jase before walking out.

Once he's gone, Jase closes the door behind him, then stalks over to me. Grabbing the bag of food out of my hands, he drops it onto the counter, then spreads my legs wide and situates himself between them. He cages me into the corner, his hands landing on the wall on either side of my head. His lips come down and meet mine for a passionate kiss that has my toes curling and the apex of my thighs squeezing around him. With his face only a hairbreadth from mine, he murmurs, "I almost canceled my appointments this morning. Leaving you, laying in my bed, in nothing but my shirt…it almost killed me." His nose brushes against mine. "I was worried I might not see you again, Dimples."

"Why?" I breathe.

"I was afraid once you woke up and the weekend was over, you would disappear." His lips brush against mine, then linger momentarily, as if he needs to touch me in some way to believe I'm really here. I swallow thickly. I need to tell him the truth. He needs to know I'm graduating from high school and leaving to New York in a few days. But today, all I want to do is spend the day with Jase. I want to watch him do what he loves. These few days may be all I get with him before he either hates me for lying or I graduate and move. Both of those possibilities leave me feeling sick to my stomach. I have no clue how this happened. How I fell so quickly for this guy, but I did. I'm falling and my only hope is that Jase will be at the bottom, ready to catch me.

"I'm here," I say softly. "Could I...maybe hangout for a little while? I'll stay out of the way."

Jase's face lights up. "That would be great." With one last kiss, he backs up and takes the bag off the counter. He dishes out the food and grabs us both a cup of coffee. While we eat, we talk about his upcoming appointments. It's obvious from how animated he is, he loves his job.

Shortly after we're done eating, his next appointment comes back. He's an older gentleman named George, looking to get his late wife's name inked on his arm. He shares that they were married for forty years and she passed away six months ago from cancer. He explains what he would like, and after Jase draws up the image and George approves it, Jase gets to work. The tattoo gun buzzes a low humming sound, but it's drowned out by George's voice. He shares memories of his life with his wife while she was alive. He talks about how they met and fell in love, and how he knew the moment he saw her that she was the one.

As he reminisces, I can't help the tears that fall. This is what I want. An entire life full of memories with Jase. A few days...a week...a month isn't enough. And then it hits me. This is what my mom wanted with my dad but never got. It's why she's chosen to live in the same trailer in the same town my entire life. She knows what it feels like to fall in love and refuses to let go of that feeling, in hope that one day the man she loves might come back and love her in return again. And while I never understood it before, I now get it. Because if I can feel this strongly about Jase after only one weekend, I can't imagine how my mom felt after being with my dad for months.

An hour later, Jase wipes George's arm down and hands him a small mirror. Tears leak from his eyes as he nods slowly. "Thank you," he whispers. Jase runs through the same speech he did with his other client about caring for the tattoo. When he's done, George turns to me with a sad smile and says, "I see the way you two look at each other. It reminds me of the way my Melinda and I used to look at each other." And with a wink, he stands and walks out of the room.

The rest of the day continues much the same—although, thankfully, not as emotional. All types of people come in and out of the shop to get tattooed. Some have back stories, others just want something fun or cool or pretty. I can see why Jase is booked up. He treats each tattoo like it's going to be a masterpiece. It doesn't matter if it's a simple butterfly or a remembrance piece, he gives each person one hundred percent of him. He makes them feel as though what they're getting tattooed isn't just ink, but rather a piece of them, and through extension, a piece of him.

Lunchtime arrives, and Jase orders in for us. He breaks for lunch, and we spend the hour kissing, talking, eating, and laughing. I can't remember a time when I felt this content.

When my phone buzzes, I check it and see it's Nick. It's already five o'clock, and he's asking where he should pick me up. I text him back to pick me up near the movie theater. It's only a couple blocks away, and he won't piece it together that I was here.

"Everything okay?" Jase asks. I look up and notice his latest client has left.

"Yeah, but I have to get going." I frown. "I promised Nick I would hang out with him."

"All right," Jase says. "Will I see you later?"

My heart skips a beat at his question. He wants to see me later. "Yeah." I nod. "I'm not sure how late I'll be, but you will definitely see me later."

"Good." He gives me a searing kiss goodbye, and I take off to meet Nick. He's waiting for me at the theater where we agreed and thankfully doesn't ask me any questions. We head straight to the mall, where he helps me pick out my first set of Louis Vuitton luggage—a gift from his family for my graduation—as well as some new outfits and toiletries I'll need to get me started once I'm over there.

Once we're done shopping, we head to dinner, and then afterward Nick drops me off at home. I quickly change my clothes and pack a bag. Since my mom isn't home, I leave a note that I'm spending the night at a friend's house, and then take a taxi over to Jase's. When I arrive, he's already home from work and greets me at the door with a kiss.

The next few days continue the same way. During the day, while Jase is at work, I hang out with Nick—he keeps me company while I pack for New York, we have lunch with Killian on campus since he's finishing up the last of his finals, and I even join him at the gym, since he's insistent he gets some training in, even though he's in his off-season.

My nights are spent with Jase. We hang out with his brother and sister just long enough to not be rude—usually ordering in dinner—and then we excuse ourselves to bed, where we spend the rest of our night kissing and cuddling and making love.

Now it's the day of my graduation rehearsal and my time has run out. I've spent the entire morning with Jase in bed since his first appointment isn't until this afternoon. Just like every morning before he leaves for work, he leans down to kiss me and asks, "Will I see you later?" But unlike every morning when I tell him yes, I can't say that. Because tonight after my rehearsal, I have a family dinner with Nick's family and my mom, and then tomorrow morning is my graduation.

I open my mouth to explain all of this to him, but I can't do it. There's a good chance he's going to be pissed that I've lied. Tomorrow. I'm going to tell him tomorrow. Once I've officially graduated. We'll sit down and I'll be honest with him. *But then what?* I ask myself. He loves his job. He has an entire life here. He isn't going to follow me to New York. I shake the thoughts from my head. We'll figure it out.

"Celeste?" He says my name, getting my attention. "Will I see you later?" he repeats.

"No." I shake my head. "I have this family thing I have to do tonight and tomorrow. How about tomorrow night? I can come by after you get off work."

Jase looks like he wants to ask for details but instead nods. "Okay. Tomorrow night."

Pulling him down to my level, I wrap my arms around

his neck and kiss him hard. I'm not sure why, but it feels like I need to somehow convey every feeling I have for him into this kiss. So when I tell him the truth tomorrow night, he'll be understanding.

Once our kiss ends, we say goodbye and Jase leaves for work. After I shower and get dressed, I text Nick to see if he can drive me over to NCU to my rehearsal, since it will cost me a fortune to take a cab there. He, of course, says yes. Since the theater is too far of a walk, and I don't want to bug Quinn to drive me, I have him pick me up at the corner store around the block from Jase's place, using the excuse that I spent the night at a friend's place. I'm not sure if Nick buys it, but he at least doesn't question it. I'm not even a block away from Jase's apartment and my heart and body are already missing him.

We arrive at NCU and head straight over to the auditorium where the graduation is taking place. The teachers and administrators walk us through how everything will go tomorrow. When my row is called up, I walk across the stage, along with everyone else in my row. It's only the rehearsal, but for some reason it all hits me hard. Tomorrow I graduate, and then I'm supposed to get on a plane and fly five hundred miles away from Jase. This wasn't supposed to happen. I wasn't supposed to fall in love a damn week before leaving. Hell, I wasn't supposed to fall in love at all. I have a dream, a goal. I've had a vision of what my future is supposed to look like since I was a kid. And nowhere in that future, am I supposed to fall in love with Jase.

"What's going on?" Nick asks as he turns onto his parents' street.

"Nothing." I shake my head.

"Don't lie to me, please. I've known you your entire life. Something is going on with you. It's like you're lost or something…"

"Lost?" I question.

"I don't know…I can't explain it. Something is off with you." He's not going to let this go, and he, of all people, deserves to know what's going on with me.

"I don't think I want to go to New York," I blurt out. Nick's head whips around to look at me. The car swerves a tad, but he quickly straightens it.

"What's going on? Are you scared? You know Killian will be in New York too. He's leaving right after his last exam."

"Killian hates me, and no, I'm not scared."

"Then what is it?" Nick parks the car but doesn't get out. "This is what you've wanted your entire life. Talk to me."

"I—I don't know what's going on with me." And that's the truth. Nick is right. I've wanted to be a model my entire life. I'm being given the opportunity of a lifetime. I can't just give that up for a guy I *might* be in love with. A guy I've only known for a week. But maybe once I talk to him, we can figure it out. Maybe he'll be willing to do the long distance thing or be willing to move with me. I need to talk to him. I won't know anything until I tell Jase the truth.

"Celeste," Nick says, "you're going to be amazing. You always are. Every modeling ad you've been in over the years…"

"Those were nothing," I whisper. They were just local shoots for department stores.

"Every play and musical," he continues, "everything you do, you excel at. You're going to take New York and the modeling world by storm. Okay?" He smiles at me.

I nod once, unable to speak. It means the world to me that Nick believes in me. I can't let him down. He put himself on the line by asking for this opportunity for me. I have to go. This is my future.

"You got this," he says with conviction. "And you know I'm always here for you, right? It doesn't matter if I'm hundreds of miles away. I'm here."

"Thank you." Nick pulls me into a hug, and the tears fall.

The minute we walk through the door, Victoria tells us that dinner is being served. We sit at the dinner table and make small talk while we all eat. When my mom is around Victoria, it's the only time she attempts to clean herself up and stay sober. She's dressed in a pair of jeans and a blue off-the-shoulder sweater. Her brown hair is brushed and straightened, and her makeup is done nicely. She also doesn't look like she's high or drunk. When my mom cleans up, she's beautiful.

"Are you excited for New York?" Victoria asks as she sips her coffee while we each have a slice of apple pie for dessert.

"New York?" my mom asks, confused.

"You didn't tell her?" Victoria chides. I was meaning to, but since I found out, I've either been with Jase or Nick every day. And when I have stopped home, she wasn't there. It seems we just keep missing each other. "Nicholas got her an internship in New York with Elite Modeling. She's leaving in a few days."

My mom's eyes dart from Victoria to me. "Wow, so you're leaving." It's not a question. She knows I am. Only I'm not so sure anymore. Before this last week, I would've had zero doubts about getting on that plane and never looking back. It's crazy how quickly one's priorities can change.

"Yeah," I admit softly, "I'm leaving."

"Congratulations, pretty girl. I'm very happy for you." Mom gives me a rare, genuine smile, and it makes me feel worse for even considering not going. As much as I care about Jase, I have to go to New York. The only way I can one day take care of my mom, take care of myself, is by going.

"Thank you," I say, forcing a smile on my lips.

After a few moments of uncomfortable silence, Victoria excuses us from the table so we can go over the last minute details for the celebration that will be taking place after my graduation tomorrow. Half the senior class is invited, even though I barely talk to any of them. They heard the party was being thrown by Nick Shaw's family, and of course, accepted the invite. Nick's dad, Henry, waves us off. "Good, I need to speak to Nick about some contract stuff anyway." Henry Shaw is a well-known sports agent, who owns an agency here in North Carolina. He's also Nick's agent.

After Victoria and my mom have gone over everything twice, my mom gives Victoria a hug and thanks her. "This is very sweet of you."

"Of course!" Victoria grins. "You know Celeste is like a daughter to me." She gives me a hug. "We'll see you tomorrow."

"You haven't been home in a few days," my mom says as we make our way to the front door. Nick and his dad have stopped talking, and Nick is now giving me a curious look as he stands and walks over to say goodbye. Every day we've hung out, he's dropped me off at my house. "Will you be coming home tonight?" she asks. My mom never asks about when I'll be home. I think her knowing that I'm leaving in a few days has her suddenly wanting to spend time with me before I leave. It wasn't said, but I think we both know once I leave this town, the chances of my coming back are slim.

"Yes," I tell her, ignoring Nick's glare. "I'll ride with you."

The ten-minute drive home is quiet. When we pull up to the trailer, a couple bikers pass by, and my mom's head turns. She does it anytime a bike passes by. She's checking to make sure it's not my dad. She's been doing it my entire life.

"You were only with my dad for a couple months, right?" I ask.

She looks at me stunned. I never ask about him. "Yes, two and a half months." She smiles sadly. "But I knew I loved him the minute I met him."

"How did you know?"

"It was the way he smiled at me. Like, without even

knowing me, I was already his entire world." A single tear rolls down her cheek. "I know it seems crazy, Celeste." More tears fall. "I tried to move on a few times…when you were younger. I just couldn't." She shakes her head. "My heart just can't let go of him."

"But what if he's moved on?" I ask.

"I don't believe it. He loved me with his entire heart. I don't know why he never came back, but I refuse to believe it's because he found someone else."

"I think…I've fallen in love," I admit out loud to my mom.

"Oh, sweetie," my mom coos. "What's his name? Can I meet him?"

"His name is Jase, and I don't know. I'm leaving in a few days to New York. It's like the worst timing ever. And on top of that, I lied to him…well, kind of lied. He thinks I'm in college and older than what I am." I leave out that he also has no clue that I live in a rundown trailer park on the other side of the tracks. "And he has no clue I'm leaving soon. I doubt he'll even forgive me for not being honest."

My mom takes my hand in hers, and my throat clogs with emotion. Over the years, I've dreamt of having boy talks with my mom, and of course, when we finally do, it's over a boy I'm going to have to walk away from, while also walking away from my mom.

"You need to talk to him, Celeste. Find him and tell him everything. If he loves you, he'll forgive you. He'll put all that shit aside and focus on what matters. If it's true love, you will find a way to be together. Every day I wish I would've spoken to Snake before he left. I wish I would've gotten more information, so I could look for him. Don't live with regrets."

"I hate that you're so heartbroken, Mom," I admit. "I want more for you. For you to fall in love, again, or for you to move on. Come to New York with me," I plead.

My mom gives me a soft smile. "I can't do that, pretty girl. New York is your dream. I need to stay right here. I have to believe one day Snake will return."

"It's been eighteen years," I point out.

"I know." She sighs. "I know I'm stupid to think that maybe one day he'll return, but I just can't stop hoping. Your heart can't help who it loves. I love Snake, and I can't just stop. Now, go find that boy and talk to him. You can take my car. Follow your heart, pretty girl."

"Okay, thank you." I lean over and give my mom a hug. I hate that she's been stuck in the same place for the last two decades. I hate that love did this to her. It's the reason I never wanted to fall in love, yet somehow it found me anyway. She's right. I need to talk to Jase. I need to follow my heart. I can't end up like my mom—always wondering what if.

I pull up to Jase's apartment complex and park my mom's car. I run up the stairs and knock on the door. When nobody answers, I check the time on my phone. It's already after ten o'clock. Maybe they're sleeping. Remembering there's a key under the mat Jase told me I could use, I pluck it out and unlock the door. The apartment is quiet, and I wonder if maybe I should've called first.

My need to talk to him wins out, and I head down the hall to his room. I can hear the shower running from outside the door. A smile forms on my lips. I can join him and then talk to him. But when I open the door, joining him is the last thing on my mind. Because laying in his bed is Amaya. Her fiery red hair is fanned out across his pillow. And she's naked. My heart feels like it's just been ripped out of my chest. The bathroom door opens and out walks Jase in nothing but a towel around his waist. Because of the location of the doors, he can't see me standing here. He can't see my heart breaking into a million pieces.

I want to yell at him for leading me on, making me believe we were something more. I want to scream at him for fucking his best friend only hours after making love to me. I want to curse him for not loving me the way I've fallen in love with him. But I don't do any of it. I followed my heart and this is where it led me to.

Reality. Smacking me right in the face. I was stupid to ever consider for a second I should choose a man over my future. That I should listen to my heart instead of my head. I watch as Jase gently pulls the blanket over Amaya's naked body, and then pushes several wayward strands of hair out of her face. Unable to be here for another second, I back away from the door and walk away.

I go back to my house. My mom is already asleep, and I don't wake her up. Instead, I call for a taxi, and write her an apology note. Because tomorrow when she wakes up, I won't be here. Not at my graduation, or at the celebration. I'll be in New York. But my heart, it will still be in pieces right outside Jase's bedroom door. Because like my mom said. You can't help who your heart loves. And my stupid heart loves a man who doesn't love me back.

Five

CELESTE

The Present

"If I gain much more weight before this wedding, I'm going to have to buy a new dress." Olivia pats her growing belly and giggles. "I don't know how much more the seamstress can stretch the fabric." We've just finished having dinner and are heading over to the valet so they can bring Olivia's car around. Over the last several months, weekly lunches-slash-dinners have somehow become a thing. It was hard at first to accept Olivia's and Giselle's friendship. I've never been the kind of girl to have friends—aside from Nick—but these two women have grown on me, and now, I actually find myself looking forward to us meeting up.

"It's because you're having a girl," Giselle says. "They carry high, making you look fatter."

"Wait." I stop in the middle of the sidewalk. "You didn't

tell me you're having a girl. So she finally cooperated?"

Olivia blushes. "Yes! She spread her legs during the ultrasound!" She giggles. "We actually just found out yesterday. We were planning to announce it at brunch this weekend."

"Congratulations!" I give Olivia a hug. "She's going to be the most spoiled little girl to ever walk this earth. How's Nick doing with the news?"

"He's freaking out," she says, handing the valet her slip. "Having a boy is one thing. A girl is apparently a whole other story. He's already planning all the ways to keep her locked up once she becomes a teenager."

I laugh at that. "That doesn't surprise me. He's probably thinking of all the women he slept with in his younger years." I flinch the second the words leave my mouth. I'm obviously still getting used to this whole friendship thing. "Shit! What I meant was…well…"

Olivia laughs. "I know what you meant. And you aren't wrong."

"Do you also know what you're having?" I ask Giselle, giving her a *don't lie to me* look.

"I do!" she squeals. "We're also having a girl."

"Oh my God!" I give her a hug. "I'm going to need to make a baby clothing line just to spoil all these babies!"

The three of us are laughing when Olivia says, "Hey, isn't that Jase?" My eyes follow her gaze, and sure enough, Jase is standing on the sidewalk hailing a cab. My mind goes back to a few months ago when I ran into him on Giselle's birthday at the tattoo shop. I never imagined in a million years I would ever see him again, let alone in the same city I'm living in. It's been well over a decade since I last saw him. Since I saw Amaya in his bed and him in nothing but a towel. I wish I could say the years have been bad to him, but that would be a lie. Jase looks nearly the same as he did all those years ago. The main difference being, he now looks less like a boy and more like a man. He's filled out, his muscles now more defined. His skin dons several new tattoos, and his face looks harder. No less beautiful. Just more guarded.

I stood in the middle of the tattoo shop frozen in place while Quinn spoke to Killian, who she apparently knows because he gets all of his work done here. And then Jase spoke. He made eye contact with me and asked if I was going to get a tattoo... as if it completely escaped his mind that over ten years ago he stole my heart then destroyed it.

"Are you going to finally let me mark this flawless skin of yours?" His finger runs up my arm, and I visibly shiver at his touch. His voice, a bit deeper than it was all those years ago, but no less smooth and captivating. And then I remember how it was that same smooth voice that made me fall in love with him. Only to have him break my heart shortly after.

"Don't touch me," I snap, finally gaining my composure.

Giselle and Olivia ask if I'm okay, both concerned with the way I'm suddenly acting. Olivia even suggests they go somewhere else. Then Nick speaks up, introducing Olivia to Jase.

"Nice to meet you," Jase says. "I've heard a lot about you." All these years, Nick and Jase have been keeping in touch? Nick has never mentioned him once.

Nick explains they played high school and college ball together.

"Did you go to school with them?" Giselle asks me.

"No, I went to public school," I tell her, trying to get my shit together. My heart is beating quickly. It's hard to breathe. I can't believe I'm standing here with him right now. Is this his shop? Does he own Forbidden Ink? How ironic is it, that in the end, we ended up living in the same city?

"You met him at the party I took you to, right?" Nick asks, shaking me from my thoughts. "I forgot about that. Do you two...know each other?" His eyes volley between Jase and me. I never told Nick about Jase. When I didn't show up to my graduation, Nick called me, and I told him I needed to go. I was ready to start my new life and didn't want to wait another second. My mom and Victoria were both upset, but eventually got over it. To this day, nobody knows why I left early.

"Yes, I did," I admit to Nick, "but I don't know him." Even to my own ears I sound like a woman scorned. I need to get myself composed. I am not that woman. Jase did me a favor that night. I should be thanking him. He reminded me that love is nothing more than a wasted emotion. Because of his indiscretion, I got off the plane in New York a hundred times more motivated to make something for myself. I would never become my mother. A brokenhearted woman pining over a man who clearly never loved her the way she loved him. I'm stronger and wiser because of Jase.

Quinn sneers. "Oh, that's rich! What's wrong? Is my brother not worthy of your memories? Did you block out everything that happened before you ran your stuck-up ass to New York? What are you even doing slumming it in East Village? It's a far ride from the Upper East Side."

"You know what"—I step into Quinn's face. She has no

89

idea what really happened—"I don't need to take this shit from you. I didn't know you guys worked here, and if I had, trust me, I never would've come."

"Well, now you do know. And FYI, my brothers don't just work here...they own the place. Don't let the door hit you on the way out," Quinn says before turning her back on me. I consider outing her brother. Telling her he's the reason I ran to New York, but I don't. For one, admitting he cheated on me will open up a can of worms that I'm not prepared to deal with. And two, I don't owe anybody an explanation.

As I'm about to leave, Jax appears, introducing himself to everyone. "Celeste, it's good to see you again," he says giving me a kind smile. "Although, with those billboards of you all over New York, I feel like I see you every day." He winks playfully, and I can't help but smile back at him.

"Great, if we're all done with this reunion, how about we figure out who's getting inked?" Jase says, sounding annoyed. I want to snap at the cheating asshole. Because fuck him!

"I want the nice guy," Giselle says, pointing to Jax. "It's my birthday. Livi, you can take the cranky one." Everyone laughs, and Jase cracks a small smile. One that makes the butterflies in my belly flutter. Damn him for giving me butterflies. He's a cheater, I remind my heart and head.

"I might be the crankier one, but I'm still the better artist. Ain't that right, Dimples?" He looks my way, and I shoot daggers at him. How dare he use the nickname he gave me. He lost all right to use that name when he chose to fuck another woman.

"Bullshit!" Jax laughs. "I'm older, wiser, and a better artist."

"Nah." Jase cackles. "Just older." He gives me another look, and I know I need to get out of here. My body and heart aren't accepting what my head knows. Jase is bad for me. He's a lying, cheating, asshole.

"I really need to get going," I announce, turning for the door. I give Giselle a hug and wish her a Happy Birthday. Olivia tries to stop me, but I tell her I have an early morning meeting and promise we'll do lunch this week.

Then I give Jax a quick hug. I'm not sure why. I think maybe it's because he's the only person in his family not acting like I'm in the wrong. "It was nice to see you again," I tell him before I run out the door. Nick, of course, follows after me, demanding to know what's going on.

"I'm just upset that I didn't know Jase works here!" I hiss.

Nick gives me a confused look. "You just said in there, you don't know him, so why would you even care where he works?" He's right. I know he is. I'm being ridiculous and throwing this way out of proportion. I know I am. But I can't help it. Every emotion, every painful feeling I've worked my ass off to bury is being dug up, and I can't stop it from happening. For every shovelful I throw back into the grave, two more are flying out and landing on my feet.

"We…" The need to confide in Nick is so strong, but I can't do it. It would mean admitting that I went against everything I believed in and fell in love. It would mean admitting that Jase broke my heart. I'm too worked up. I just need to get away from here. Thankfully a cab pulls up. "I need to go," I tell him, rushing to get into the cab and get away before he can call me out on my obvious lie.

Thinking back to that night in Forbidden Ink, a thought niggles in the back of my mind. I didn't put the pieces together before. I was too upset. But now, the way Jase is acting…it all makes sense. He has no idea that I know he cheated. I mean, how could he know? I left his apartment without making myself known. I switched out the ticket Nick had bought me as my graduation present and took the next flight out, never looking back. He probably thinks I left for New York without saying goodbye.

"It is Jase," Olivia says, answering her own question. And she's right, it is in fact Jase Crawford, standing on the edge of the sidewalk, waving his hand in the air as he tries to snag a cab. With the memory of what he did to me still fresh in my mind, I stalk over to him. It's about damn time he knows I'm aware of what he did to me all those years ago.

"Hey!" I scream over the blaring horns and people chattering about on the busy sidewalk. "Jase!" I yell to get his attention. He turns his head toward me, a slow smirk creeping up on his lips. My only thought is that I'm going to knock that damn smirk square off his face. This conversation is years overdue.

"Oh my god! Dad! It's Celeste Leblanc!" a tiny voice squeals. I look down, and for the first time, notice Jase is holding hands with a young girl. Because of his size, she was being blocked by his body. She grins wide, and letting go of Jase's hand, steps in front of me. "I am seriously your biggest fan!" Her green eyes glimmer with happiness. "Do you…do you know my dad?" She points back at Jase as I finally absorb her words.

Dad. She called Jase dad. He's her dad. I can't help as I trail my eyes over her. Red fiery hair. Emerald eyes. It might've been over ten years since I've seen her, but I'll never forget what *her* eyes and hair looked like. The girl standing in front of me is Amaya's daughter. No, correction. She's Amaya *and* Jase's daughter. While she has her mother's eyes and hair, she's naturally tan like Jase. She's dressed in an adorable red crop top that shows just a hint of her belly and black skinny jeans with rips in the knees, and she's sporting a pair of...are those Burberry rain boots?

"Hello?" She tilts her head to the side. "You *are* Celeste Leblanc, right?"

My name out of her mouth has me snapping to attention. "Yes, I am Celeste." I muster up the best smile I can.

"Do you know my dad?" she repeats.

"I..." I will myself not to look at Jase. "I do know your dad."

"Eeeek!" she squeals again, and I force myself not to flinch. Once in a while, I will come across a college-aged woman asking for an autograph, but I've yet to have someone this young recognize me. My clothing, jewelry, and makeup lines are mainly geared toward women in their late twenties and older—the businesswomen and the wealthy who can afford the price tag that comes with my brand.

"I am *literally* your biggest fan." Her eyes sparkle, and for a second I forget who she's standing with. "When I grow up I want to be just like you. I want to be a model and travel all over the world. I've watched every episode of America's Elite Model," she gushes. Last year I guest-starred on a television show where dozens of women competed to get a modeling contract with Elite—the same modeling company that gave me my start when I was eighteen. The winner was also given a spot in my clothing line launch a few months ago in Paris.

"Thank you," I tell her. When I give her a closer look, I notice she's wearing makeup, and it's done beautifully. I wonder if her mom did her makeup, and my heart drops at the thought as I remember who she is...who she belongs to. I suddenly want to get as far away from here as humanly possible, but instead I take a deep breath. It's not her fault who her parents are.

"My name is Skyla." She extends her tiny hand to shake mine. She's petite yet tall—all legs—so I can't tell how old she is, but she acts more like a young adult than a child. If I had to guess, I would say she looks to be about twelve... maybe thirteen years old. I do the math in my head. Did Jase know he had a daughter and not tell me? I take her hand in mine, and it's then I notice my hands are shaking. "Could I...could I get your autograph?" she asks, suddenly shy.

"Sure," I tell her, taking my hand back. "Do you have something for me to write on?" She looks back at her dad, and my eyes lock once again with his. He's frozen in place. He probably never imagined the two separate parts of his past would one day collide. We were only together for a short time. I doubt he's even thought about me over the years. I was probably nothing more than a blip in his radar. A week-long fuck. *Although, he did remember the nickname he gave me...*

Flustered, I begin to dig through my purse to find something to write with, or write on, when a hand taps my shoulder. I look over and Giselle is handing me a cocktail napkin. She smiles softly, and I silently thank her. When I look back to Skyla, she also has something in her hand.

"It's my sketch pad. I want to design clothes one day...like you. Will you sign it?" Oh, the irony of this situation. I take the book from her and open it up. The first page is a sketch of a gorgeous ballgown. The details so intricate and perfect, it looks like something an artist would draw.

"Did you draw this?" I ask in awe as I continue to flip through the pages of exquisite drawings, each one more beautiful than the last.

"I did," she says. I glance back up at her and she's beaming with pride.

"They're amazing. Keep it up and one day everyone will be wearing your designs."

Skyla's smile brightens even more, if that's even possible. "Thank you." She hands me a pen.

I sign my name on the inside cover with a couple words of wisdom, then hand it back to her. She opens it up and reads what I wrote. When she makes eye contact with me, she frowns, and I worry maybe what I wrote wasn't the right thing. I've never signed something for a young girl before, so I simply wrote to always follow her dreams.

"Could you sign something for my mom as well?" she asks softly. "I wish she were here to meet you."

"Umm... sure," I say, trying and failing to keep my voice light. I can feel everyone's eyes on me, especially Jase's, but I don't chance looking anywhere but at Skyla. If I look at Jase, I might just lose it. He still doesn't know I saw him with Amaya. Using the napkin Giselle gave me, I sign my name.

"Can you make it out to Amaya?" she says. "That's her name."

"Sure." I write her name on the top then hand it to her. When the napkin passes from my hand to hers, I make the mistake of looking at Jase. And I'm shocked to find that he's glaring at me. Glaring! Like I'm at fault here. What in the ever-loving fuck! He's damn lucky his daughter is standing here or I'd give him a piece of my mind.

"It was very nice to meet you," I tell Skyla, and with one last fake smile, I turn to walk away. Giselle and Olivia are both staring at me. I walk past them and can feel them on my heels. I don't even need to look back to know they're chomping at the bit to ask me questions. "Not now," I say as we walk back over to the restaurant.

Thankfully, the valet brings Olivia's car around and opens the door, forcing them to get in. I tell them I'll see them tomorrow and then take off. Only instead of taking a cab home, I decide to walk. It's only a few blocks away, but I take a detour through Central Park to clear my head. Tomorrow night is the bachelor-slash-bachelorette party. It was going to be hard enough to go knowing Jase might be there. But now that I know he's still with Amaya and they share a child, possibly one he had while he was hanging out with me… I'm strong, but I don't know if I'm strong enough to face that. Will Amaya be there? Nick and Olivia have never once mentioned her. I would've remembered her name being said. Maybe they're no longer together.

As soon as I get home, I change into a pair of my silk pajamas. Then, after pouring myself a glass of wine, head out onto my balcony. I want to text Nick and ask him about Jase and Amaya, but I know if I do, he'll come back at me with an entire slew of questions. So instead, I sit outside and drink my wine with the hope that once I'm drunk enough, I'll no longer think about Jase. And drunk I do get, but not even the insanely large amount of alcohol in my system can stop the thoughts of Jase.

The cab stops in front of Olivia's beautiful two-story home in Park Slope, complete with a white picket fence. I swipe my card, thank the cabbie, and get out. I glance around and take in my surroundings. I can't imagine ever not living in the city. Why live in New York if you can't experience the hustle and bustle of what makes New York, *New York?* But then again, I don't have children, nor will I ever. As I'm straightening the creases in my skirt, I spot Giselle and Killian walking down the street toward me. They live two houses down from Olivia and Nick. Giselle waves and gives me a knowing grin, telling me that she and Olivia are going to interrogate me the moment the three of us are in the same room. When I roll my eyes at her smile, Killian's lips curl into a half-smile. Ever since he and Giselle got together, he's been friendlier toward me, which is both strange and nice at the same time.

I wanted to meet them at the club where the party is being held, but Olivia insisted we meet here, have dinner, and then ride over together. I know this is just her way of cornering me about yesterday, but I have a hard time saying no to her. She's just too damn sweet. My suspicions are confirmed the minute we walk inside and Olivia starts in on me. "Okay, you've had enough space. I even gave you twenty-four hours, now spill."

"Yeah, the chemistry between you and Jase was so thick, I could barely breathe," Giselle adds.

"I think you're confusing chemistry for tension," I mutter.

"Oh no, there was sparks," Giselle says. "Sure, there was tension too, but the chemistry was definitely stronger."

"Did something happen between you two?" Olivia asks.

"Did something happen between who?" Nick questions. My eyes swing over to him. He's holding his son in his arms—Reed's head resting on his daddy's shoulder, his eyes barely open. Nick must be about to put him to bed before we leave. My mind goes to Jase. He's a dad. Does he live in the city, or in the suburbs? Does Amaya live with him? Does he make sure he's home every night to put his daughter to bed? I can't even remember a time when I was little that my mom put me to bed.

"We ran into Jase when we were leaving the restaurant yesterday," Olivia says. "He was with his daughter. She's apparently a fan of Celeste's."

"Oh, Skyla? She's a sweet kid," Nick says. "I can see that. From what Jase has said, she's really into fashion."

"You knew he has a daughter?" I snap, and instantly

regret it, knowing my harsh tone is going to make Nick ask questions.

"Yeah…" Nick gives me a confused look. "I *am* friends with him."

"I know," I say dumbly. "I need a drink." As I'm about to head to the kitchen, Nick's hand lands on my shoulder.

"Celeste, what the heck is going on?" I open my mouth, about to say something—what, I have no idea—but Nick adds, "And don't you dare say nothing. First you lost it at Forbidden Ink, and now you're acting like I committed a sin by not telling you a guy you barely know has a daughter. I want the truth. Did something happen between you and Jase?"

When I divert my eyes, they land on Killian, who's glaring intently at me, like he's waiting to hear my answer as well. So much for him being nicer…

"It doesn't matter what happened," I say. "It was a mistake. One I'd rather not think about ever again." And without waiting for anyone to ask me what I mean, I stalk out of the room and into the kitchen. I pluck a bottle of white wine out of the fridge and pour myself a glass. Giselle walks in after me, pulls a bottle of Patron out of the freezer and pours some into a shot glass.

"You might want this instead." She hands me the shot. When I eye her quizzically, she says, "Jase confirmed he will be at the party tonight."

Just. Fucking. Great. I set the wine glass down and take the shot from Giselle. Tilting my head back, I throw back the entire shot, reveling in the burning trail the alcohol leaves behind as it goes down my throat.

I'm sitting in the plush booth of the M Lounge, one of New York's most exclusive nightclubs, watching everyone I'm here with dance with someone else. Olivia and Nick are swaying to the music with their arms around each other. Giselle and Killian might as well be getting it on right there in the middle of the dance floor. My good friend, Mercedes—who is also a model—and her husband, Brandon—who plays for the New York Brewers—are grinding against one another. Several other friends of Nick and Olivia are dancing as well. All with someone in their arms. Me? I'm alone, sipping on a strawberry Mojito, while waiting for Chad to arrive. He's late. Again.

My eyes, of their own accord, find Jase and Jax, who are both leaning against the bar, each nursing a beer. We have a VIP area roped off with several booths to accommodate everyone who's here to help celebrate Olivia and Nick's upcoming nuptials—complete with our own waitress. While I'm sitting in one of the booths, sipping my drink, I notice that Jase hasn't once come near where I'm sitting since he initially showed up and said hello to everyone but me.

As I'm taking another sip of my drink, a cool pair of lips brush against my cheek. When I look over, I see Chad is here, still dressed to the nines in his three-piece suit he wore to work. It's not that I saw him leave for work this morning, it's just that he wears the same version of this suit every day. He sits next to me and grants me with a quick "hello" before he pulls his phone out from his jacket pocket and starts typing on it. I eye him for a long minute, annoyed as hell that he's already back to business, but too exhausted to argue about it. Instead, I down the rest of my drink and look back out to the sea of people on the dance floor. Only this time another couple has been added to the mix. Jase is holding hands with some blond-hair skanky-looking woman as they make their way to the middle of the club. She immediately turns her back on him and starts grinding her ass against his front. Her arms go up, raising her already short shirt to just below her tits. My eyes scan down her body. She might be dressed like trash, but there's no denying she's hot—in a two-bit stripper sort of way.

Before I can look away, Jase's eyes lock with mine, and for a brief second, it feels as if we're the only two people in the room. Only we aren't, and the woman rubbing all over him is proof. He doesn't smile, but he doesn't glare either. I can't quite pinpoint the look he's giving me. Is it apologetic? Regret? Maybe it's indifference. I'm not sure, but I have to force myself to look away before any of the emotions I've managed to keep hidden, surface.

"Dance with me," I murmur into Chad's ear. He glances up from what he's looking at and eyes me speculatively. "Please," I add for good measure.

He releases a frustrated sigh. "In a few minutes. I'm in

the middle of an important chat with a client in China."

"No, now," I demand, fully aware I sound like a bratty teenager.

Chad's brows furrow as he takes me in. "Are you drunk, Celeste?" he asks.

"No," I snap. "I just want to dance with my boyfriend. Is that too much to ask?" I stick him with a hard glare.

He sets his phone down on the table, but I notice he's still in the group chat. "What's gotten into you lately?" he questions. "You're acting like a petulant child."

"Because I want the man I'm dating to pay attention to me?" I huff.

"You've never acted like this before," he accuses, his tone a mixture of confusion and annoyance. He stares at me for a long second before he says, "You've changed. What's going on with you?"

I scoff as if I have no idea what he's talking about. Even though he's right. I have changed. And I hate it. I don't want to feel this way. I want my company and success to make me feel complete. I want my beautiful high-rise condo to not feel so lonely. I want my wealthy, hard-working boyfriend to be enough. But I can't stop all of my emotions from breaking through. I've felt myself changing for a while now, but I ignored it. And then I saw Jase, and every raw emotion I've kept buried deep, surfaced without my permission.

"I can't do this anymore," I whisper.

"What?" he asks, tilting his head to the side in confusion.

Unsure if his response is because he can't hear me over

the music, or if he doesn't understand what I'm trying to say, I repeat myself, this time louder. "I can't do this anymore." Then I add, "I'm not happy."

This time his eyes widen, indicating he heard and understood me. "What is it you want, Celeste?" he asks, clearly aggravated. Chad is a businessman. When there's a problem, he fixes it. But he can't fix this. He can't fix me. He can't fix us.

"I want..." I glance out at all the couples still dancing. Olivia has her head thrown back in laughter as Nick whispers into her ear. Giselle's eyes are filled with a mixture of lust and love as Killian holds her close to him, his fingers digging into her ass possessively. Even Mercedes, who isn't much different from me, is smiling as her husband holds her tight. My eyes land on Jase, who now has his back to me. The woman he's dancing with has her arms around his neck and her face plastered against his chest.

"Celeste," Chad says, bringing my attention back to him. "What do you want? What will make you happy?"

"Love," I say softly, yet loud enough for him to hear. "I want to be in love." Tears prick my eyes as memories of Jase holding me in bed surface. Of the way he made love to me. The way he would hold my hand and kiss me. It might not have been love on his end, but it was on mine. And while I have no desire to ever be with that two-timing asshole again, I want to feel what I felt when I was with him, again. I want to feel the butterflies attacking my belly and my heartstrings being tugged. I want someone to look at me the way Nick and Killian look at Olivia and Giselle.

Chad blinks slowly, his face completely devoid of all

emotion. He knows there's no fixing this problem. Our relationship has never been about love, and Chad isn't capable of loving anything but his business. No words need to be spoken to know we're over.

Six

JASE

I'm standing in the middle of the dance floor while a woman, who I'm not the least bit attracted to, grinds and shakes her ass all over the front of my body, while I chant over and over again in my head not look back and make eye contact with Celeste. The woman turns around and her arms snake around my neck. Her head falls to my chest and her thigh pushes through the middle of my legs as she attempts to rub her knee against my dick. I've had enough. When she asked to dance, I had just witnessed—who looks to be—Celeste's white-collar, rich-as-shit boyfriend approach and kiss her. He was sporting a suit, one that screams wealth and power, but looks douchy-as-fuck when worn in a club.

Needing to take my mind off them, I accepted this woman's proposition to dance, but now I'm regretting it. Because the longer I stand here and smell her cheap perfume, the more I crave the sweet scent of Celeste. It's been over ten years, and I only had her for a week, but I can still remember how she smelled—a perfect mixture of her natural scent, that sweet, rose lotion she would rub all over her body, and me. I've been with several women over the years, but not one of them smells like Celeste did. And that makes me wonder, if I walked over to the booth and dragged her away from her boyfriend, would she still smell the same? Or would it be different because she's no longer with me? She's no longer in my bed, in my clothes. She's older now, more refined, but just as fucking gorgeous as she was back then. Maybe the smell I remember is only because she was with me. If I brought her home and forced her to stay in my bed all weekend, could I get her to smell like I remember, again?

Unable to take another second of my back toward her, I peel the woman's arms off me and back away, turning my body toward where Celeste is sitting...only she's no longer there—and neither is the guy she was with.

"I need a drink," I tell the woman. Her face lights up, taking my words as an invitation to join me. "Alone," I add. Her lips turn down into a frown, but I don't care. I'm too annoyed to care.

"You sure?" She flutters her fake eyelashes. "I can give—"

"I'm sure," I say, cutting her off, not giving a shit what she can *give* me.

I stalk off the dance floor and over to the bar where my brother, Jax, is still nursing his beer. I lift my finger and the bartender comes over. "Double shot of Johnnie Walker

Black," I request.

"You got it." She gives me a flirtatious wink before sauntering away to make my drink.

"Damn, what's with the hard shit?" Jax asks.

When I shake my head, he says, "It doesn't happen to have anything to do with that brown-haired, legs for days, bombshell I saw sitting across the room with her uptight boyfriend, does it?" My gaze flies over to Jax, and he's grinning ear-to-fucking-ear. "Guess so."

"How do you know he's her boyfriend?"

"I don't. I just wanted to see if I could get a rise out of you." Jax laughs. "When are you going to admit she's the one that got away?"

The bartender lays a napkin down in front of me then sets my shot on top. Before it even touches the paper, I snatch it out of her hand and throw it back. "She didn't get away," I snap, slamming the glass down. "She left. And she was nothing more than a fuck."

Jax's eyes go wide, but he isn't looking at me. He's looking just past me. When I turn to see who or what he's looking at, I see Celeste standing there, frozen in place. I could be wrong, but I'm almost positive she has tears in her eyes. But before I can confirm it, she takes off back to the table, clearly having heard what I said. Although, I'm not sure why that upsets her. She chose to leave. And without even so much as a goddamn goodbye.

Seven

CELESTE

"She was nothing more than a fuck." The words pound against my heart, shattering what little is left of it, piece by piece. I would've thought his words wouldn't be able to hurt me. Once the heart is broken, it shouldn't be able to break again. It's not as if it's been fixed or even repaired. It's been damaged for the last ten years, just hanging together enough to continue to beat—enough to keep me alive. But it's not in any shape to do any other type of job like hold love. At least I didn't think it was…until now. Because as I walk back to the table, tears burning my eyes, I realize that my broken heart was intact enough to still feel. I was just simply protecting what was left of it. But his words…they were like a hammer to crystal. My fragile heart didn't stand a chance against that force.

I always assumed he felt that way about me. If he felt

more, he wouldn't have hooked up with Amaya while with me, right? But hearing the actual words come from his mouth, confirming what I always suspected, hurt worse than any assumption. *"She was nothing more than a fuck."*

When I get back to the table, Nick and Olivia are sitting in the booth, their limbs wrapped around one another. Her adorable baby bump hitting the side of the table. They're smiling and laughing, and I need to get away. I can't ruin this night for them. Next week they're going to get married and they deserve, more than anyone I know, to be happy and not be brought down by me. I'm about to grab my clutch and leave, figuring I can make an excuse through text, when Nick looks up and spots me. His brows furrow in confusion, then all too quickly, his eyelids form into thin slits, his entire face morphing into anger. I'm not sure what he sees, until my hand comes up to my cheek and I feel the wetness. I'm crying.

"What the hell happened?" he demands, which makes Olivia turn toward me as well. Her look isn't one of anger but sympathy. She's worried.

"Nothing," I say, reaching for my clutch. Nick eyes it and snatches it before I can.

"Celeste, don't fucking 'nothing' me," he growls. "What's wrong?"

"Nothing. Give me back my clutch."

"No, tell me what's wrong."

"Are you guys excited for your big day?" I ask, changing the subject.

"Yes, you know we are. Don't try to change the subject." Nick glares.

"How are classes going?" I ask, moving onto another safe topic.

"He graduated!" Olivia squeals, then throws her hand over her mouth.

"Brown-Eyes," Nick groans to his fiancée, "you weren't supposed to tell anyone." He's trying to sound mad, but everyone knows, in Nick's eyes, Olivia walks on water.

"Sorry." She bats her lashes playfully.

"Hey, don't apologize!" I shoot daggers at Nick. "We're best friends and you don't even tell me you've graduated? Why wasn't I invited to the ceremony?" My feelings are seriously hurt right now. When Nick announced he was going back to school to get his degree in literature, I was one hundred percent supportive. Why would he hide that he graduated?

"Nobody was invited," he admits. "I didn't want to make a big deal out of it." He shrugs. "Besides, it's not like I saw you graduate." He sticks me with a pointed look.

"Yeah, well…" I take a deep breath, not wanting to remember why I didn't attend my graduation or party afterward. And then it hits me… Needing to move our conversation into safer waters, I blurt out, "I'm going to throw you a graduation party once you guys get back from your honeymoon."

"Oh, yay!" Olivia claps excitedly. "And we can also celebrate that—"

"No more changing the subject," Nick says, cutting her off. "What's going on?" It's clear in his voice he's not going to let this go, but I really don't want to have this conversation.

"Should we do it at a restaurant or your house?" I ask Olivia, ignoring his questions.

Before she can answer, Nick says, "Stop. I'm not fucking kidding, Celeste. You don't cry. Ever."

"Give me back my clutch," I demand.

"After you tell me why you're upset enough to shed tears."

Unable to have this conversation sober, I down a shot that's sitting on the table. It burns like a bitch, but I more than welcome the discomfort. After I repeat this two more times, Nick pulls the tray out of my reach.

"You've had enough to drink," he chides. "Now tell me what's wrong."

I've never told anyone about Jase. No one. I left for New York without looking back and kept everything that happened between us to myself. But suddenly, as I look at Nick and Olivia looking at me, I feel like the weight is too much. I need to tell someone, and if I'm going to trust anyone to know my truth, it's them.

"I fell in love," I admit with a harsh breath as I fall into the chair across from them. Their eyes go wide, and Olivia moves from next to Nick over to me.

"With Chad?" Olivia asks, confused.

"No, we actually broke up tonight," I admit. "When I was eighteen. I fell in love...and then he broke my heart. And I...I just don't understand why I wasn't enough."

"Celeste," Olivia coos, reaching over and giving me a side hug. "You are enough. I don't know who this guy was, but fuck him." A burst of laughter comes out at Olivia's choice of words. She isn't one to just curse on the regular.

111

"I'm serious," she says, "and if he was here right now, I would tell him that myself."

I shift uncomfortably in my seat, and Nick eyes me curiously. He's probably putting the pieces together. Jase and me meeting ten years ago, me getting upset at the tattoo shop…

Giselle and Killian come over and sit next to Nick, both of them eyeing the situation, probably feeling the tension. "What's going on?" Giselle asks, concerned.

Before I can stop Olivia from talking, she says, "Some dickhead broke Celeste's heart ten years ago, and I was just telling her that if I ever see him, I'll punch him in the arm for hurting her." She glares, and I stifle my laugh at how adorable she is. Olivia wouldn't hurt a fly.

"Ten years ago…" Killian muses. His head tilts to the side slightly and then his gaze goes over my shoulder. I don't need to look back to know who he's looking at. He knows who broke my heart. How? I have no clue. But he knows. I saw it in his gaze when we were at dinner and Jase got brought up.

"Yeah, when she was eighteen," Olivia adds.

"I need another drink," I tell no one. Reaching over, I snag a shot from the tray and down it in one gulp. Giselle's brows raise. She knows too. She's perceptive. She saw the way I reacted to Jase coming tonight.

"What was his name?" Nick asks. "The guy who broke your heart."

"It doesn't matter," I tell him, but my words come out in a slur since I'm now well on my way to being drunk. Both Killian and Giselle eye me speculatively, but I ignore them.

"Give me back my clutch," I say to Nick.

"Give me a name."

"Fine. Keep my clutch!" I huff. "I'm going to go dance." Standing slowly, so I don't wobble or trip, I turn on my heel and walk away, not waiting for anyone to respond. The music is pumping through the speakers and the crowd has filled in. The club is now hopping. I head straight for the middle, where I saw Jase and that skank earlier, and find a guy who isn't attached to dance with.

One song blurs into the next. I have no clue how long I've been dancing for, but the alcohol has officially made its way through my body and I'm drunk and sweaty. The guy I've been dancing with pulls me into his body and whispers, "You're fucking sexy. Let's go." I attempt to shake my head no, but because of how drunk I am, I'm not sure it actually moves.

"Yes," he insists, taking my hand and pulling me off the dance floor.

"Ummm…" I begin, my fuzzy brain working too slow. "My clutch is over there." I turn to find where everyone is sitting, but the room spins slightly, and I stumble on my own two feet. I squint my eyes to find the table, but everything is kind of blurry. The guy ignores my attempt to speak, pulling me along, not even slowing down when I stumble once again.

"I…I need to find my friends," I slur, trying to pull on his hand to stop him—with no success. His grip is too tight. I have no clue where we're going or where we even are, but suddenly my body flies backward and hits a hard…wall? No, that can't be right. From the force of being pulled back, my

113

hand is yanked out of the guy's. When he notices, he looks back and his eyes go wide. I tilt my head to the side to see what's going on, and that's when I see him. Jase.

"What the fuck, dude," the guy hisses.

"She won't be going anywhere with you," Jase growls, and without even waiting for the guy to respond, he grabs my hand and pulls me in the opposite direction. I stumble slightly, but unlike the other guy, Jase notices and instead of ignoring it, he stops walking and turns around, then lifts me into his arms, bridal style. If I were sober, I would yell at him to put me down. He's the last guy I want to carry me. The last body I want to touch me. But I'm drunk, and his warm body feels good, even comforting. So, I just go with it, wrapping my arms around his neck. The room is now spinning, so I close my eyes and nuzzle my face into his chest. Taking a deep breath, I inhale his scent. He still smells the same as he did all those years ago. All man and comfort and warmth. I should be pushing myself away from him instead of snuggling closer. Being this close to him is not going to bode well for my emotional or mental health once I'm sober. But drunk me doesn't seem to care. So, instead of freaking out, I release a long sigh and allow the vibration of his body to lull me to sleep.

Eight

JASE

As I carry Celeste through the club, toward the VIP section, so I can get her shit and take her home, anger is emanating through my veins at the fucking asshole who thought he would take advantage of a drunk girl, at Celeste for putting herself in that situation in the first place, at her friends for not keeping a closer eye on her, and most of all, at me. Because there's no doubt in my mind that she's drunk because of the lies I spoke to my brother. Because even after all these years, I'm still butt hurt over her walking away without even so much as a fuckin' goodbye, like what we shared, what she gave me, didn't mean shit to her.

The second her friends spot her in my arms, they jump up to come to the rescue—too late, I might add. Nick and Olivia start spitting out questions, and Celeste's model friend—I can't remember her name even though we were introduced earlier—Benz, Cadillac, or some shit like that—reaches for Celeste, as if she's going to carry her, herself. With her still in my arms, I shake my head, not bothering to speak. It's too loud for anyone to hear me, and right now, I know if I do talk, shit will come out that I might regret later. I have one goal right now: to get whatever she came with and find out where she lives. My eyes lock with Nick's and he frowns. I'm not sure if it's at me, Celeste, the situation, or at himself, but right now it doesn't even matter.

"Is she okay?" Olivia asks. All I can do is shake my head. "She only had a few shots over here. I saw her dancing with that guy, but I don't think she had any more to drink."

"We can get her home," Nick offers. I shake my head again, still unable to speak without freaking the fuck out.

"Okay," Olivia says, "let me get her purse." She scurries around the table while everyone stays standing in place, unsure of what to do or say.

"She can come home with me," Mercedes—that's her name!—offers, and her husband nods in agreement. I simply shake my head again.

Olivia places her tiny purse on Celeste since my hands are currently full, then says, "I'll have Nick text you her address." She moves a few damp strands of hair from Celeste's face, but she doesn't even stir. She's out. "Can you please let us know when she's home safe? Maybe I should go too and stay with her." Olivia's eyes fill with tears. "I knew she was drinking, but I didn't know…"

"Hey," Nick says, "Celeste just doesn't drink…like ever." He gives me a hard stare. "She's a lightweight. We

116

should've cut her off. She was upset, so I didn't stop her. She's okay," he says to Olivia. "Jase will get her home and make sure she's okay. Right, man?"

"Yeah," I grunt. "I'll let you know," I tell Olivia.

"Okay, thank you. I'll go by and see her in the morning."

With one last nod, I carry her out of the club. Even though she weighs no more than a buck twenty dripping wet, because of her being out cold, she's like dead weight in my arms. So I'm grateful when I spot a cab parked in front of the club, and I'm able to sit down with her still in my arms. She shifts slightly, and I take a breath I didn't know I was holding. Pulling out my phone, I find her address in a text from Nick. I relay it to the cab driver and he takes off. When we arrive, we're in front of a huge building directly in front of Central Park. I double check the address and throw a twenty at the driver, not needing change. I walk through the lobby and the concierge eyes me cautiously. Something I'm used to. It doesn't matter where I go. With the tattoos covering my body, I get noticed.

"I need to bring her up to her place," I tell him. "I imagine she has a key in her purse, but I can't grab it."

He nods once. "What's your name?" I give him all my information, glad Celeste lives somewhere safe, somewhere that cares about her well-being. Once I'm done, he scans his card so the elevator opens, gives me Celeste's floor and number, and hands me a spare key to her place.

"Thank you."

Once I get us inside, I take her straight to her room. The

doors are all open, so it's easy to spot which one is hers. I lay her in the middle of her big bed and she looks so tiny. Pulling off each of her heels, I drop them to the floor. She's dressed in a tight black dress, and I can't imagine it's comfortable, but I'm not about to take her clothes off. Instead, I pull the blankets out from under her and cover her. Celeste stirs, her eyes opening slightly.

"Stay, please," she slurs. "I don't want to be alone." Her eyes are already closed, and I doubt she'll even remember what she said, but I still stay. I use the excuse that I need to make sure she's okay before I go. I spot a chair in the corner of her room, but it's too far away to see her in the dark. So, I toe off my shoes and climb into the bed next to her. I watch her sleep for a few minutes before she stirs once more.

Her eyes flutter open once again. "Jase?" she croaks.

"Yeah, I'm here." I run my fingers through her hair and her eyes roll back slightly.

"What does she have?" she whispers.

"Huh?" I question, unsure of what she's talking about.

"I could've given you it," she slurs, "whatever you wanted." I have no clue what she's talking about, but now isn't the time to ask. She's drunk and barely conscious.

"Shh…go to sleep, Dimples."

Her lips turn down into an adorable pout as she mumbles, "But I don't want this dream to end." I continue to play with her hair until her breathing evens out and I know she's back to sleep. Pulling my cell phone out, I send a text to Jax and Quinn to let them know where I am and that I'll be home before Skyla wakes up. And then for the next few hours I watch Celeste sleep and wonder what our life would be like had she not left me.

"Dad! You're home!" Skyla bounds toward the front door, her errant red curls bouncing along the way. She wraps her arms around my waist and gives me a hug. "Where were you? It's not like you to be out all night." She smirks slyly. "Were you...out on a date?" She waggles her eyebrows playfully.

My little girl is growing up too damn fast and is becoming way too perceptive. My hope was to get home before she woke up, but when I sat down on Celeste's bed to watch over her, I ended up passing out. I woke up to my phone going off with a text from Quinn, letting me know Skyla was up and asking questions. After leaving a bottle of water and two Advil on Celeste's nightstand, I left her sleeping to come home. Since the day Skyla became mine, I've done everything in my power to provide a stable home for her and that includes being home every morning when she wakes up and being the one to put her to bed every night. At thirteen years old, she technically doesn't need me to tuck her in, but I still want to be there.

"No, I wasn't out on a date. A friend of mine wasn't feeling well, so I was taking care of her," I tell her, trying not to lie too badly. Quinn comes from around the corner and gives me a curious look but doesn't say anything.

"If you're good, I'm going to head out," Quinn says.

"Sky, your pancakes are ready." She shoots my daughter a wink, and Skyla heads straight to the kitchen to eat her breakfast, leaving Quinn and me alone.

"Jax already told me you took Celeste home," Quinn says, judgment evident in her tone. "It's been what...ten years since she left you, Jase?"

"Eleven," I murmur. "It's been eleven years. And I was just making sure a woman who drank too much got home safe," I say nonchalantly, but even to my own ears, I sound like I'm full of shit. "How did everything go here?" I ask, changing the subject.

"Good. We hung out and watched a movie. Skyla insisted we watch Pirates of the Caribbean, so..." She shrugs a shoulder.

"Yeah, I'm sure." I laugh. "More like, you begged and my daughter took pity on you." Quinn is obsessed with the Pirates of the Caribbean movies. The woman has probably watched all of them a hundred times. She even has a tattoo of Jack Sparrow on her thigh.

"Semantics." She rolls her eyes playfully, knowing it drives me nuts. Especially since my daughter does the same thing, having had picked up on it from her aunt years ago.

"I need to get home. Rick flew in this morning, and I want to make him breakfast." She winks, then grabs her purse off the couch as I playfully gag at her insinuation of what she really wants to do with him. Rick is her boyfriend of about six months. I'm not happy with how fast things are moving with them, but my sister is a big girl, and I have to let her make her own mistakes. When we first moved to New York, Quinn, Jax, and I all lived together in a small apartment. But once the shop started to make decent money, we moved into a bigger home in Cobble Hill—a smaller, less busy neighborhood in Brooklyn. While Jax still lives here with Skyla and me, a few months ago, Quinn and her boyfriend decided to get their own place—an expensive high-rise condo in the Upper East Side. He's some type of corporate mogul, who owns several businesses all over the world. It seems like he's gone more than he's home, but Quinn doesn't ever complain, so I keep my opinions to myself. Plus, while he's traveling, Quinn will often spend the night here with us, so that works out well for me, and Skyla loves spending time with her Aunt.

"Dad, your pancakes are getting cold," Skyla yells.

"Coming, Sky," I shout back. "Thanks for keeping an eye on her," I tell my sister.

"Any time," she says. "Oh!"—she stops in her place and turns around—"Rick has to fly out next weekend for a last minute business deal, so he won't be able to attend the wedding with me after all." She frowns. "Would you mind if I tagged along with you?"

Olivia and Nick's wedding is at the Yacht Club in the Hamptons, and they both insisted Skyla was more than welcome to join. So I thought it would be a nice weekend getaway. It's the summer in New York and the place we're staying at has a nice pool Skyla will love to swim in.

"Of course," I tell her. "Jax is leaving Gage to run the place, so we can all drive over together." Gage is one of the tattooists that works for us. When the shop took off, Jax and I couldn't handle the place on our own any longer, so we hired two other artists—Gage and Willow. Quinn has also been helping us out while we look for a fulltime receptionist. She's building up her photography company, which means she's able to make her own hours.

After Quinn leaves, I head back into the kitchen to join Skyla for breakfast. She pushes the butter and syrup my way, and when I look up, she's smiling nervously.

"What's up?" I ask, knowing my daughter. That smile means she wants to ask me for something.

"I was thinking, once school is out for the summer, we could go visit Mom. I really want to give her the signed paper Celeste gave me. I still can't believe I met her. She said she knew you… How do you know her? Why didn't you tell me? That's something super important. She's the best model in the industry…in the entire world."

I tune out her rambling, stuck on the words that she wants to go visit her mom. It's been a little over a year since the last time we went to visit Amaya. While I would never stop my daughter from visiting her mom, I hate going there. I hate Skyla seeing her mom in that state. Every time we go to visit her, she ends up afraid and upset, asking questions I don't have the answers to. In the past, because she was so young, once we were back home, she would forget how scared and upset she was and ask to visit her mom again. Now, though, she's getting older and I'm not sure whether she'll be scared and upset or understand and be okay. It shouldn't be this way. No child should have to visit their mom in that condition. But it's out of my hands. I can't control the decisions her family makes. I'm just grateful that, for the most part, they leave Skyla and me alone.

"Dad…" I'm not sure how many times Skyla has said

my name, but by the annoyed look on her face, it must've been a few times.

"Sorry, yeah, we can go visit your mom," I tell her, ignoring the second half of her question about how I know Celeste. I'm not ready to go there, especially not with my daughter. "I'm not sure when, but we'll go for sure this summer."

"Thanks, Dad." Skyla jumps out of her seat and comes around the table to give me a hug.

Nine

CELESTE

"Thank you, again, for coming with me." I squeeze Adam's hand and he smiles softly at me, knowing how much him being here truly means to me. I met Adam several years ago when he was just beginning his modeling career. We clicked immediately and a wonderful friendship blossomed. Over the years, Adam's and my friendship has turned into so much more. He's like a brother to me. When Chad and I broke up and I knew I was going to have to attend this wedding alone, Adam insisted he join me so I wouldn't be alone. His boyfriend, Felix, is one of the top photographers in the business and is away on a shoot, so it worked out perfect.

"You know I wouldn't be anywhere else." Adam leans over and gives me a kiss on my cheek. "Now, get your butt inside and get dressed. I can't wait to see you walk down the aisle." He shoots me a flirty wink and I laugh humorlessly.

"Take pictures. It will probably be the only time I ever walk down an aisle." I roll my eyes, trying to play my insecurities off, and Adam frowns.

"If I didn't know better, I would think the idea of you *not* getting married is what's upsetting you. Has my little ice queen thawed?" He gives me a quizzical look, but I don't answer him. Instead, I turn to head to the room where all the women in the wedding are getting ready.

"See you soon!" I call out over my shoulder.

"This conversation isn't over," Adam yells back through a laugh.

I'm dressed in a simple royal blue V-neck halter gown with a floor length charmeuse skirt that has a slit running up the side. It's tasteful and elegant. I must admit, Olivia did a fabulous job when she chose my dress. I've seen enough wedding designs to know most bridesmaids end up in something ugly because the bride is too afraid to be outdone. The other women are in something similar, each dress varying slightly. Olivia, of course, looks absolutely stunning in her wedding dress. It's a white strapless gown with a fitted bodice and a wide, full tulle skirt that shows off her adorable baby bump. She truly looks like a Disney Princess. Giselle and Corrine, her stepmother, dote on her while the hair and makeup team finish getting her ready. I use this time to slip out and visit Nick. I knock once on the door and Killian opens it.

"Celeste," he says politely with a curt nod. "You look beautiful." I'm not sure I will ever get over the shock of Killian being nice to me. So, after I stare at him stunned for a second, I smile and thank him.

"I'll give you two a moment alone," Killian says before making himself scarce.

"Celeste," Nick says, giving me a hug and a kiss on my cheek. "You look gorgeous as always." He hands me a small box. "Thank you for doing this."

"Of course," I say back, taking in his fitted tuxedo. His tie is royal blue, matching the bridesmaids' dresses and the jewels in Olivia's princess tiara. As I stare at my best friend, I can't help but get choked up. While I'm extremely happy for him, I'm also sad. It wasn't too long ago Nick and I were engaged and I was planning our wedding. I know we never would've worked out, and I don't view Nick as anything more than a friend, but being with him kept what's left of my heart safe. I didn't run the risk of it being stomped on or broken any more. Now it feels as though the tiny slivers of my heart that are still left intact are out there for anyone to take and destroy.

"Thank you," he says softly, and I give him a confused look.

"You already thanked me." I laugh.

"Not for bringing Olivia my wedding gift." He shakes his head. "For being my best friend. For being you." His eyes gloss over with unshed tears. "You know

I'm always going to be here for you no matter what, right?"

"I know." I nod. "I'm so happy that you found your one." Tears of my own surface and I blink several times, willing them away, so they don't ruin my makeup.

"You know it's time, right?" Nick says. "To find yourself someone to love."

"I don't think I can do it," I admit quietly. "I don't think I know how to."

"You do," Nick says with a small smile. "You just have to let go of all that hurt."

"How?" I ask. "How did you let go of it all?"

"I had no choice," he says, his smile widening. "I had to make room in my heart for Olivia and Reed."

"Yeah, well, my problem is a little different," I blurt out. My heart isn't just filled with hurt. It's damaged beyond repair. Nobody wants something that's been used and abused, when they can have something new and shiny and perfect.

"How?" he questions, and I shake my head.

"It doesn't matter." I flick away a traitor tear and plaster on a smile. "Today is your big day. Don't let my problems bring you down." I shake the box he handed me. "I will make sure Olivia gets this."

I turn to walk away but Nick catches my wrist. "Was it Jase, Celeste? Did he break your heart?"

The tears I worked so hard not to let fall, do, as I nod my head once and whisper, "Yes."

Nick turns me around to face him, and with a deep frown asks, "What happened?" I can see it in his features, hear it in his tone, he isn't going to take a brush-off. We're no longer in a crowded, loud club surrounded by our friends. It's just Nick and me, and my truth.

"I-I fell in love with him. It was stupid, really. It was only a few days, and I was young…" I try to downplay my feelings, but Nick's head tilts slightly and I know he isn't buying it. "Anyway, I was going to give up the summer internship to stay with him." Nick's eyes widen at my words. "But when I went to talk to him about it, I caught him with another woman." I shrug.

"Fuck, Celeste." Nick pulls me into a hug. "Say the word and he's gone."

"No, it's okay," I tell him as we pull away. "It was a long time ago and clearly all the feelings were one-sided. What's done is done."

"Except it's not," Nick points out. "Whatever happened between you two has been lingering and festering for years. Maybe it's time you two talk and get some closure."

"You're right," I tell him. And he is. I've spent too many years allowing my broken heart to steer my life. I meant what I said when I broke things off with Chad. I want to find love, and in order to do that, I need to have a whole heart to give someone, and I can't do that as long as I allow mine to remain broken. Now, I just have to work up the courage to talk to Jase.

After giving Nick one last hug, I head back over to Olivia's room to give her Nick's gift. It's a beautiful necklace with a charm of an open book on it.

On the back is their wedding date with an inscription

that reads: *This isn't the epilogue... it's the first chapter of a new book.*

The wedding was beautiful, full of happy tears and laughter. Happy tears, when Olivia and Nick said their vows, promising to love each other as they continue to write their story. Laughter, when Reed insisted on joining them at the alter as they kissed.

Once they were pronounced husband and wife, we spent the next hour taking pictures, and then came the reception. So far—through the couple's first dance, the sit-down dinner, the toasts and speeches, and cutting of the cake—I've managed to successfully avoid Jase. Nick and Olivia have announced their departure, thanking everyone for joining them, and I've just taken a deep breath, feeling confident that I might make it through the wedding *and* reception without running into Jase. But apparently my confidence was premature, because I haven't even finished exhaling, when I spot a beautiful red-head, dressed in a pale pink shift dress, heading straight over to me. She locks eyes with me, grinning wide, and I know my luck has run out.

"Celeste!" Skyla screeches, and Adam gives me a curious look. "You're here! Wow! Your dress is gorgeous. Not quite as beautiful as your spring couture line, but still gorgeous, especially for a bridesmaid's dress. Have you seen some of the ones brides pick out? I swear they design them ugly on purpose, so they can't outdo the bride." She shivers dramatically, her nose scrunching up in disgust, and I giggle, having thought the same thing earlier. "It *is* possible to go simple *and* pretty without outshining the bride." When she stops speaking, her eyes find Adam and she smiles, as if she's just now noticing I'm not sitting alone.

"Hello," she says, lifting her chin a tad and extending her hand. "I'm Skyla." Adam takes her hand in his, and I notice her nails are done. They aren't fake, but they're long and neat, and she's sporting a french manicure.

"Skyla, this is my friend Adam. He's a model."

"I know." She nods. "I've seen you in ads for Ralph Lauren, Tom Ford, Gap, and for Celeste's new clothing line," she says matter-of-factly. Adam's eyes light up, and I grin. Girl knows her stuff.

"I was," Adam says, extending his hand. "It's nice to meet you. Are you a model?" he asks.

"Not yet," Skyla answers. "Dad says I'm too young"— she rolls her eyes—"but I plan to be. I also want to design jewelry and makeup and clothes like Celeste does, but I'll have a children's and teen line as well." She nods matter-of-factly. "You have no idea how hard it is to find stylish clothes when you're a kid, and being a teenager isn't much better. Designers don't seem to understand that not all teens want to dress trashy." Taking a closer look at Skyla's outfit, I notice the tiny gold tulle layers and the embellished gold sequin flowers on her dress. Then my gaze goes down to her matching pale pink ballet flats. I'm not sure who she's wearing, but I know her outfit isn't cheap. The girl seriously has good taste in fashion.

I can't help the laugh that escapes when I think about how ironic it is that Jase's daughter is the exact opposite of him. I can't even imagine how he deals with her. Then it hits me... he probably doesn't. It's probably all her mom... Amaya. And with that sobering thought, my laughter comes to an abrupt halt.

"I agree," Adam says to Skyla. "Class over trash any day."

When he shoots me a confused look, silently asking who this girl is, I say, "Skyla is *Jase's* daughter." It takes him a second, but I can tell when it all clicks. He's one of the few people who know my entire story. "Is your dad here?" I ask Skyla. The last thing I need is to run into Jase...and his date.

"He's getting us another piece of cake." Skyla frowns. "I wish my mom could be here. Red Velvet is her favorite."

"Why couldn't she be here?" I ask before I can stop my nosiness.

"She's sick," Skyla says with a frown. Then, as if she's just remembered something, her face lights up. "My dad said I can give her the paper you signed. We're going to visit her this summer, once school's out." She smiles softly. Her words swirl in my head and it hits me that she said they're going to visit her this summer. They must not be together after all. If they were, they wouldn't be going to visit her. Well, serves him right. But then I feel bad because, if they aren't together, that means Skyla is part of a broken family, and I wouldn't wish that on any child.

"Will you be in Paris for Fashion Week?" Skyla asks.

"Leblanc will be participating, but I won't personally be there. I'm actually partaking in a new fashion show, right here in New York."

"Oh! The Global Fashion Extravaganza?" she asks. "I heard it's going to be amazing! That it could even possibly replace Fashion Week."

Adam laughs. "Well, look at you! All in the know. You should be interning at Leblanc." He gives me a knowing look, which I ignore.

"I'm still in school," Skyla says with a shrug.

"You're right," I tell her, "It is the Global Fashion Extravaganza, also known as GFE, but we're hoping, not to replace Fashion Week, but give fashion four seasons instead of two. There's also a huge charity fashion show on the last day."

"I'm planning to live-stream it the entire week," Skyla says, excitedly. I almost tell her I could get her tickets, but remember Jase is her father, and the last thing I want to do is weave my life in with his—even if his daughter is completely amazing.

"Skyla, there you are!" Quinn exclaims. She glances from her niece to me and glares. "You can't take off on your own."

"I'm not a child." Skyla scoffs. "I'm thirteen." Thirteen... I quickly do the math in my head, but it doesn't add up. That would mean Skyla was two years old when I met Jase. He had a daughter and didn't mention it? He introduced Amaya to me as his *friend*...so what were they? Friends with benefits? They had a daughter together, but weren't together... *Just sleeping together apparently*...

"Celeste," Quinn says curtly, knocking me out of my thoughts.

"Quinn," I say back. Then to Skyla, I say, "I need to use the ladies room before I leave, but it was wonderful to see you again. Enjoy your cake, sweet girl." I stand and bend at the waist to give Skyla an air kiss to each of her cheeks. She reciprocates, acting more like an adult than her real age of thirteen. And as I walk away, I can't help but wonder what it would be like if Skyla was mine and Jase's instead of Amaya's and his.

With that thought, I change course, suddenly in need of a stiff drink. The champagne is delicious, but with the thoughts swirling around in my head, I need something stronger. I tell the bartender I don't care what she brings. When she returns, she sets down the shot and says, "One red-headed slut." I bark out a loud laugh at the name. How fitting. I down the alcoholic beverage and ask for another.

Before she walks away, a good-looking gentleman approaches and says, "Make that two."

"But you don't even know what I'm drinking," I sass.

"If you're drinking it, I'm sure it's top shelf. I can't imagine you wasting your time on anything less."

A minute later, she returns with our drinks. "Two red-headed sluts." She grins and the gentleman laughs with a shake of his head. We each take a glass and clink them against each other before we throw our shots back.

"Real nice," I hear a voice hiss. When I turn around, I spot Jase. At one point he must've been in a suit, but now, his jacket is missing and his powder blue button down shirt is rolled up at the sleeves, exposing all of his sexy-as-sin tattoos. His hair is gelled neatly to the side and peeking out of his collar are a few more intricate tattoos. He screams sex and bad boy and cheater. "You are aware my daughter is a redhead as well," he points out.

"And you do know she isn't the slut I would be referring to had I actually picked the drink." I wave him off. The bartender, God love her, brings me over another shot, which I down as quickly as the last two before I add, "She picked the drink, not me, but I must say it is rather fitting."

I slam the glass down and walk away from Jase. I don't realize he's following me until I enter the ladies room and hear the door close and the lock click behind me. When I whirl around, Jase is standing there with his arms crossed over his chest, his muscular forearms on display.

"Jealousy doesn't look good on you," he says with a smirk.

"Fuck you," I spat.

"Tsk, tsk, that's not very ladylike, Celeste. What would all your admirers think if they heard you talking like trailer trash instead of high class?" They would probably think it makes more sense since that's where I come from...

"For your information," I hiss, ignoring his question, "I'm not jealous."

"As you shouldn't be." Jase shrugs nonchalantly, but when he speaks, his words are anything but. "You have everything you could ever want, right? Money, fame, status. You achieved every dream you ever dreamt." He steps closer, and I back up, my butt hitting the edge of the marble counter.

"Maybe you should focus on your perfect little family and not worry about what I have." I wait to see if he confirms or denies what I'm implying, but he does neither, giving nothing away.

Instead, he simply laughs, but it comes out all wrong. It doesn't sound melodic and carefree and beautiful like I remember it sounding all those years ago. No, this laugh is devoid of all humor and happiness. He places his hands on either side of my body, caging me in. "The perfect family?" He chuckles darkly. "You have no fucking idea what you're talking about, Celeste." When the coolness of his breath hits my ear, I let out a shaky breath. It's been too long since I felt Jase's body against mine. He's so close. His groin rubs against my front, and I shiver in response. *Damn traitor body.*

"It's been eleven years, yet your body still responds to mine," he murmurs, backing up slightly, his hazel eyes meeting my onyx ones. Then his eyes travel a few inches south, landing on my mouth. His tongue darts out slightly, wetting his lips. He's going to kiss me. I can feel it in my bones. I should stop him. Push him away. But I don't. And just as I predicted, seconds later, his mouth crashes against mine, roughly. Our tongues meeting and dueling with one another. Jase's fingers dig into my sides as he lifts me onto the counter. My legs wrap around his waist as my fingers grip the back of his hair, pulling him closer to me.

As our kiss deepens, moans release from the both of us, echoing in the otherwise silent bathroom. His hands glide up my thighs, my dress bunching up at my waist. I release his hair, undoing his button and zipper. Using my heel, I push his pants and boxers down as Jase pulls my lace panties to the side, pushing his fingers into me. A loud sigh escapes my lips as my head goes back, hitting the mirror. His lips find my neck, and as he trails soft, wet kisses across my now-heated flesh, he pulls his fingers out of me, jerks me forward, and thrusts his entire hard length into me. He feels so good, but different…something about him is different. Is that…Is he…pierced?

"Fuck, Celeste," Jase growls, pushing my thoughts away as he fucks me hard and deep. His fingers are digging into my sides. It should hurt, but it only adds to the pleasure. I feel my orgasm building with every thrust of his hips, and then he hits my sweet spot.

"Yes, right there!" I scream. Jase listens, hitting it again and again. And before I know it, my entire body lets go, and I come harder than I ever have before. My body shakes as my orgasm continues to rip right through me. Jase nuzzles his face into my neck, his lips sucking on my sweaty skin as he follows right behind. My eyes are closed, and I take a deep breath, enjoying the moment of pure bliss I feel.

But then he stills, his now semi-soft dick still in me, and reality hits. I just let Jase fuck me…without a condom. I'm on the pill, but that's not really the point. I'm about to say something when Jase speaks first.

"Fuck, this was a mistake." I might've been thinking the same thing, but fuck him for saying it first. I push him back and his dick slides out—the mess of what we just did drips out of me.

I can't help the maniacal laugh that escapes my lips as Jase stares at his cum dripping down the inside of my thigh. Reaching over, I grab a paper towel to wipe it up.

"That shouldn't have happened," Jase says. "I don't cheat." And with those words, I snap my head up to give him my full attention, my focus on cleaning up no longer a priority.

"Good to see you now have morals," I say, laughing even harder, "but you don't have to worry." I jump down off the sink and throw the paper towel into the garbage. "My boyfriend and I broke up last week."

"And the guy you're here with?" he questions.

"Just a friend."

I turn around slowly and lock eyes with Jase, realizing I just had sex—granted, it was hate sex, but still sex—with the man who cheated on me and broke my heart. And then his words sink in. He said he doesn't cheat. I assumed he was referring to me being in a relationship, but he could've been talking about himself as well. I don't even know if he's with anyone. Does he have a girlfriend? A fiancée? Oh my god, is he married? Suddenly, I feel cheap and dirty and want to take a long, hot shower to get Jase off my flesh.

"And what about you?" I whisper. If he could cheat on me, who's to say he wouldn't do it to someone else. We might be older, but there's a reason for the saying: once a cheater, always a cheater…"Are you with anyone?" Based on what his daughter said, I assumed he was single. But you know what they say about people who assume…especially with his track record. I quickly glance down at his left hand, relieved that there's at least no ring on his finger.

"What if I am?" His brows rise to his hairline.

"Then it wouldn't surprise me that you have no problem fucking someone else." I shrug my shoulders with all the confidence I don't have and walk out the door.

Ten

JASE

"Then it wouldn't surprise me that you have no problem fucking someone else." I can't get Celeste's words out of my head. They don't make any sense. Why would she believe I would ever be okay having sex with someone while with someone else? I wanted to chase her down and ask her what she meant by that, but when I got outside, she was nowhere to be found. My daughter and Quinn were, though, and while Quinn kept giving me a knowing look, like she could tell something went down, she couldn't voice her suspicions because of Skyla being with us. During the elevator ride up to our room, Skyla went on and on about how she ran into Celeste and met her model friend Adam. She didn't even notice that, while I was gone for a while, I didn't return with the cake I originally set out to get us.

After Skyla showered and went to bed, I grabbed a

bottle of Johnnie that the resort keeps in stock to purchase and took it out onto the terrace with me before Quinn could start in on her interrogation. My thoughts couldn't escape what Celeste and I did...what she said afterward. Over the years, I've had my fair share of one-night stands. I've even been in a couple short-term relationships. But not once have I ever went in raw. No glove, no love. Every man knows that rule. Sure, when we were together before, she was on birth control, but I don't know her situation now, and I definitely don't know who she's been with.

Yet, I didn't even think twice about going in without a rubber—just like all those years ago. From the moment I laid my eyes on Celeste at that party, it's as if she somehow bewitched me. I don't think logically or rationally when she's near me. My dick and my heart seem to be the only two organs that function when she's around.

The longer I drink, the more my mind replays tonight. The way Celeste felt with her legs wrapped around me. The way she tugged on my hair, and the way her tight cunt clenched around my cock as I fucked her deep. I couldn't even tell you who initiated it, probably me, but I can tell you that, even though it's been eleven damn years since I've been with her, it felt as if no time had passed.

While her body is less girl and more woman, her soft, pouty lips haven't changed a bit. The way she kissed me, as if everything of mine was hers for the taking. She owned my body, heart, and soul all those years ago, and tonight, I realized she could easily take it all again. But the question is, could I let her? Would I even have a choice? First things first, I needed to find out why she left me all those years ago without even so much as a goodbye. The way she's acted every time I've run into her, it's as if I'm in the wrong, which makes no sense. She's the one who lied about her age, and where she went to school, and about her damn modeling gig in New York. Hell, she's the one who got a plane and left me.

I should be the one that's pissed—and I am. But at the same time, all those damn feelings I had are coming back in full swing. No woman has ever affected me the way Celeste does. With a single look, a simple touch, she knocks me off my game. Over the years, I thought Skyla being so into modeling was God's way of laughing at me, mocking me. Of all the things my daughter could be into, of course she has to be into fashion—sketching, drawing, designing, modeling. She loves it all. And for most kids, that would mean observing the latest trends from afar. But for Skyla, because her grandparents are ridiculously wealthy, it means she's able to enjoy the luxuries of name brand clothes up close and personal. Some days, my daughter puts on outfits that cost more than the monthly payment on the mortgage for the townhouse we live in, which is something I try not to think about. Because, despite me not wanting my child to wear shit like Burberry and Ralph Lauren, Amaya's parents, Monica and Phil, asked that I accept the gifts they send her every month. It was one of their stipulations when I told them I wanted to move to New York. Most grandparents would ask to visit every so often, or to receive phone calls, but not them. Their way of showing love is through materialistic possessions. While I didn't agree with it—still don't—it meant getting to leave with my daughter without them putting up a fight. I've learned over the years to pick my battles with them.

Their other stipulation was for Skyla to attend private school. Since there was no way I could ever afford to send her to one myself, and I'm man enough to admit that, I agreed. Being a father comes first, and if that means allowing her grandparents to pay for her schooling, then so be it. Skyla loves her school, and I love that she's getting a top-notch education. There's even an art club she's part of there. Several days after school she also attends a STEM program for kids, which allows her to learn technology through fashion design. My daughter has a bright future ahead of her.

"You drunk yet?" Quinn asks, stepping out onto the terrace.

"Not enough," I murmur, taking another swig.

"I saw Celeste storm out of the bathroom..." When I don't acknowledge her words, she adds, "And you storm out right afterward."

I nod in affirmation, but still don't speak. What is there to say? Quinn was there the day I found out that the girl I could see a future with had lied to me then skipped town. She was there the day I saw Celeste on the stupid modeling show and threw my phone at the screen, shattering it. And she was there the day my daughter announced Celeste was her role model and wanted to be just like her. And I had no choice but to smile and nod and agree that Celeste is beautiful and talented. Which she was...is...but it still hurt like hell admitting out loud.

One week was all I had with her. She should've been nothing more than a blip on my fucking radar. I've been with dozens of women since her, and I couldn't tell you half their names. But Celeste, if I close my eyes and focus hard enough, I could tell you everything about her. The way she smelled like the beach and roses. The way she moaned softly every time she came because she was young and embarrassed, but it felt too good for her to hold it in. I could tell you how soft her skin was and point out where every freckle she has is located because I spent hours learning every inch of her body while she slept—and while she was awake. I could tell you the adorable way she scrunched her nose up when she wasn't sure of something. The way she blushed when I said something crass—which I did just to see her cheeks flush pink.

So while she should've been nothing more than some chick I fucked a few times—okay, several times—she was more than that. Through my daughter, I watched Celeste's career explode. From her modeling to the startup of her company. I watched her grow and blossom into one amazing woman who chased her dreams and held onto them like they were her lifeline. I watched her become engaged to Nick...and then I watched it end. All while assuming she probably wouldn't even recognize me if she saw me in person. Until she walked into my shop and recognized me. And in that moment, I thought maybe she would apologize for leaving, or at the very least, explain. But she did neither. She snapped at me and acted like I was the bad guy. And then after hugging my brother, who she barely fucking knew, she walked out the door once again.

"Jase, are you going to tell me what happened?" Quinn asks. When I raise a brow, she rolls her eyes. "I didn't mean those details. I meant what's going on with the two of you. I know she's always been the one who got away…"

"She didn't get away. She ran," I say, repeating the same words I said to my brother at the club. After taking another swig of my drink, I add, "And I don't want to talk about it. There's nothing to say." I stand, and without another word, head into my bedroom and close the door behind me.

Want to know why parents don't get drunk as often once they have kids? It's not because they're more responsible or mature. No, it's because the next day, when those kids wake up at seven in the fucking morning, demanding breakfast and to go to the pool, there is nobody to save your hungover ass because you're the damn parent. Which means, even with a pounding headache that won't go away, you have no choice but to drag yourself out of bed, take a shower, order room service, and pray she doesn't pick today to talk too much or ask too many questions.

"Dad, come in the pool with me!" Skyla screams way too loudly. I've taken several aspirin, but nothing is helping the throbbing pain that feels as if my head was smashed into a cement wall instead of me drinking a bottle of Johnnie last night.

"Alright, alright." Taking my shirt off, I throw it onto the chair, kick my sandals off my feet, then head over to the steps to slowly work my way into the pool. With my aviators on, the sun is slightly dulled. When my feet touch the water, I thank whatever pool God is up there for the pool being warm.

"Yes!" Skyla screeches, and I do my best not to flinch at her voice. It's not my daughter's fault that her father thought it would be a good idea after she went to bed to get stupid drunk in an attempt to temporarily forget the woman he fucked bare in the bathroom of their friends' wedding.

"Celeste!" Skyla yells, and my head whips around so fast it feels like a million nails were just hammered into my skull. "Over here!" she continues. When I finally spot where Skyla is looking, I see Celeste standing next to a lounge chair in a tiny-as-fuck black and white string bikini. She's bending over as she pushes her shorts down her tanned, toned legs, and her tits, the same ones I was kissing all over last night, are on display. She stands back up, and it's then I notice her flat stomach is donning a belly-button ring, which is glittering in the sunlight. Her hair is pulled up into a messy bun and she's smiling at Skyla hesitantly, trying to decide whether to come over or run away since I'm standing right next to my daughter.

"Celeste, come in!" my daughter yells. "It's warm in here." Celeste's eyes land on mine, but she can't make out my expression because of my shades. She places her shorts on the edge of the lounge chair and kicks off her flip-flops. She's obviously stalling, and I'm secretly enjoying her feeling of uneasiness. She doesn't want to say no, but she also doesn't want to come anywhere near me. But then when my daughter adds in a "please" in her cute-as-fuck innocent voice, I know she's got her. And I grin, despite myself, because I know all too well how hard it is to say no to her when she uses that voice.

"Okay," Celeste says with a nod. After she applies sunscreen to her front, she hands the bottle to her friend, who applies it to her back. And it takes everything in me not to stalk out of the pool, rip the bottle out of his hands, and demand he not touch her. *Friend, my ass...*

I watch as Celeste fixes her hair into a low ponytail and grabs a huge, floppy hat from her bag, tugging it on so it shades her entire face. The hat is so big, it should look ridiculous, but on her, it looks fucking adorable. A complete contrast to her barely there skimpy bikini. She glides through the water and stops in front of my daughter, making it a point not to look my way.

"Hey, Skyla! Did you enjoy your cake last night?" She smiles so wide, it lights up her entire face.

Skyla frowns and looks at me. "Dad, you never brought me cake." She pouts.

"Sorry," I say quickly, "I didn't see any more." I shrug. Thankfully, Skyla doesn't question it because the last thing I want to do is dig myself into a deeper hole. Technically, I'm not lying. I never made it over to the cake to see if there was any more. I hate lying to my daughter, even if it's something as little as a piece of cake. I was lied to by my dad growing up, and I swore I would never be anything like my father. Even if it hurts, I will always tell Skyla the truth.

I see Celeste's lips twitch, and I know she's thinking about why I never made it to see if there was any more cake. But thankfully she doesn't call me out on it. Instead, she keeps her attention on Skyla. "Are you having fun in the pool?"

"We just got here. Dad woke up with a bad headache and took forever to get out of bed." Skyla rolls her eyes dramatically, and Celeste's lips twitch again. "He said we can only stay for a little while and then we have to go home. I have school tomorrow." Skyla groans.

"Well, school is important," Celeste replies.

"I guess so." Skyla shrugs. "I just want to be a model and design clothes. I don't know why I have to go to school for that." Her nose scrunches up in annoyance.

I'm about to give my standard Dad speech—the one I give every time Skyla says this—but Celeste speaks first. "Skyla, school really is important," Celeste says seriously. "It's where you'll learn how to do the math you need to design your clothes. Would you want to wear a shirt that has one arm longer than the other?" Her eyes go wide, and Skyla giggles with a shake of her head.

"No!" Skyla exclaims.

"It's also where you'll learn how to use a computer. You need to know how to use programs like PowerPoint and Excel for meetings, and that's just the beginning."

"What about geography?" Skyla counters. "Why do I need to know that?"

I stifle a laugh, almost positive my daughter has stumped her, when Celeste says, "Where's Milan?"

Skyla shrugs. "I think…isn't it a country?"

"Wrong," Celeste says. "It's in Italy. I just got back from there last month. If I didn't know my countries, how would I be able to sell my clothes and jewelry and makeup all over the world." She raises a brow, and Skyla's shoulders slump in defeat.

"I get it," she mutters. "I am in the STEM program," she adds.

"What's that?" Celeste asks.

"I'm learning how to use science and technology to design clothes. I can draw them on the computer."

"Wow!" Celeste exclaims. "That's amazing. It was so hard for me to learn how to use the programs. Sometimes I still have trouble." She frowns, but I can tell it's exaggerated for my daughter's benefit. "I didn't go to college, but I wish I would've. I could've learned so much more. Instead, I needed a lot of people to help me."

"I can help you!" Skyla beams. "I'm practically a genius on the computer."

Celeste smiles warmly. "I would love that." The grin I've been sporting suddenly disappears as I take in the huge smile on Skyla's face. The conversation went from hypothetically designing clothes one day to Skyla helping Celeste. It's not Celeste's fault. I don't even think she realizes what she implied, but that won't stop my daughter from taking it that way.

"Hey Sky…" I start to say, knowing I need to nip this conversation in the bud quickly. But I know I'm too late when Skyla ignores me and asks, "When?" And Celeste's eyes bug out in realization of where the conversation has led to.

"Umm…" she sputters, and for the first time, her gaze goes to me, begging me for help.

"Sky, Celeste is really busy," I say. Celeste's brows furrow and her head tilts to the side slightly. I didn't mean it in a bad way, but she's clearly taking it as such. I'm just trying to get her out of the hole she unknowingly dug herself into.

"Oh," Skyla whispers, disappointment dripping in those two letters. She nods once and my heart plummets. I should've figured out sooner where this was leading to, so I could've put a stop to it.

"Actually," Celeste says with defiance clear in her tone, "I'm not that busy at all. I would love for you to come and help me." She plasters on a smile, but I can see through it. It's all false bravado. The woman is so far out of her element right now, but fuck if she isn't trying. And her trying is only making her that much fucking hotter. Because the fact is, she doesn't have to try. Skyla is nothing to Celeste.

"Celeste," I begin, about to tell her she doesn't have to do this, but before I can get the words out, Skyla cuts me off.

"Really? That would be awesome!" Skyla shouts in excitement. "Oh! Since you aren't busy, can you come to my career day next week? It's the last day of school." Oh, Jesus…

"Sky," I groan. "Leave her alone, please." I glance over at Celeste, who is now chewing on her bottom lip nervously. My guess is she jumped the gun when she invited Skyla to help her, out of spite, and now she's realizing all that she's agreeing to.

"Can you?" Skyla repeats.

"Umm…I think so…" She nods once. "I would have to check my calendar, but I think it would be okay…" She bites down on her lip again.

"Yes! Dad did you hear that? Celeste is coming to my career day!" Skyla closes the gap between her and Celeste, pulling her into a hug. Wrapping her arms around my daughter, Celeste's eyes close briefly, and when she opens them, I'm almost certain her eyes are glossed over with tears. But she turns her face away from me quickly, so I can't confirm.

"Sky, she said she'll try," I point out. The last thing I want is for my daughter to get her hopes up and then to be let down. She's been let down enough in her life.

Their hug ends and Celeste says, "I'm going to give your dad my business card so he can text me the info."

Skyla nods and claps her hands together in pure bliss.

CELESTE

"I've been waiting for over a week for the photoshoot proofs, so I can approve the winter mockups, and my email still has nothing from you!" I yell into the speaker at Vince, my photo editor who works with Adam's boyfriend, Felix. He remains silent on the phone—I'm sure shocked as to why I'm snapping at him, when technically the proofs aren't due until the end of the day today, and he's never once, in all the time he's worked for me, been late.

When I stop yelling to breathe, Margie takes my cell phone off the desk and presses the speaker button. "Please excuse Celeste. She's currently having an out-of-body experience. Aliens, dressed in Gucci and Marchesa, have taken over. We'll be on the lookout for your email later. Ciao." She hangs up and gives me her attention, her head tilting slightly to the side while I glare at her, annoyed at her making jokes while I feel so annoyed and agitated I'm about to rip my skin from my own body.

"This sudden little outburst doesn't have anything to do with a handsome, tattooed man or his sweet daughter, does it?" She smirks knowingly, and I let out a growl.

"Adam!" I yell at the top of my lungs, knowing he's somewhere close. He was scheduled for a photoshoot today and we're supposed to have lunch when he's done. "Stop talking behind my back!"

I hear a light-hearted chuckle but no response. My phone rings and Margie looks to see who's calling, then hands it to me. "It's Victoria Shaw."

I answer it, praying nothing has happened to my mom. Ever since Nick and I called off our engagement last year and he disowned his parents after they tried to ruin his relationship with Olivia, Victoria and I have been somewhat on the outs. It was as if a line was crossed, and I chose to side with Nick and Olivia. She was in the wrong, but refuses to see it. Therefore, she hasn't once called me unless it's been regarding my mom.

"Victoria," I say, putting the phone on speaker. I do it out of habit, so Margie can take notes.

"Celeste," she says, her voice formal, "I'm calling because I thought you should know your mother has lost her job." My heart plummets into my stomach. While I pay all of my mom's bills, she continues to work at the diner for one reason.

"The diner closed," she adds. "She's been sitting outside of it every day…" She doesn't need to finish her sentence for me to know why. In case Snake shows up.

I let out a long sigh, unsure of how to handle this. "Thank you," I tell Victoria. "I'll...figure something out." We hang up, and that's when I notice Adam has joined us in the office.

"Your mom needs help," he says, stating the obvious.

"She doesn't want help," I counter. "She wants a man, who, if I wasn't alive as proof, wouldn't even believe exists."

"When's the last time you searched for him?" Margie asks. She, too, is aware of my mother's entire situation.

"I haven't."

"What do you mean, you haven't?" Adam gives me a shocked look. "You have more than enough money to hire a private investigator." When I don't say anything, he searches my face for several seconds before he adds, "You're afraid."

I drop my eyes to the floor, not wanting to be further analyzed. "I'm not afraid..." But even to my own ears, I can hear the lack of conviction.

"Yes, you are," he argues. "You're afraid of what you might find. That maybe he's not really your dad, or he's dead. He might be some asshole who isn't everything your mom has made him out to be." I flinch at his words, but he doesn't stop there. "Or worse, you're afraid that you'll find him alive and that would mean he left because he didn't want your mom...or you." I don't bother to argue. He's hit the nail straight on the head.

"Celeste," Adam says, putting his hands on my shoulders. "You need to find out what happened to him. Your mom needs closure, and so do you." He raises a brow. "Are you seriously going to let her die never knowing what happened because you have daddy issues?"

"You're right," I admit softly. "I'll look into finding a PI."

"Felix's best friend from college is one. I'll give him a call."

"Thank you." I give Adam a hug. I don't have a lot of friends, but the few I do have are nothing short of amazing.

"So what time is career day?" he asks, and I groan. Margie, of course, laughs. When I don't answer right away, Adam gives me a look of disappointment. "You're not going to let that girl down, are you?"

"You don't understand…" I start to say.

"That you're in love with her father?" he cuts in.

"No!" I exclaim.

"Yes!" Adam argues.

"What?" Margie squeals in shock.

"Oh, yes, girl." Adam pulls Margie onto the couch. "She totally banged him in the women's bathroom at the wedding." Margie giggles. Damn traitor. You can't even pay for loyalty anymore.

When she spots me glaring, she stops abruptly. "You're going, right?"

"Yes, of course." I pull up the single text message Jase sent me late last night. It's the address to Skyla's school along with the time I need to arrive. He might've waited until the last minute to let me know the details of the event, but luckily, I didn't wait to get things ready. Skyla only mentioned me having to speak, but I wanted to do something extra to make it memorable, for her so when I returned to my office the next day, I got to work putting together a surprise I think she's going to love.

Every day, I've checked my phone, waiting to get the details from Jase, and day after day, when nothing came in, I started to wonder if maybe Skyla changed her mind about the invitation, and it pissed me off that Jase couldn't even take a second to let me know. Yesterday, I considered calling Nick to get Jase's number to ask him, or looking up his address so I could at least mail the surprise to Skyla, so she could give them to her classmates if she wanted to. Then, last night, as I was deciding what to do, Jase's text finally came through. Annoyed that he waited until the last possible second, I didn't even bother to respond. It was immature, but on the other hand, so was him waiting that long. I just hope Skyla doesn't think my lack of response means I'm not coming. Surely, if Jase thought that, he would've texted again to make sure. Right?

Glancing at the current time on my phone, I tell Adam to call us a car, then have Margie help me grab the box of goodies. Today is about Skyla, not Jase, and if he thinks texting me at the last minute is going to ruffle my feathers, he better think again. I'm Celeste-fucking-Leblanc, and I'm about to show Jase he's messed with the wrong woman. I didn't get to where I am today by letting people screw with me.

Twelve

JASE

My alarm goes off, reminding me that I need to head over to Skyla's school for career day. Originally I was supposed to be the one speaking for her. That was until she invited Celeste. Now Celeste is the one representing my daughter. One might take offense that his daughter would rather have a woman she barely knows speak instead of her own dad, but I'm not offended in the slightest. Skyla has never shown any interest in tattoos. Her entire life, since she was barely old enough to pick out her own clothes, has been about fashion. I know how important today is for her. While she may not know Celeste personally, my daughter has grown up following her career and worshipping the runway she struts down.

So, no, I'm not offended, but I am worried. Because last night when I finally got the guts to text Celeste the address and time of Career Day, along with an apology for waiting until the last minute, she didn't text me back. Not even a simple "OK." I have no idea if she will even be there today. Several times, I've considered texting her to ask, but pride is a funny thing. But now, as I shut down my station and head out the door, I wish I would've. I could have prepared Skyla properly.

Since Skyla's school is located in Lower Manhattan, I snag a cab. I rarely drive my own car in the city, especially since Skyla rides the bus to school, and it's quicker for me to ride the subway or grab a cab to work. Mostly it just stays parked in the driveway, unless I take it for a drive out of the city, like when we went to the wedding in the Hamptons. I should really consider just getting rid of it, but I love my car and I'm not ready to part with it yet.

After checking in with the front office to get my visitor pass, and getting a mixture of odd looks, from lust—the secretary, who I'm sure is imagining what it would be like to fuck a "bad-boy with tattoos"—to disgust—the Headmaster, who is scrunching up her nose, that a parent, even dressed in a white button-down dress shirt and black slacks, looks like I do—I make my way to the auditorium where career day is being held.

I step in quietly, since there's a parent currently at the front discussing his career as a Bankruptcy Attorney, while lecturing the kids on not putting themselves in a situation where they accumulate too much debt. I spot my daughter immediately, her head moving from side-to-side as she looks around for someone. When our eyes lock, I know right away, it's not me she's looking for, it's Celeste, and judging by the pitiful frown she's sporting, Celeste isn't here yet. Fuck! Maybe she didn't get my text. Maybe I texted the wrong number. I pull up the message and pull the card out of my pocket. They match. I copy and paste the message and click send again, watching intently for the bubbles to pop up, indicating she's texting back. Nothing.

A few minutes later, Skyla's name is called, and she stands to introduce the person she's brought. She speaks softly into the microphone. "My name is Skyla Crawford, and the person I brought with me is…" She stops speaking and her lips curl into a bright smile. "The person I brought with me is Celeste Leblanc. She's not only one of the highest paid models in the industry, but she also owns her own company, Leblanc, Inc., which includes several fashion lines from jewelry to her most recent, clothing. My dream is to be just like her when I grow up."

I glance around to find Celeste. My daughter wouldn't have announced her if she wasn't here. And that's when I spot her. She's dressed in a form-fitting navy blue and white pin-striped suit with heels that clack along the marble floor as she sways her ass up to the podium with all the confidence in the world. When she gets to the front, she gives Skyla those stupid air kisses to each cheek like all the famous people do, then addresses the audience.

Skyla remains standing next to Celeste as she discusses her career. She laughs, and smiles, and of course is completely fucking captivating. With her on stage, I'm able to admire just how damn beautiful Celeste is. Her auburn hair is down in waves and her makeup is barely there. She holds her head up with confidence, and not for a single second, does she ever show one ounce of fear or nervousness. And even though to this day, my heart tightens over the loss of this woman, I can't help but grin, because she did it. She achieved the goals and dreams she made. And while I thought for the longest time that my daughter looking up to her was a curse, I have to admit that if she's going to worship someone, I'm glad it's Celeste. She's strong, independent, and hard-working. She's everything Skyla's mother wasn't and everything I want my daughter to be.

"…and now to conclude my presentation, my assistants will be passing out friendship bracelets I've designed for today. They are inspired by my new friendship with Skyla and a preview to my new jewelry collection called Friendship. Each box contains a bracelet with an inspirational quote written on it for you to give to a friend who inspires you."

A man—the one I recognize from the wedding—and a woman begin to pass out tiny gold-colored boxes to each person in the room. When the guy goes to hand me mine, I shake my head. He nods once then shoots me an exaggerated wink before moving on to the next person. *Did he just flirt with me?*

"Thank you so much for coming!" Skyla throws her arms around Celeste. Career day has ended, and since it's the last day of school, we were told that we can take our kids home with us now if we choose to. Of course Skyla wants me to.

Now we're standing in the parking lot with Celeste, saying our goodbyes.

"You're welcome," Celeste says. "It was my honor."

Skyla nods in response, her cheeks turning a light pink, which is an indication she's embarrassed. Why is she embarrassed? "I was wondering..." she begins, her voice slightly off. She's not embarrassed; she's nervous. "I was wondering if you would wear my friendship bracelet."

"Only on one condition," Celeste tells her. "You wear mine." She pulls a box out of her purse and opens it, handing it to Skyla. Skyla takes the silver bracelet in her hands and reads the quote: "You are amazing. Remember that." Then she turns the charm over and glances up. "Dad, look." She shows me the charm. "It's a dandelion. Just like the one you have a picture of in the shop. Like the one grandma used to wish upon."

My eyes meet Celeste's, and for the first time, I can see her confidence waver.

"Put it on me, please," Skyla requests, and I do.

"It's beautiful," I tell my daughter.

"Thank you," she tells Celeste. "Do you want me to put yours on for you?"

"Please." Celeste holds her wrist out and Skyla locks the clasp.

"Thank you for coming today," Skyla says again. "It's the last day of school. Every year, on the last day, Dad and I go to the FIT museum and then to dinner. Would you like to join us?"

Celeste's eyes go wide. I should reprimand my daughter for inviting someone out without asking me first, but for some reason, I'm not ready to let Celeste go yet, and if having dinner with her and my daughter gives me more time with her, I'll go with it.

"Please," Skyla adds, and I don't even have to look at her to know she's giving Celeste her signature pleading look she always gives to my sister and brother when she wants to get her way because she knows they don't stand a chance against it. I, on the other hand, have a special dad forcefield that shoots up the minute her lower lip juts out to protect myself, and wallet, from that look.

"Sure." Celeste nods. "I would love to."

"Yay!" Skyla exclaims. Because it was the last day of school, she doesn't have a backpack or anything. After Celeste introduces us to her assistant, Margie, and me to her friend, Adam, since apparently my daughter already knows him, I call for a car service to pick us up. Because we're at Skyla's school, there's no way to snag a cab. We could walk to the subway, but I doubt Celeste will want to walk that far in her heels. It's a bit of a hike.

When we arrive at the museum, Skyla grabs Celeste's hand and starts to drag her around to each exhibit. Celeste doesn't complain once, instead she gives Skyla her complete attention the entire time. They ooh and ahh over everything, while I follow them around, joining in occasionally. We spend the next couple of hours there, until Skyla begins to slow down and complain she's hungry. Then we head a couple blocks over, on foot, to Jake's Burger Joint. It's Skyla's favorite place to eat, and it has a decent arcade she used to like to play games in when she was younger.

While we sit at the table, eating our food and sipping on

our milkshakes, Skyla keeps the conversation flowing. But then she spots a couple friends from school, leaving Celeste and me at the table alone while she goes to hang out with them.

After a few minutes of awkward silence, Celeste says, "So…any summer plans now that Skyla is out of school?" Great, cue the awkward, forced conversation.

"I still work, so she goes to a bunch of different camps, but we're planning a trip to North Carolina." I cringe the second the words are out of my mouth, hoping she doesn't ask what for. She knows I don't have any family there. My only family are my brother and sister and they both live here in New York.

"Skyla mentioned that…going to visit Amaya, right?" Her tone has changed from awkward and soft to…snippy?

"Yeah." I nod.

"Well, make sure you tell her hello from me." I look up in time to see her roll her eyes as she says the last word. *Great! Another woman in my life who relays her emotions by rolling her eyes up into her head.* She only met Amaya once during the time we spent together, so I'm not sure why the mention of Skyla's mom has her attitude changing. I don't usually tell people about Amaya's situation, but decide I should tell Celeste, in case it gets brought up by Skyla in front of her.

"Amaya does live in North Carolina," I start, but Celeste cuts me off.

"I don't really wish to hear about her. I was just trying to be polite." She takes a sip of her lemonade and it hits me…Celeste thinks I was—or am—with Amaya. And she's jealous.

"We're not together," I tell her.

"I didn't ask if you were," she quips.

"No, but your tone indicated you were thinking it."

"No, it didn't. Obviously you're not together still, or she would be living in New York." She looks everywhere but at me as she speaks. "I still don't want to hear about her."

"She's in a coma," I tell her bluntly. The hand holding her cup stills and she sets it down.

"Excuse me?"

"She's in a coma. When Skyla was four years old, Amaya was found unconscious. They were able to revive her, but she slipped into a coma."

Celeste's hands go to her mouth, her eyes wide with shock. "I'm so sorry. I didn't know...She asked for an autograph for her...I assumed..."

"Every year we go to North Carolina to visit her. When Skyla was younger, the nurses would say that her mom could hear her when she talks, so every time we go, she talks to her mom like she's still alive...well, I guess technically she is, but..." I let out a frustrated sigh. The whole situation is just so damn fucked up.

"Wow, Jase." I look up and see tears in Celeste's eyes. "I'm so, so sorry."

"You were just rolling your eyes over the mention of her...now you're crying..." I sound like a dick, calling her out on it, but I don't need her false sympathy.

"Excuse me for having emotions." She huffs. "No, I didn't particularly like the woman I found in bed with the guy I thought I was in love with, but I wouldn't wish that on anyone, even my biggest enemy."

"In bed?" I question. What the fuck is she talking about? There's no way Amaya and Celeste ever ran in the same circles, let alone slept with the same guy…unless it was back before Celeste moved. But even then, Amaya was a year older than me, so she was way older than Celeste. "Who do you know that slept with Amaya?"

Celeste hits me with a hard glare that has me backing up slightly. "Are you serious right now?" she sneers.

"I didn't even know you two knew the same people."

"We knew the same *person*," she snips.

"Who? Me?" I ask confused as fuck. And then it's like a lightbulb comes on. She thinks I slept with Amaya because I'm Skyla's dad. But why is she so mad about that? Skyla was born years before I even met Celeste.

"I didn't sleep with Amaya," I say, and Celeste rolls her eyes.

"So, Skyla was what? Created out of immaculate conception?"

I glance around to make sure Skyla isn't near us, then I lean in and murmur, "Skyla isn't biologically mine. But she doesn't know, so please don't repeat that." I've never admitted that to anyone but my siblings, but for some reason, I feel the need to defend myself to Celeste.

"You still slept with her." She glares.

I open my mouth to argue, when Skyla comes running over. "Look at this adorable stuffed bear I won."

"Wow, it is adorable," Celeste says as she stands. "I have to get going."

"So soon?" Skyla pouts.

"Skyla," I warn. "Celeste has given you all afternoon.

You know she has a company to run."

"I know," Skyla murmurs. "Thank you for coming. Do you think I could visit your work one day this summer?"

Celeste nods. "Absolutely. Your dad has my cell phone number. Have him text me and we'll set something up."

"I have my own," Skyla says, pulling her iPhone out that her grandparents bought for her so they could reach her without having to deal with me. Celeste laughs as she rattles off her number to Skyla.

"Text me and we'll figure it out." She winks and then gives Skyla a hug before walking away. Skyla and I spend the next half-hour in the arcade playing Pacman before we head home. When we step inside, we find Jax sitting on the couch watching television. Skyla gives him a quick hug and shows him her friendship bracelet before taking off to her room.

"Shop closed?" I ask, sitting next to him.

"Nah, Willow and Gage both have clients. Gage is going to close up. My last appointment had to reschedule, so I came home." He pauses the show he's watching and turns to face me. "How was career day? I take it by the way Sky was talking, Celeste showed up…"

"Yeah." I nod absently, unable to get Celeste's accusation out of my head.

"So, what's up?"

"Celeste and I were talking and things got a little heated…She mentioned Amaya…" I shake my head. "I don't even remember all that was said now. But what's got my head reeling is that for some reason Celeste is under the impression Amaya and I slept together."

Jax snorts. "You and Amaya? Where the hell would she

get that from?"

"I don't know." I scrub my hands over my face. This is going to drive me nuts until we finish our conversation. "Hey, would you mind watching Sky for me?"

"Yeah, sure," Jax agrees.

"Thanks."

Not having the slightest clue as to where Celeste might be, I decide it's best to take my own vehicle. About halfway to her house, I figure showing up unannounced probably won't go over well with her, so I give her a call. She answers on the third ring.

"Hello?" Her voice is timid, unsure as to why I'm calling.

"Hey, it's Jase," I say stupidly. She obviously knows it's me.

"Yeah, I know," she says. "Everything okay with Skyla?"

"Yeah, but I need to talk to you."

"Now?"

"Yeah, are you at home? I can come by."

There's a sound of papers shuffling. "I'm about to leave the office. I can meet you there."

"See you in a few," I say before I hang up.

After finding a parking spot, I pay the meter, then head inside Celeste's building. The doorman must recognize me from when I brought Celeste home because he says, "Sorry, but she's not home."

"I know. We're meeting here," I tell him as the door opens and Celeste saunters inside.

"Mr. Walters, how are you?" She gives her doorman a

sincere smile.

"I'm good, Miss Leblanc." He tips his hat to her.

Celeste walks straight to the elevator and the doors open. We both step inside, neither of us saying a word. When we arrive on her floor, I follow her to her door and then inside.

"Coffee?" she offers.

"No thanks."

"Wine?"

"I'm good."

"Cognac?" She holds up a bottle of brandy.

"How about a beer?" I counter, and she scrunches her nose up.

"I'm just kidding," I say through a laugh. I knew she wouldn't have any beer. Celeste rolls her eyes.

"Thank you for coming today," I tell her, sounding like my daughter. I think between Skyla and me, we've now thanked Celeste at least ten times.

"I didn't do it for you." She pours herself a glass of white wine and takes a dainty sip.

"I know, but I'm still thankful." I shrug. We're both standing in her living room, facing each other. She hasn't offered me a seat, and I'm pretty sure she's not going to.

"You asked to come by... So, how can I help you?" I guess we are getting straight to it.

"What you said at dinner, about me sleeping with Amaya. I never slept with her."

Celeste scoffs. "It's been over ten years, Jase. There's no reason to lie...I saw you."

"You saw me in bed with Amaya?" I ask slowly. There's

no way. It never happened.

"Well…" She shifts from one foot to the other. "I didn't see you *in* bed with her. You were coming out of the shower and she was naked in your bed." What the fuck is she talking about? Has she lost her damn mind?

"And when was this?"

"The day before…" She swallows thickly. "I came to see you. I came over to talk to you, and when I opened the door, I saw Amaya in your bed. She was naked, and you were in a towel, stepping out of the bathroom. Your hair was wet like you just got out of the shower." And suddenly it all comes back.

"So, let me get this straight. You saw Amaya in my bed, and because she was naked and I was in a towel, you assumed I had fucked her?"

Celeste releases an exasperated sigh. "Yes, it was obvious."

"Wow." I shake my head slowly. "You must've had zero faith in me. You saw the first thing that might've *looked* like I was cheating and you ran." I step closer to Celeste. My body is on fire. All these years and she just assumed I cheated on her. She didn't even have the decency to confront me. She was right fucking there. She could've spoken up. Yelled, screamed. And I would've explained. Instead, she ran.

"I meant so little to you that you didn't even stop for a single fucking second. You saw what you wanted to see so you could leave without feeling guilty." All the puzzle pieces finally fit together. All these years I wondered why she left without saying goodbye. Now I know.

"Guilty for what?" She sets her glass of wine down and

puts one hand on her hip.

"For playing me like a fool, for one. For lying to me about your age and where you went to school. For not telling me you had a fucking internship waiting on you in New York!"

Celeste gasps in shock. "How did you know?"

The Past

I haven't heard from Celeste in two days. She was supposed to come by last night, but she never showed up. I thought maybe I misunderstood her, but when she didn't show up tonight either, I knew something was up. I went to text her and realized I never got her number. So, I emailed her, only it bounced back. It didn't bounce when I sent her the image of the tattoo, which means the account has only recently been deleted.

Unsure of where to go from here, I call Nick to get her info, but he doesn't answer. Without leaving a message, I hang up and jump in my car to head over to NCU. While I'm scouring the huge campus that is almost empty since exams are pretty much over and everyone is leaving for the summer, I spot Killian juggling a couple of boxes.

"Hey, man!" he yells from a distance. "How's it going?"

"Good." I grab one of the boxes from him so they don't fall. "Finally done?"

"Don't you fucking know it. This is the last of my stuff.

I'm heading out to New York tonight. Just dropping this shit off at my parents' place before I take off." Killian was picked up by the New York Brewers as a first round draft pick.

"Congratulations," I tell him. "You deserve it."

"Thanks." We start to walk together in, what I'm assuming is, the direction of his vehicle. "So what are you doing on campus?" he asks.

"I'm looking for a girl…actually you might know her." Killian and Nick are good friends, so it would make sense he also knows Celeste. "Her name is Celeste. She's friends with Nick."

Killian stops in place. "Yeah, I know her. But why are *you* looking for her?"

"We hung out." I shrug. "Forgot to get her number."

For a good thirty seconds, Killian gives me a hard stare, and then he says, "She's no longer here. She moved to New York a couple days ago."

What. The. Fuck. "You sure?" I question. I was just with her a couple days ago.

"Yeah, she actually left earlier than planned. She was supposed to be at her graduation, but didn't show up. Nick said she skipped it and left for New York early. He got her an internship at some modeling agency."

"She graduated from college?" Why wouldn't she tell me she was graduating. We hung out for days, talking and getting to know each other. Her graduating from college seems like something she would've mentioned.

"Umm…no…" Killian looks at me confused. "Celeste is eighteen. She graduated from high school." Jesus fucking Christ. I try to think back to our conversations. There's no

169

way I would've missed her telling me she was a fucking senior in high school. Holy fuck, she's younger than my little sister. I just spent the last week fucking someone six years younger than me.

"You okay?" Killian asks, but I'm in too much shock to answer him. "Look, I don't know what happened between you two, but it's probably for the best if you don't find her. Celeste…well, there's no nice way to put this, so I'll just say it. She's a gold-digging bitch." He shrugs, and I have half a mind to punch him in the face for calling her that. "I'm not saying it to be mean, but it's the truth. Unless you have money, she isn't wasting her time on you. If you want, I can get her number from Nick…"

"No, that's okay," I choke out, flabbergasted by these turn of events. It's like I didn't even know Celeste. I spent the week falling for a woman who was playing me for a fool. But why? She had to know I have no money, yet she still acted like she was falling for me just as hard. She gave me her virginity, spent the week in my bed. We hung out with my family, went to the movies…she even came to see me at the shop several times. None of it makes any sense. But it really doesn't matter because she left. She got on a plane and flew over five hundred miles away without so much as a goodbye.

Thirteen

CELESTE

"Did you really think you would leave and I wouldn't go looking for you?" Jase asks. "You disappeared. I was scared out of my fucking mind that something happened to you. Then I ran into Killian and learned, the girl I was falling in love with was nothing more than a liar and a coward." Jase takes another step toward me. "What was I to you, Celeste?" My name comes out as a sneer. "Something to pass your time with while you waited to graduate and go to New York? An experiment…you wanted to see how the other side live?"

"You know nothing about me!" I shout, unable to hear another word out of his mouth. "The other side? I am the other side! I lived in a two bedroom piece-of-shit trailer that more times than not didn't have any working electric or water!" I throw my hands up in frustration. My hand hits my wine glass and it topples to the ground, shattering into pieces as it hits the wood floor. I flinch but leave it alone. I'll deal with it later.

Lowering my voice several octaves, I admit, "I was embarrassed to tell you where I lived. I didn't want you to know I was trailer trash."

"But you knew I wasn't rich," Jase says. "I told you my story."

"I know," I tell him, "but you also told me you hated your father for lying, so I was afraid to tell you the truth."

"So instead you just continued to lie?"

"No." I shake my head. "I never lied…I omitted the truth." Jase opens his mouth to argue, but I put up my hand to stop him. "I know that's still lying, but I'm just pointing out that I never actually gave you my age or where I lived or where I went to school. You assumed it, and I allowed you to. I knew it was wrong, and I was going to tell you the truth. But the night I came over to, I saw Amaya in your bed naked and I ran away."

Jase takes one last step toward me, bridging the gap between us. Lifting my chin with his thumb, he forces me to look him in the eyes. "I never slept with Amaya." He doesn't blink or speak for a long moment, giving me time to absorb what he's saying. "She came over drunk and high and threw up all over me before she passed out. I got her out of her soiled clothes and laid her in my bed so I could get out of my filthy clothes and shower. Once I got out, I dressed her in one of my shirts and let her sleep it off."

Oh my God. Oh. My. God. All these years I assumed he slept with her, assumed he cheated on me. That he wanted her and not me. I close my eyes at how stupid I was.

"Celeste," he murmurs, and I open my eyes. "I didn't sleep with her," he repeats. "You were all I wanted."

I nod slowly. He wanted me and I left. Tears burn my lids. All these years wasted because I assumed. I should've talked to him, but I didn't. His words from earlier fill my head.

"You saw what you wanted to see so you could leave without feeling guilty."

Maybe he's right. Maybe I saw what I wanted to see so I could take the coward's way out and leave. I could've walked in and yelled at him. I could've asked questions, demanded an explanation. But instead, I got on the first flight out and left. I was so terrified that he would tell me he couldn't go to New York, or worse, that he didn't want me to stay. I was so scared he would break things off, I ended what was going on between us on my terms.

"I think you're right," I whisper, and Jase gives me a quizzical look. "I think I saw what I wanted to see so I wouldn't have to put my heart on the line."

"What do you mean?" he asks.

"That night I was coming over to tell you about New York. I was going to ask you to go with me." A huge lump fills my throat.

"You were going to ask me to go?" Jase's eyes lock with mine.

"Or…" I swallow thickly. "I was going to tell you that I wasn't going to go." The tears burning behind my lids slide down my cheeks.

"Dimples." My nickname leaves Jase's mouth like a prayer. "I never would've let you go." He brings his hand up to the side of my cheek and my face tilts slightly into it, my eyes closing, as I lose myself in his touch and in his words. I don't know if he means he wouldn't have let me go to New York, or if he wouldn't have let *me* go, but either way, his words are my breaking point.

With my own hand, I cover Jase's—the one still holding my face—and lean in to kiss him. Our lips touch, softly at first. I'm scared he's going to push me away. But when I feel his tongue run along the fleshy part of my lip, my confidence soars and I throw myself completely into the kiss.

Jase removes our hands from my face and pushes me back against the wall. Only breaking our kiss long enough for our shirts to come off, we strip out of our clothes as if they're on fire until we're both completely naked. Then picking me up, Jase walks us through my condo, our kiss not once faltering. My fingers tug on his hair, not wanting our kiss to ever end. I know when we've made it to my room because Jase drops me onto my mattress. His lips remain seared to mine as he crawls up my body. Gathering my hair, he fists my locks tightly, tilting my chin up. He kisses me long and hard, with reverence, before tilting my head to the side so he can move downward. His soft yet masculine lips rain kisses down my neck.

Needing to feel him, I reach for his dick to stroke it, and that's when I feel something foreign. Something metal… I knew I felt something when we had sex the night of Olivia and Nick's wedding, but I was too far gone to give it much thought.

"Jase," I murmur against his lips, "did you have this the night we…"

"The night I fucked you on the sink in the bathroom?" He chuckles, his lips suckling on the soft spot just below my ear. "Yeah." He kisses along my collarbone, sending chills of pleasure down my spine.

Needing to explore, I push his chest back lightly. He pouts slightly, but it quickly turns into a grin as my hand wraps around his shaft and I stroke his hard length. Folding at the waist, I kiss the tip of his dick before slowly taking him all the way in my mouth. I count the number of barbells as my lips touch each one. Four in all. They're cold to the touch, and I make it a point to give each one special attention, running the tip of my tongue along each one.

I feel Jase lean forward, his tight abs brushing against the top of my head as he reaches for my backside. He massages circles along my butt and then gives one side a stinging slap.

"Jesus, woman," he grunts. "That ass. This mouth…" He grips my hair once again, pulling me off his cock and pushing me onto my back. His mouth crashes down on mine, his tongue parts my lips and explores, stroking and tasting and worshipping. With his free hand, he lifts my leg up high, resting it above his forearm, and then sinks inside me. The feel of Jase filling me up is like being lost and then finally finding my way home. I feel full, complete, whole. If possible, even with all the years we were apart, the connection between us has intensified. With deep yet frenzied strokes, he works my body over.

His fingers release my hair so he can lean on both hands to go even deeper, and I pull his face down to mine, not wanting to lose any part of our connection. Our tongues move frantically against each other. My nails scrape lightly along his back, my orgasm starting to build. My fingers slide across his damp skin. We're both working up a sweat. Jase's thrusts get harder, rougher, more demanding.

"Jesus, you feel so good," he murmurs against my lips. "Fuck." His head drops to my chest, and his lips wrap around my hardened nipple. When his teeth clamp down, my climax rips through my body. My walls clench around his dick, and I can feel the barbells massaging my insides as Jase finds his own release.

He moves his arm, and my leg drops down onto the bed, but he doesn't pull out. Instead, he spends the next several minutes nuzzling my neck. Kissing my fevered skin. Licking my nipples. His dick throbs, reminding me he's still inside me. I've never felt so completely worshipped in my life. When he finally pulls out, he lowers his body until his face is up close and personal with my pussy.

"Jase," I groan. We're no longer in the heat of our passion. I don't want him hanging out down there…

"Shh…" He gives the hood of my pussy an open-mouthed kiss. "I need to get fully reacquainted with your perfect cunt."

"Jase…" I moan as he pushes his fingers into me. They make a slurping sound, reminding me that we just had sex without a condom. "What are you doing?"

His answer is to grab the backs of my thighs and flip me over. Before I can lay my head down against the cotton sheets, he entwines my hair around his fist and pulls me up onto my knees, tilting my head to give him access to my neck. He enters me from behind, his other hand gripping the curve of my hip, his lips sucking on the sensitive spot below my ear. Unlike last time, which was rough and frenzied, this time he makes love to me nice and slow.

With my body already sensitive, I feel my orgasm surfacing once again. He releases my hair and pushes down on my back. My ass pops out farther and he sinks himself into me deeper. My cheek presses against the sheets and my eyes close as I get lost in all that is Jase.

As my eyes flutter open, the tickling sensation I feel causes my heart to expand. I breathe out a soft sigh as I allow myself to remember the last time I woke up to Jase drawing across my skin. The last time I thought it was a bug crawling on me, but now I know it's the feeling of the pen running along my flesh.

The tickling stops, and then I feel Jase's warm lips press a kiss to each of the dimples just above my ass. "Morning, Dimples," he murmurs, the sound of his voice like a soft velvet blanket I want to grab ahold of and cuddle with.

"Morning." I roll over and come face-to-face with Jase. His hazel eyes are playful and his day old stubble has me wanting to rub my cheek along his. His lips press to mine for a chaste kiss before he backs up and sits upright.

"I need to head home," he says. "My brother is keeping an eye on Skyla, but he needs to head into the shop. He has an early appointment." He runs his fingers down the side of my cheek in such a loving way, my body shudders. Jase notices and smirks. "I love how responsive your body is to me." I bring myself into a sitting position, and he kisses me again before standing to get dressed. I can't help the pout my lips make at the thought of leaving this bedroom, but I know he's a man with responsibilities. Especially since he's a single dad.

"What made you move to New York?" I ask, curiously. I never would've imagined him moving here.

"Quinn originally wanted to work in a museum. She got picked for an internship at the MET."

"So you all moved here?" I knew they were close, but wow.

"I had recently gotten custody of Skyla and felt we all needed a fresh start. She was almost five and ready to start school, so I figured it was a good time to move."

I quickly do the math in my head. "You've been living here for the last eight years." It's a huge city, and it's not like we mingle in the same circles, but I can't believe he came here only a couple years after me, and this entire time I never knew it.

Jase nods. "Of course, Quinn didn't end up loving the position and quit shortly after." He rolls his eyes, but I know behind his mock annoyance, there's a sibling bond he can't hide. "She realized she loved photography, so she took a job working under some well-known photographer, and after a few years, branched out on her own. She mostly takes family portraits and shoots wedding and stuff, but she loves what she does."

"I thought she works at the shop with you guys?"

"She does part-time, but only until we get around to finding someone permanent."

Jase pulls his boxers up, tucking his beautiful dick inside, and I frown. He, of course, sees and laughs. "Don't give me that look or I'll never be able to leave."

"Is that supposed to be a threat?" I ask half playfully-half seriously, and Jase laughs again.

"Woman, you're going to be the death of me."

I giggle at his playfulness. "I was so shocked when I walked into that tattoo shop and learned it was yours. I mean, I always knew you would open up your own shop, but I never thought it would be right here in New York."

"Yeah," he agrees, "getting custody of Skyla changed everything. Our dream took a little longer than we originally planned. We worked at another shop for a few years, while we continued to save, and then about four years ago, we finally took the plunge and opened Forbidden Ink."

He pulls up his jeans, zippering and buttoning them.

"It's a beautiful shop."

"Thanks." The corners of his sexy mouth curl into a boyish grin. "I love it there. It's like home away from home. I love that Skyla can be there and we can make our own hours. There's nothing like working for yourself." He gives me a lopsided grin. "I'm sure you can understand that."

"I do," I admit. "It gives me a sense of control I never had growing up."

Jase comes over and sits on the edge of the bed, his fingers finding the curve of my hip. I'm briefly distracted by the view of his taut muscles and rock-solid abs on display, but quickly shake myself out of my haze and remember the subject we were originally discussing.

"If you didn't sleep with Amaya, how did you end up as Skyla's father?" I wanted to ask him this last night, but instead ended up jumping his bones. Jase opens his mouth to speak, but I put up my finger to stop him. Reaching down, I grab his shirt off the floor and hand it to him. "Put it on, or I won't be able to focus on anything you say."

He throws his head back in the most beautiful laugh but does as I say. "Amaya came to me when she found out she was pregnant. She had no idea who the dad was. She had been partying a lot and it could've been several guys. She asked me to help keep her sober. She wanted to do right by her baby.

"So I moved her in with me and helped her the best I could throughout her pregnancy. Unfortunately, her staying sober only lasted a few months after Skyla was born. She was colicky and Amaya just didn't have that maternal gene."

I swallow thickly. I know all about lacking that gene. I can't even imagine, if I ever got pregnant, what I would do with a baby. Sure, financially I can afford one, but money can't parent. It can't nurture and love and protect. Nick's mom was rich and lacked every maternal gene. My mother was poor and wasn't any better.

"So you took care of her?" I ask. It wouldn't surprise me. Jase's heart is so damn big. I only knew him for a short time but could feel how deeply he cared for those around him.

"No." He frowns. "We got into a fight over her choosing drugs and alcohol over her daughter. I came home from school one day to find she had taken off with Skyla.

I'm not sure what happened to her during those next two and a half years. I tried to find her but had no luck." His eyes gloss over with emotion, and my heart squeezes for him and Skyla.

"She came back when Skyla was three years old." Jase is quiet for a moment, then adds, "It was actually the day you met her. She asked around and found out where we had moved to." He shakes his head. "She told me she was back and apologized for taking off. She said things would be different. She wanted to get herself cleaned up."

He takes a deep breath then continues, "The night you saw her in my bed, she had come over high and drunk. She had Sky with her. Quinn took care of Sky, feeding her and giving her a bath, while I tried to take care of Amaya. After she threw up and passed out, I laid her in my bed and watched over her to make sure she was okay. When she woke up, she begged me to be with her. Told me she needed me in order to stay sober. I told her that I could only be friends with her, but I offered to take her and Sky back in. I hated that she had her daughter around all those druggies she hung out with. She left upset, taking Sky with her. She said if I didn't want her in that way, then she would find someone who did."

"That poor baby," I whisper.

Jase nods in agreement, then continues, "I begged her to let me keep Sky but she refused. About a week later, I got a call from Child Services. Amaya was in the hospital in a coma after overdosing. The guy who called it in, handed Sky over saying she wasn't his. Apparently Amaya had put my name on the birth certificate as the father."

I hear myself gasp at his admission. "So, you what? Showed up and claimed her?"

Jase nods once. "I felt so damn guilty, Celeste. I thought if I wouldn't have pushed her away, maybe she wouldn't have overdosed…"

"You can't think like that," I say. "She had serious issues. Unfortunately, more than likely, something along those lines would've happened eventually."

"I know," Jase says solemnly, "I've, for the most part, come to terms with it all over the years."

"Is that why you took Skyla? Out of guilt?" I ask, not trying to judge him, but trying to understand.

"No." Jase shakes his head. "Amaya's parents are rich as fuck, but they're older and flat out said they couldn't handle raising another child. Hell, they barely raised Amaya. They said they were going to hire a full-time nanny, but I couldn't let that happen. They chose their freedom, Amaya chose drugs…Sky needed someone to choose her." He shrugs like it's no big deal, when it is in fact a very big deal. He took on a three-year-old who wasn't biologically his. He loved her and nurtured her, providing a home for her.

"Monica and Phil, Amaya's parents, didn't even put up a fight. A couple years later, when I told them I was planning to move to New York, they just asked that they be allowed to financially provide for Sky, including her education." Now it all makes sense. The expensive clothes, the private school. "I could've argued, but it was a small price to pay to get full custody of her and be able to move. They could've fought me, and with the money they have, they would've won."

"What you did is so selfless, Jase." I climb into his lap,

wrapping my legs around his waist. "Moving for your sister, taking on a little girl who wasn't biologically yours. I don't know anybody who would've done such a thing...well, except Nick. He has a big heart."

Jase's brows dip down. "Then you're associating yourself with the wrong people. Speaking of Nick..." He lets his words linger, but the way his brows shoot up tells me he's asking about our engagement.

"It was all fake," I admit. "We made a stupid pact that, if we didn't find love by the time Nick turned thirty, he would give up on love and marry me."

Jase's lips turn down. "You were going to marry him without being in love with him?"

Hesitantly, I nod. "We made the pact before I met you...before I fell for you. And then after I saw you and Amaya...well, after I *thought* I saw you and Amaya, I was done with love."

"Celeste." Jase sighs. "You were so young. You're telling me, you didn't once find love in the last eleven years? I've seen you dating."

"So, you've been keeping tabs on me?" I joke to lighten the mood.

"Damn right, I have," he admits with conviction. "I was so pissed you left, but I was also so damn proud of your success. I watched you grow and blossom into this beautiful, successful businesswoman. I just figured along the way you would've found love too."

"I wasn't looking for it," I tell him. "I didn't want it. To be honest, in a lot of ways, you're the reason I'm where I am today. When I got on that plane, I was driven and determined to succeed on my own. And since you, I've only dated guys I knew my heart would be safe with."

"Why?" Jase asks, his voice free of judgment. "That doesn't sound anything like the woman I fell for all those years ago."

"Actually, the woman you met never planned to fall in love," I admit. "The only guy I wanted was one who could help me climb up the proverbial ladder. Someone with a daddy in a fortune 500 company who would take over one day. Until I met you, I only saw myself with a rich guy who would take care of me."

"Why?" Jase asks.

"Well," I begin, "you now know I grew up in a trailer with my mom." I avert my eyes out of embarrassment, but Jase tips my chin with his thumb so I have no choice but to look at him.

"Don't do that," he says. "Don't hide."

I nod once and then tell him the story of my mom and dad. Aside from the few people I'm close to, Jase is the first person I've ever told. When I'm done, he asks, "So, have you found him?"

"I haven't called the PI yet," I admit sheepishly.

"Call him," Jase says. "You're a lot stronger than you give yourself credit for. No more hiding behind your fears. You're not alone anymore. I've got your back. Okay?"

"Okay," I agree.

Gripping the back of my head, Jase pulls me in for a kiss, then he asks, "What kind of guy do you see yourself with now?"

"Huh?" I ask, confused.

184

"You said when you were younger, you wanted a rich man to take care of you... until you met me. What kind of man do you want now?"

"One who will love me," I admit softly.

C~

"Let me get this straight," Giselle says, taking a sip of her coffee. "You hooked up with Jase when you were eighteen, but then thought he was also sleeping with Amaya, who is Skyla's baby momma, but he wasn't."

I nod once, and Olivia shouts, "Can you please verbally speak? I'm on Facetime, in case you forgot." I roll my eyes, and Giselle giggles. Olivia is currently at Disney on her honeymoon, but insisted on not missing our weekly get together, so we're using my laptop to Facetime with her from the coffee shop Giselle and I are sitting in. We usually do lunch or dinner, but I was only able to meet early this morning, so coffee and pastries it is.

"Sorry," I say through my laughter. "Yes, I was with Jase when I was eighteen."

"I can't believe this!" Olivia chides. "I feel like I never really knew you." She pouts, and sitting back, rubs her belly.

"Oh, stop, nobody knew about Jase and me."

"So, are you guys back together now?" Giselle asks.

"I-I don't know." I shrug. "We didn't talk about it..." After I told him I wanted a man who would love me, his phone rang, reminding us he needed to get home to his daughter.

"Because you were too busy having s-e-x." I laugh at Olivia spelling the word. Reed repeated one word he shouldn't have, and now the woman spells everything she doesn't want him to repeat.

"Jesus, Liv," I hear Nick say from the background. "I don't want to hear about Celeste fucking…" The lady sitting at the table next to us glances over and I lower the volume a tad while Giselle laughs.

"Nick!" Olivia shouts, turning around to, I'm sure, glare at him.

"Sorry." He groans. "I don't want to hear about her f-u-c-k-ing Jase!" I can't help my laugh. These two are fucking nuts.

"Thank you." She sighs then turns around. "We'll be discussing this further once I'm back."

"Oh!" Giselle clasps her hands together. "Speaking of which. Do you remember that yacht rental I won at the fundraiser?" Olivia and I both nod. A few months ago, Olivia and Nick threw a fundraising event to announce their expansion of Nick's charity, Touchdown for Reading, into Touchdown for Reading and the Arts. Killian, thinking he was hilarious, bid on the yacht rental in Giselle's name, and won.

"Well, since it's nice out, we've made a reservation to do a day trip the second week of July. We have no clue when we will find the time to go once Killian's football season has begun, on top of us having this little girl"—she pats her growing baby bump—"right in the middle of the season."

"Oh, yes! That will be so much fun," Olivia says. "I'll

have my parents watch Reed."

"And you should totally invite Jase." Giselle waggles her eyebrows.

"Agreed!" Olivia adds.

"Yeah, yeah. It's time to say goodbye. See you when you get home. Give Reed a kiss from me."

"Bye!" Giselle waves at the screen.

"Bye!" Olivia smiles. I press the end button and she disappears.

Once I close the screen, Giselle leans in, and with a big grin, says, "Okay, now that Olivia and Nick are gone, I want all the juicy details. He looks like a bad boy with all those tats. Please tell me he fucks like one." She lifts one brow.

"I'm not kissing and telling," I say, "but I have two words for you: pierced dick."

$$\mathcal{C}_\mathcal{D}$$

"So, what can you tell me about the gentleman you're interested in locating?" It's Saturday evening, and I'm working from home. Adam texted me a few minutes ago, asking if I've contacted the PI yet, which I hadn't, so I figured I should call him now before I chicken out.

"Unfortunately, the only info I have on him is that he went by the name Snake, his last name is Leblanc, and he met my mom in Piermont when he was having dinner at the diner she worked at," I tell Duncan, the PI Adam referred me to.

"Okay, well that's a start. Why don't you email me all

the details you have, including the dates they were together and any description of him you know of. Ask your mom if she can recall any specific tattoos."

"I'm not telling my mom," I say. "I don't want to get her hopes up. If you're able to locate him, I will then decide what to do with the information."

"Gotcha." He gives me his email and lets me know, once I send him all the info I can think of, he will start immediately. I thank him for his help and then we hang up.

As I'm setting my phone on the coffee table, it rings, Jase's name popping up on the screen. We haven't spoken since we parted ways the other morning, aside from a good morning and good night text.

"Hello," I say, answering the phone. I have to admit, I was getting worried that maybe Jase regretted what happened between us. Neither of us are the same people we were all those years ago. While I'm still—if not more—attracted to him, I'm not stupid enough to believe we can just pick up where we left off. We're in a different city, both running businesses. Jase is a dad! I swore I would never have kids. I don't know where we stand, and I'm starting to wish I would've asked him when he was here the other day, but at the same time, I don't think I'm ready to put a label on us. It's all just too new, yet not. Ugh! It's so confusing.

"How are you?" Jase asks, his voice smooth like the finest silk. I don't realize it, until I release a harsh breath, that I was even holding my breath. The way he speaks doesn't sound like a man who regrets being with me.

"I'm good," I say nonchalantly. "You?"

"Aside from missing a certain auburn-haired woman

like crazy, I'm okay." And there goes my heart.

"Oh yeah?" I squeak out like a school girl with a crush. Damn it! How does Jase always manage to turn me into such a girly-girl?

"Yeah," he says, his voice husky. "My sister is having a sleepover with Sky at her place tonight, so I was thinking you could come by the shop and hang out and then I could show you my place."

"What about Jax?" He mentioned before that, while Quinn moved out and lives with her boyfriend, Jax still lives with him and Skyla.

"He's having a sleepover too…with some chick he tattooed earlier…at her place." He coughs out a laugh. "So, what do you say? "

"Should I, umm…" I clear my throat, suddenly nervous. "Should I pack a bag?"

"Hell, yes, you should," he growls, and I let out an annoying giggle.

"Okay, I'll see you soon."

Fourteen

JASE

For the last ten years, my life has been about my daughter and our future. I have spent hours upon hours learning how to navigate being a single father to a little girl with a sad past while also trying to grow a business. When I first got her, she was malnourished and mute. She didn't talk or smile for almost a year. The day she smiled at me for the first time, I swear I cried for an hour straight. And then when she finally spoke, I fucking lost it. Over the years, my focus has been on building a thriving relationship with Skyla, and later, it shifted to building a thriving business that would provide for Skyla.

Because of that, no-strings type of sex became my go-to. On the nights my sister or brother would watch my daughter, I would meet up with different women. Some, I hung out with a few times to see where things might go, others, it was nothing more than a one-time thing. But there was never a single woman I met that I could imagine bringing home to meet my family, to meet my daughter. Skyla had been through enough in her first three years to last a lifetime. When I wasn't working, I was taking her to the doctors, including several children psychologists. And then once she was finally on the right path and blossoming like the beautiful flower she is, I wasn't about to risk any set-backs. So I made it a point to keep my family life and my private life separate.

But now, for the first time, I can see those two parts, I worked so hard to keep from touching, merging together and becoming one. The house, the family, the marriage. Spending my days doing what I love, my evenings with my family around the dinner table or on the couch watching a movie, taking family trips to amusement parks, and my nights…I can see them vividly. In bed, getting lost in one woman—Celeste. The problem is, I'm almost positive, if I told her any of that, she would most likely run for the hills…or the runway. Sure, she said she's looking for a man to love her, and at the time, those were the best damn words I could've been told. Until I started to think about how different our lives are.

Celeste's life is glamorous and consists of traveling to different countries and designing clothes for the rich and famous, while mine is spent tattooing and parenting. We're complete opposites in every way, but she's who I want, and without spooking her, I need to show her we can work. It's why it took me a couple days to work up the courage to call her. I wanted to give her time in case she decided one night was all she wanted. In case she was caught up in the moment and didn't mean what she said about wanting to be loved. Or maybe she meant it, but didn't mean by me specifically. Or maybe she meant me at the time, but didn't think about what it would entail to be with a guy like me. Yeah, I'm fully aware that I'm overthinking the hell out of her simple five words, but I can't help it. It feels like I've been given a second chance, only everything has changed. We're no longer the carefree individuals we once were, lying in bed, wrapped around one another, with only the *thought* of our dreams and futures ahead of us. Now, we're *actually* living them.

So, with all that said, I planned to give Celeste more time, but then my sister asked to take Skyla and I couldn't wait any longer to call her. When I asked her if she wanted to come over, I listened for any hesitation, but didn't hear any. She did sound nervous, though, which tells me I need to take things slow.

"All right, Gilbert. Take a look and let me know what you think?" I hand him the mirror so he can look at the tattoo I just finished.

"Damn, man, it looks fucking dope." He grins. "It's done, huh?"

"It is." I nod, satisfied with my work. It's a huge, intricate tattoo that covers his entire back, made up of different pieces that all interconnect into one large canvas.

"Thank you." He pulls a wad of cash out of his pocket and shakes my hand, slipping me several bills. "I'll give you a call when I'm ready to start my sleeve."

"Sounds good." I apply the ointment to the newly inked area and cover it with cellophane. "You know the drill. Take care of it so it heals well."

"You got it." We walk down the hall toward the front. I'm the last one here this evening—Willow and Gage both finished up earlier, so I offered to close up shop. After we shake hands, I open the door for him to exit, then pull out my phone to text Celeste. I don't want to lock the door until she gets here. There's movement from the left that has me whipping my head around, and that's when I see her leaning against the pool table. She's donning a simple beige dress that's clearly business attire, yet it's still cut low enough to hint at how perfect and perky her breasts are, and still short enough to show off her tanned, sexy legs which are currently crossed at her ankles. She's wearing matching heels that are tall enough to be considered weapons. But the only thing they make think of in this moment is how they would feel digging into my back as I fuck her on that pool table.

"You really shouldn't leave the door unlocked this late at night," she tsks. "Anyone can wander in without you knowing."

"I left it unlocked for you," I say, locking the door and then walking over to her. "You ever play pool?" I ask, nodding to the table she's leaning against.

"No." She shakes her head. "Is this the part where you offer to teach me how to play?" She smiles coyly.

"Do you want to learn how to play?"

She laughs. "I can only imagine how many times you've used that pick up line on a woman." She runs her hands along the fabric. "I bet you've taught *many* women how to play, haven't you?" She smirks playfully, but I can see it in her eyes, the hidden insecurity. She's asking, without asking, if I've been with a lot of women.

Gripping her hips, I set her on top of the pool table and spread her creamy thighs, so I'm standing between them. Her dress rises, showing off more of her skin. "I've never used that line before, and I've never been with a woman in here," I tell her. I'm not going to beat around the bush. I'm a thirty-five year-old man, and I don't want to play games with Celeste.

Pulling her face toward mine, I give her a hard kiss. It's only been a couple days, but fuck if I haven't missed the hell out of her. The longer we kiss, the deeper it goes. My hands skate along Celeste's thighs as hers tug on my hair, pulling me closer. I can feel her heat pressed against my crotch. She's grinding against me, trying to get herself off.

Breaking our kiss, I push her legs farther apart and drop to my knees, so my face is parallel to her pussy. Running my hands up her thighs, I find her panties and tug them down her legs. She lifts, pushing her dress up to her waist and exposing her bare cunt. It's glistening with want, and just the thought of tasting her has my dick hardening in my jeans. I lean in and take my first lick right up her slit. Celeste's body shivers and goosebumps pop up across her skin.

"Jase," she murmurs softly, "what if…what if someone sees us?" Her question would be one of concern, if her tone didn't come across like the thought of someone watching us turned her on.

I glance up at her and notice her cheeks and neck are

slightly pink. Her chest is rising and falling like she's out of breath. "What?" I ask, confused. Nobody is in here but us. I made sure of it.

"Out there." She nods. When I glance back, I see a couple walking by. It appears as if they're looking into the shop, but really they're only looking at their reflection.

"It's a one-way mirror. We can see out, but they can't see in."

"Oh," she says, her voice breathless, confirms my suspicions.

"Does the thought of them watching us turn you on, Dimples?" I push my fingers into her tight center and she's dripping fucking wet. I don't need for her to answer. It obviously does.

"I-I don't know." Her cheeks turn a brighter shade of pink.

"Oh, you know," I murmur, adding another finger to the mix. "I think it turns you the fuck on to think about someone watching me as I fuck this tight cunt." Celeste gasps and her muscles constrict. Apparently dirty talk also turns her on. While fingering her, I spread her lips with my other hand and take another lick of her sweet pussy. When I get to the top of her clit, I bite down on the swollen nub.

"You know what I think?"

"What?" she asks, the word stretching out through a soft moan.

"I think you should get this pussy pierced." I flick my tongue over her clit and her entire body shakes with pleasure. "And nobody would ever know," I add, remembering that her excuse for not being able to get a tattoo was because she wanted to be a model.

"I don't know if—" Her words are cut off with a loud moan when I lean back in and suck her clit into my mouth, my teeth scraping along the sensitive flesh and my tongue darting out to lap up her juices. I continue to fuck her with my fingers while my mouth devours her. Her fingers pull on my hair to the point of pain, telling me what I'm doing feels good. Another few licks of my tongue and pumps of my fingers and she's coming hard. Her juices flow down my chin and onto the pool table like a beautiful fucking waterfall. When I glance up, her head is thrown back and her back is arched as she rides out her orgasm.

After a few seconds of watching her, I pull my fingers out and yank her toward me. She comes willingly—her entire body limp from her orgasm—and I grab the back of her head, bringing her lips to mine. When she releases a low groan into my mouth, I know she's tasted herself on me. Reluctantly breaking our kiss, I back up and grab her panties, placing each heeled foot into a hole and pulling them up her legs.

When she gives me a confused look, I lift her off the table and set her down. "We have my place to ourselves. I'm not fucking you here. I need to take my time with you." I kiss her pouty lips once more and then walk over to the wall to flick off the lights so we can head out.

"This is really cool," she says, eyeing the wall I painted years ago when we first bought the place. It's the name of our shop, Forbidden Ink, graffitied, and to the right is a large gloved hand and tattoo gun. It's painted 3D to look lifelike.

"Did you draw it?" she asks.

"Yeah." I nod, admiring the image.

"You're so talented," she says with awe in her voice.

"Talented enough to tattoo you?" I shoot her a wink and she rolls her eyes.

"Not a chance." She scoffs. "I have a reputation to uphold." She grabs a bag from the corner and hands it to me to carry. It must be her overnight bag. "Now, if you would've asked me earlier, while your tongue was"—she waggles her brows playfully—"down there…I probably would've agreed to let you do whatever you wanted to my body."

"Good to know."

I swing the door open so Celeste can walk out first, but when she walks by, she purposely rubs her hand along my still-hard dick. Gripping her wrist, I pull her back into me, swiping her hair to the side, so I can place a kiss to her neck. I don't know what it is about this woman, but I'm fucking addicted. I can't even go five damn minutes without needing to touch her in some way.

"Jase," she says through a moan. "We'll never make it to your place if you keep that up."

After setting the alarm and locking up, we start walking down the sidewalk. I hit the unlock button on my key fob and my headlights flicker on and off.

"Is this your car?" Celeste asks as I pop open the trunk and toss her bag inside.

"It is." I slam the trunk closed then walk over to open the door for her.

"It looks like one of those cars in that Fast and Furious movie." She eyes the car further.

"You've seen those movies?"

"Nick made me watch one once." She slides into the car, and I close the door once she's all the way in. She puts on her seatbelt, and I start the car. When the V8 engine rumbles to life, Celeste's brows rise, impressed.

"It's a 1967 Chevy Camaro Z28," I tell her, even though she probably has no clue what any of that means.

"It's sexy." She runs her hand along the dashboard as I pull out into the heavy city traffic to head home. "I've never been in a car like this before. It's very…manly." Her hand leaves the dash and lands in my lap.

"That's because you date those rich twats," I point out. "They prefer town cars and limos."

She rubs the top of my pants, awakening my dick from its slumber. "True," she agrees. "But I prefer a car like this."

"Celeste," I warn, "we'll be to my place in twenty minutes."

"I'm not sure I can wait that long." She unlocks her seatbelt and edges closer to me. Her lips find my ear, and she licks the lobe before kissing down my neck—the entire time, she's stroking my cock through my pants.

And then her hand dips into my jeans, under my boxers, and she squeezes my dick. A car pulls out in front of me, and I slam on my brakes. "Jesus, woman, you're going to get us into an accident."

"You're the one driving." She giggles into my ear. Her fingers grip my shaft, stroking me root to tip, and her mouth trails kisses along my jaw.

"Oh! I forgot to tell you. Giselle invited us to go on a

yacht they're renting. Want to go?" She's talking to me like she doesn't have her hands all over me. Meanwhile, I can barely think straight.

"Yeah, whatever you want." I let out another groan. Fuck! We're stuck in traffic. Damn New York!

Unable to handle another second of her touch without being able to reciprocate, I make a sharp right turn onto a side street. The alley is empty, but even if it was full of people, I wouldn't give a fuck. After unbuckling my seatbelt, I push my pants and boxers down, and my dick—still wrapped up with Celeste's hand—springs free. Leaning over, I grab her hips and pull her on top of me, her legs landing on either side of my seat. Wanting to be inside her, and annoyed that her panties are in the way, I rip the thin material off her body and pull her down onto my hard length until I'm so deep inside her, I bottom the fuck out in her tight cunt. She releases a loud moan, and then with her arms wrapped around my neck, raises her body slightly and then lowers herself down onto me once again.

She grinds her cunt against me, her clit rubbing friction against my pelvis. "Oh my god, Jase." Her eyes roll upward into the back of her head. I was prepared to take charge, to fuck her until we both came, but instead I sit back and watch as my woman rides me. As she explores, like it's her first time finding her own release, and fuck if it isn't the hottest thing I've ever experienced.

"I've never...Jesus...This feels so good." Her words come out breathless. She's close. So fucking close. "Oh...Oh...Jase!" Her walls tighten like a goddamn vice grip as she comes all over my dick right before I come deep inside her.

"Turn around so I can clean your back," I say. Celeste smirks, knowing the last thing I want to do is clean her. When we got to my place, I attempted to give her the full tour, but once we arrived at my bathroom, she insisted, as she stripped down out of her clothes, she could see the rest of my place later. Without waiting for me to agree, she turned on the shower and got in. So, I did what any selfless host would do and joined her.

I've just spent the last ten minutes cleaning her front, which included sucking her pink, pebbled nipples, kissing my way down her flat stomach, and licking her clit until she came all over my tongue. Now, I'm just trying to wash her, but she, for some reason, thinks I'm kidding.

"I'm serious," I insist.

"Uh huh," she says coyly. "That's what you said about my front."

"Well, unless of course you're okay with some backdoor action" —I waggle my eyebrows playfully, and Celeste's eyes widen— "I promise you I'm just going to wash your sexy back."

"I've never done anything like that before," she admits, taking this conversation in an unexpected direction. I was just messing with her, but hell, if she wants to discuss anal,

I'm down. "Does it hurt?" she asks.

"Not if it's done right," I tell her honestly.

She bites down on her bottom lip and then says softly, "Does it feel good?"

"It can definitely feel good."

She nods once slowly, and then shocking the shit out of me, turns around, and with her back to me, says, "I think I want to find out." And fucking hell, she doesn't have to tell me twice.

Taking a step into her space, I tell her to put her hands on the wall, and she complies, placing her tiny hands flat against the tile. "Spread your legs," I say next, and she does. Opening the shower door quickly, I lean over and open the cabinet to grab the baby oil, then close the door.

"Celeste, baby, I'm not going to fuck your ass tonight."

"Why not?" she asks sounding disappointed. What's that saying? Lady in the streets, but a freak in the sheets. Yep, I think that about sums up my woman. First, she likes the idea of being watched. Then she rides me in my car in an alley, and now she wants to know what it's like to be fucked in the ass. I'm pretty sure I'm the luckiest damn man in the world.

"Remember when you lost your virginity to me?" I ask. "How tight you were?"

"Uh huh."

"Well, your ass is just as tight, and on top of that, I'm pierced." I pour the oil onto the top of her ass, then set the bottle down on the ledge. Spreading her ass cheeks, I rub it along her crack. "Tonight, we're going to start small. Tell me if anything I do hurts, okay?"

"Okay," she whimpers as I push my finger into her puckered hole slowly, one knuckle at a time. With my other hand, I come around to her front and tweak her nipple. Celeste moans in pleasure, and her ass pushes back, forcing my finger to go all the way in.

"How does that feel, baby?" I ask, pushing my finger in and out of her tight hole.

"Like…I need more," she says. Chuckling softly, I pull my finger out then push two back in. "Oh…Oh my god, Jase," she groans, pushing her ass back. "Can you…add another?"

"I don't want it to hurt, babe." I move my hand that was pinching her nipples down to her pussy and start massaging circles against her clit.

"Okay, but can you maybe…go deep?" she says breathily. I do as she says, picking up the speed and fingerfucking her ass deeper.

"How does it feel now?"

"Oh, fuck, so good." Her ass is now meeting my fingers thrust for thrust. I watch as my fingers glide in and out of her tight asshole. I'm not even doing anything at this point. It's all her. She's fucking my fingers, working herself higher and higher. I glance up in time to see one of her hands leave the wall and go to her nipple, taking over what I was doing.

"Jase, I'm…I'm so close." She moans loudly. I apply some more pressure to her clit and then she detonates. Her clit throbs, her hole tightens, and her legs shake as she orgasms.

Needing to be inside her, I pull my fingers out and push into her warm cunt. Her walls are still contracting as I grip her hips and fuck her from behind. I feel it as her orgasm rolls into another. I thrust into her a few more times before I can't take it anymore and release my seed deep inside her.

"Jase." Celeste giggles as I pull out of her.

"Yeah?"

"My body feels like Jell-O."

Laughing, I turn her around and help her wash up. Then, after wrapping a towel around her body, I pick her up and carry her into my room.

"I think I really like butt stuff," Celeste says through a playful smile as I set her down on the bed.

"I think I really like doing butt stuff to you," I say with a wink.

C~

"Dad, I'm home!" Skyla's voice rings out through the townhouse. It's two stories with the living room, dining room, kitchen, and half-bath downstairs, and the three bedrooms and two more bathrooms upstairs. I'm currently laying in my bed, but even one floor up, I can hear my daughter yelling for me as her feet stomp up the stairs.

"Dad!" she shouts as if I'm down the street, even though she's almost to my room. I glance over at the clock and see it's already ten in the morning. I'm usually an early-riser, but I didn't get to bed until almost four in the morning because Celeste couldn't keep her hands—Holy shit! Celeste is here. In my room. In my bed. I sit up, my gaze flying to the naked woman who's lying next me with only a thin sheet covering the swell of her ass. The sound of Skyla's feet pad down the hallway, and I fly out of bed to stop her before she plows into my room.

Thankful I fell asleep in my boxers, I rush to the door to lock it, but I'm a second too late. The door swings open, smacking me in the forehead, and Skyla enters the room before I can stop her.

"Oh no! Dad, are you okay?" Her tiny hands reach up to check my forehead.

"Yeah, I'm good," I say, trying to push her out the door. She hasn't noticed Celeste yet. "Let's go get you breakfast. Is your aunt here?" I press my hand to her back, guiding her out of my room, when Celeste, completely oblivious to what's going on, calls out my name. Her voice is raspy from sleep, and if my daughter wasn't currently standing in my room, it would have me wanting to sink deep into her so I could hear her call out my name in that same voice over and over again. But my daughter is, in fact, in my room and now aware of Celeste laying in my bed.

"Celeste, you're here!" my daughter squeals, too excited that her role model is in her home than to put the pieces together as to why she's here in my bed. My eyes swing over to Celeste, who flips over, shocked, and shoots up into a sitting position, her bare breasts on display.

"You're missing your clothes," Skyla points out, the corner of her mouth quirked up into a knowing grin, before I can say something.

"Oh, shit!" Celeste gasps when she realizes my daughter is here and staring at her, naked. She pulls the sheet up to cover herself and then stumbles out of bed, running straight into the bathroom.

"Yo, bro!" Quinn calls out. "What's for breakfast?" She enters the room and looks from Skyla to me. "Were you still in bed?" She eyes me in my boxers and scrunches her nose up in sibling disgust. "Get dressed. I'm hungry."

"Dad was in bed with Celeste and she was naked!" Skyla exclaims through a fit of giggles. Quinn's eyes go wide, her gaze darting around the room in search of the aforementioned woman.

"Skyla, why don't we head over to City Donuts?" Quinn suggests, and I've never been so thankful for my sister's quick thinking.

"But Celeste is here." Skyla pouts. "I didn't even get to say hi." Only my daughter would be more concerned about seeing Celeste than finding her naked in my bed.

"She's in the shower," I tell her. "By the time you get back with the donuts, I'm sure she'll be out and then you can see her."

"Fine." She huffs. "Can you go ask her what kind of donuts she wants?"

"Surprise her," I say, trying like hell to remain calm, when I'm really freaking the hell out on the inside. I've always been careful so that my daughter would never witness anything like this. And she's not a baby anymore, so I imagine she's put the pieces together on her own as to why Celeste was naked in my bed. But now what? Do I talk to her about it? Try to deny it? Admit to it? I have no idea how the mind of a thirteen year old even works. Is sex on her brain? Fuck! The thought of having to have a sex talk with my daughter makes me feel sick. This is why I'm so careful, why I never bring women home. But for some reason, when I'm around Celeste, all reasoning seems to fly out the window, leaving me to think with the wrong damn head.

"Okay," Skyla agrees then skips out of the room past my sister, who gives me an apologetic look.

"I'm sorry," she says.

"For what?" I shrug, pissed off at myself.

"I should've called. You've never…" She nods toward the bathroom door. "I didn't even think about it."

"I should've warned you. It's my fault."

"So, Celeste, huh?" She raises one brow.

"Aunt Quinn, c'mon!" Skyla yells from downstairs.

"We'll continue this conversation later," Quinn threatens before she shuts my door behind her.

"You can come out now," I say once I hear the front door slam closed. Celeste steps out of the bathroom, the sheet still wrapped around her like an oversized towel. I can't help but pull her into my arms.

Her head falls against my chest. "I can't believe that just happened." She groans.

"It's okay," I say, not wanting her to feel bad. None of this is her fault. "It happens."

"How many times has it happened?" She looks up at me with a scowl on her face.

"Well, never, but I'm sure other kids have walked in on their parents in the bedroom."

Celeste's eyes bug out, and she backs out of my arms. "But I'm not her parent," she states matter-of-factly. I'm not sure what's going on with her. While I may know Celeste on a very sexual level, there's still a lot I don't know about her. I've never seen this look in her eyes before.

"Celeste, what's going on?" I step closer to her, but she backs up again. "Talk to me."

"Nothing." She shakes her head, but she's full of shit. Her face is full of emotion I've never seen on her before. "I need to get going." She snatches her overnight bag from the floor and goes straight for the bathroom. I follow her inside, but she doesn't pay me any mind as she drops the sheet to the ground and then quickly dresses. She brushes her hair and then teeth, not once saying a word. I don't know what to say. She's obviously upset, but it feels like it's about more than Skyla walking in on us.

"Talk to me," I repeat.

She gathers up her stuff, shoves it all into her bag, throws the sheet back onto the bed, thrusts her bag over her shoulder, then heads out of my room and down the stairs.

"Celeste," I call after her, trailing behind.

"Nothing is wrong," she insists. "I just have a lot going on. I need to get my team and line ready for GFE next week. I'm usually working hundred hour weeks at this point, but I've been..." She doesn't finish her sentence, but I know what she was about to say. She's been distracted by me. She didn't get to where she is by luck or accident. She's busted her ass.

She comes to a stop in front of the door and turns around to face me. "There's a lot riding on this show," she says. "If it's a success, it can singlehandedly revitalize the fashion industry."

"That's the new one, right? Like Fashion Week but

different…Skyla mentioned how excited she is for it. She always watches them live or on YouTube."

Celeste smiles at that. "Yeah, it's a new show." She leans in and gives me a kiss on my cheek. "I'll see you later, okay?"

"All right." I don't know what else to say. Whatever has her freaking out, she's obviously not ready to talk about. She opens the door and we're met with a smiling Skyla and a frowning Quinn.

"Where are you going?" Quinn asks. "Skyla brought you donuts."

Skyla spots the bag in Celeste's hands and her smile dims. "You're not leaving, are you?" she whispers.

"Celeste has to get to work," I explain. "Fashion Week," I add, using her excuse.

"But…it's Sunday." Skyla pouts. "Please just stay for donuts."

"Sky…" I start to say, but Celeste nods once. "Okay."

"Are you sure?" I ask her.

"Yeah, she's right. It's Sunday…and there's donuts."

"Sky, go inside and pour us all a glass of milk, please." She and Quinn head inside, and I shut the door behind them. "Tell me what happened in there. Did I do something?"

Celeste sighs. "It's not you…" She seems to be warring with herself, and since I don't know why, I have no clue what to say. While I wait for her to explain, my eyes scan down her body. She's dressed in a pair of tight blue jeans with an off-the-shoulder maroon shirt. She's standing tall in a pair of black heels. The ones with the red soles that everyone knows cost thousands of dollars. Hell, they probably cost more than my mortgage payment. I suppress a deprecating laugh at the thought. Even dressed 'casual,' the woman screams power and wealth. I glance down at myself, in a pair of basketball shorts and a white T-shirt, my tattoos covering my arms and even portions of my legs. In the bedroom, when the clothes and lights are off, it feels so right, but as soon as we're dressed and in the daylight, I'm reminded of how different we are. And that's when it hits me. Why Celeste freaked out. Skyla walking in on us reminded her that I'm a single dad, while she's a single kid-less woman. I live in a townhouse, and she lives in a high-rise condo overlooking Central Park. I drive a '67 Camaro, while the guys she's used to dating ride in limos or have car services.

"Jase," Celeste says my name. "Why are you looking at me like that?"

"Finish what you were going to say. It's not you, it's me, right?"

"No…yes…I don't know." She drops her bag and brings her hands up to her face. I step forward, needing to pull her into my arms. "Skyla walking in on us was just a shock. I guess I freaked out."

"I'm a single dad, Celeste. That's not going to change." She moves her hands from her face and looks into my eyes. "I know how different our worlds are. You're this gorgeous and rich businesswoman and huge model. Hell, my daughter is a damn fan of yours. And I'm just me…a tattooist struggling to make ends meet."

"Don't do that," Celeste chides. "Don't belittle yourself. You're an amazing, hands-on, single dad who owns his own tattoo shop and busts his ass to provide for his daughter."

"Well, when you put it like that…" I grin playfully.

"When Nick and I were engaged, he found out he was going to be a dad."

"Yeah, he told me a little bit about how it all played out. One-night-stand, they went their separate ways, and then she saw him playing…"

"Yeah, but when he found out, I freaked out on him. I told him I didn't want to be a mom…ever." I still at her words. "My childhood, Jase." She shakes her head. "My mom was heartbroken and always high or drunk. We could barely keep the electric and water running."

"Your situation has changed," I point out.

"Yes, financially it has. But…" Celeste's eyes tear up, and she looks up to the sky, trying to will them away.

"Celeste…"

"Skyla already had one shit mother. The last thing she needs is another. She deserves the best."

There are so many things I could say to her right now. I could tell her she already has one up on half the parents in this world, just by knowing and recognizing what makes a parent, shitty. That the fact she unknowingly put my daughter first—even though she wouldn't make a shit mother—by simply saying what she did, speaks volumes.

After my mom died, and Jax and I were forced to be raised my Quinn's mom and my dad, I learned what it was like to be raised by parents who don't give a shit about anyone but themselves. Then I saw the shitty choices Amaya made for herself and her daughter, and how badly they affected Skyla. And it's because I've seen the difference in good and bad parenting, I've made it my life goal to be a good father to Skyla, but that doesn't make me perfect. With every decision I make, I hope and pray I'm doing what's right for my daughter.

Celeste has only been around Skyla a couple times, and she's already done more for my daughter than her own mother ever did. More than what Quinn's mom ever did for her. The truth is, Celeste would make a damn good mom, and I want nothing more than to tell her that, so she knows just how amazing she is.

But I don't say any of what I was just thinking, because that's not what she needs to hear. It's too soon for her. She's scared and freaking out. So I tell her what she needs to hear in this moment to talk her off the ledge. Because I can't let her go. I plan to keep this woman, and while she may come across strong and powerful, independent and confident, there's a piece of Celeste deep down that is vulnerable as fuck, questioning every decision she makes, scared of falling back down to where she came from.

"You're not her mom, Celeste," I tell her. "You're just you. Someone she can debate Gucci or Prada with." I give her a small, playful smirk. "I'm her only parent. I'm her dad." Her shoulders visibly sag, confirming this is what she needed to hear.

"You hang out with Olivia, right?" She nods. "But you aren't Reed's mom." Another nod. "I'm not asking you to parent her in any way. We've only just reconnected. All I'm asking is for you to give us a chance. Hang out and get to know each other." She nods once again, but this time she smiles.

"I can do that."

"But do you want to do that?" I ask.

Her smile grows bigger. "I do."

"Okay then. Let's go inside and have breakfast."

"All right, but for the record," she says in a serious tone. "Prada…it's always Prada. That's not even up for debate."

Fifteen

CELESTE

Shutting down my laptop, I press my finger against my phone screen to check for the millionth time if Jase has texted me back to confirm our dinner plans for tonight. I haven't seen him since Sunday. I ended up having to take the red-eye to California to handle some modeling issues for the shoot for my upcoming winter line. Margie was over there handling it, but when she called to let me know several of my models appeared to be on drugs, I knew I had to fly out and handle it myself.

And I'm glad I did. After threatening to have them drug tested, they admitted to using. I fired them on the spot, canceling their contract with my company, and told them if they ever wanted to model again in this industry, they would need to go to rehab. From there, I had to find four new female models available last minute and get all the clothes resized and fitted. It was an utter disaster, but once it was all handled, the shoot turned out beautifully—thanks to Felix, who handled it all like the pro he is.

It's now Thursday, and I'm back at home, and aside from a few texts, Jase and I have barely spoken. I told him all that was going on, but I know that most people can't really understand what it's like to run a business, especially one as time-consuming and demanding as mine. I should hire more people, delegate more, but it's my baby and for so long it's all I've had. But now, as I check my phone for the millionth and one time I'm wishing I did more delegating, so I wouldn't have had to go four days without seeing Jase.

My phone dings and I unlock it to check the message. It's from Jase: **I'm slammed at work**

My gut twists and my insecurities, I wasn't aware I even had, flare up like a bad rash. Does he mean that or is he blowing me off? As I'm trying to think of how to respond, another text comes through: **Sorry, I hit send by mistake. I'm slammed at work. Sky wasn't feeling well, so Quinn had to bring her home. I miss you like crazy. Raincheck?**

"What's that smile for?" Margie asks, appearing out of thin air.

"Jase," I tell her. "I thought maybe he didn't want to see me, but he's just busy at work."

"Something you can relate all too well to." She winks.

"Yeah," I agree, "and not everyone has an amazing assistant like you." As soon as the words leave my mouth, an idea hits.

"Hey Margie, I'm going to head out. Can you lock up

for me?"

"Absolutely," she says.

Snagging a cab, I give the driver the address to Forbidden Ink, and fifteen minutes later, we arrive. When I walk through the door, I find several people hanging out in the waiting area. Some are playing pool, others are sitting on the couch looking through the design books. But nobody is sitting at the front counter. Then, the phone rings and I hear Jax yell, "Someone get that!"

Walking around the desk, I grab the cordless phone and answer, "Forbidden Ink. How may I help you?"

"Yeah, I need to schedule an appointment," a guy says over the line. Sitting down on the stool behind the counter, I start searching for a calendar.

"Sure, just give me one minute, please." I press the hold button so I can find this damn calendar. There has to be one here somewhere. You can't possibly schedule four tattooists without having it written down somewhere.

"What are you doing behind the counter?" a voice asks, making me jump. I look up and into the prettiest blue eyes I've ever seen, which are a huge contrast to his harsh, spiky black hair and tatted up tan skin. Based on his question, he must work here.

"I'm looking for your schedule. A guy is on the phone wanting to setup an appointment. Any chance you know where it is?"

"And you are?" he prompts. Shit! I didn't introduce myself.

"I'm Celeste." I extend my hand to shake his. "A friend of Jase's."

The guy looks me over then smirks. "Celeste, huh? The model, right? I've heard a lot about you."

"Hopefully all good," I joke, and he laughs.

"Yeah, definitely all good. I'm Gage." He lets go of my hand. "Did Jase ask you to come in and help out?"

"Actually, he doesn't know I'm here." I shrug. "He canceled our plans and I figured he could use the help." I chew on my bottom lip, hoping I haven't crossed the line.

Gage smirks and nods. "That's really cool of you." He reaches into the drawer and pulls out four small books. "These are how we schedule. Jase likes to keep it simple." He rolls his eyes.

"How long do I block off for each appointment?"

"It varies depending on the size of the tattoo," he says. "For now, just block off three-hour time slots and highlight the appointments you make in yellow, so we can go back and double check them. Ask them what they're looking to get, and jot it down. It will help us, so we know what to expect. If they want something custom designed, you schedule a consultation and that's only thirty minutes."

"Got it," I say, repeating all of what he just said over in my head. Three hours, write down what they want, half-hour consultation.

"Oh, and if it's a piercing, let them know we only do walk-ins. They usually only take about twenty minutes."

"Okay." I nod my head once in understanding. The phone beeps, indicating there's another call coming in while the other line is on hold.

"You sure you got it?" he asks.

"Yep! You go draw and I'll handle this," I say with a

wink.

Gage chuckles. "Alright, you want me to let Jase know you're here?"

"Actually, how about we just keep it between us? I'm sure eventually he'll come out and find me."

"Ha!" He laughs harder. "Okay, you got it."

When he walks away, I answer the phone and put the caller on hold. Then I go back to the other line and schedule the appointment. Once I hang up, taking the phone with me in case it rings, I walk around the room and take down everyone's information. There are several walk-ins, but Gage didn't tell me how to handle them, so I treat them all like appointments and schedule them in.

The place is busy and time flies. I turn off the main ringer so the guys and Willow aren't bothered while they're working. Instead, it only rings on the phone I'm using. At some point, Willow comes out, and I introduce myself. She's really sweet and thanks me for helping out. I learn she handles most of the walk-ins and piercings, and when one comes in to let her know. Jase and Jax are completely booked with appointments, and Gage has a mixture of both, walk-ins and appointments.

It's seven o'clock when a pretty brunette walks in and requests Jase. She's dressed in tiny cutoff jean shorts and a barely there tank top. She has several tattoos covering her arms and legs, as well as one peeking out from the front of her top over her breast. Looking at his book, I see he's booked solid for the next week. "I'm sorry but he's booked. I can get you in with Willow or Gage in about an hour." I take a look at Jax's book. "Or Jax has availability tomorrow at five."

"Okay, well, could I just go back and see him real quick?" She winks dramatically, and it takes everything in me not to throw up all over her or smack her.

"He's with someone right now," I say politely, remembering my manners. "I can let him know you're here, though. What's your name?"

"I'm actually hoping to surprise him." She blows a bubble and it pops. I do my best not to cringe.

"Okay…You are more than welcome to wait." I point to the couch. "He should be done in the next hour."

"Thanks," she says before she saunters over to the couch and plops down, pulling out her cell phone.

For the next hour, I stay busy—ignoring the skank still waiting for Jase—scheduling some more people and organizing the desk. Margie would seriously be so proud of me right now. I also place several ads into the online classifieds for a receptionist, putting my number and email so Jase won't be bombarded with calls and emails. Once I weed out the duds, I'll give him the info of all the serious applicants.

When Willow and Gage both finish up with their last appointments for the day, they thank me for taking over, and confirm their appointments for tomorrow before they head out—leaving only Jax and Jase still with clients, and little miss skank still waiting on the couch.

When the clock hits eight and it's officially closing time, I consider whether I should go back and tell Jase or just kick her out. Figuring I should be the bigger person, I walk over to the door to lock it, in case anyone tries to come in, before

I head back to let Jase know someone is here to see him. But before I make it to the door, miss skank stands and starts heading toward the back.

"Umm…excuse me," I say with a fake smile plastered on my face. "You can't go back there."

"Oh, well, I thought you were leaving." She shrugs. "And who are you? The Jase police?" She scoffs.

JASE

Today has been a day from hell. There's no other way to describe it. First, Quinn overbooked me by accident, so I've been rushing all day to try to get ahead. Then one of my morning regulars showed up late, and at that point I knew I was screwed, so I had to cancel one of my afternoon appointments. But he didn't answer and, of course, showed up. Skyla was hanging out here with Quinn, when she, for the first time, started her period and started complaining of cramps and begging to go home. Luckily, Quinn was here to help her deal with her woman problems. But because that involved them going home, it left the shop with no one to answer the phones or greet anyone. Of course, both Jax and I had sleeves we were working on, which meant we were holed up for hours with no breaks.

I was supposed to finished by six, but didn't turn my gun off until just after eight. After applying the ointment, I walked my client out through the backdoor since he parked his bike behind the shop. Then I headed to the front to lock up. As I walked down the hall, I noticed Gage and Willow had both left, and Jax was still in with his client. I also realized the phone hadn't rang in hours.

As I walked farther down the hall, I heard two women talking. Maybe Willow is still here? But then I recognized one of the voices as Celeste's.

"You can't go back there."

Who the hell is she talking to? And why does she sound like she's pissed?

"Oh, well, I thought you were leaving," another voice says, "and who are you? The Jase police?"

I don't recognize the other voice, but when I get to the front, I recognize the person the voice belongs to. Missy. A longtime client that has wanted to get at my dick since the first time she stepped foot in here.

With Celeste's back to me, she doesn't see me as she pops her hip out and brings her hand down to her side. Damn, she looks hot in those tight jeans and those fuck-me heels. The shirt she's wearing leaves her back exposed and makes me want to bend her over the pool table and trail kisses down her spine.

"Actually, skank," Celeste hisses, and I stop in my tracks, waiting to hear the rest. "I'm the woman who's fucking Jase, so how about you turn your trashy ass around and call him tomorrow to make an appointment." I can't see her glare from behind but I can hear the possessiveness in her voice, and holy fucking shit, I've never been so turned on in my life.

"Fuck you, bitch!" Missy screeches. "There's no way Jase is fucking you. He doesn't fuck women at the tattoo shop."

Celeste laughs. Not a ha ha kind of laugh, but a maniacal, my woman might be crazy, sort of laugh. When she finally stops, she says, "That may be true. We haven't fucked here." Her shoulders rise and fall. "But he did eat my pussy out over on the pool table."

Damn, my woman is scrappy as fuck! Figuring I better stop this before it turns into a full-blown cat fight, I step forward to make my presence known. Missy notices me first, her face lighting up. She obviously has no idea I just heard their entire conversation. "Jase!" she screeches, causing Celeste to turn around. Unlike Missy who looks delighted to see me, Celeste looks pissed as hell.

"Jase," she says, her voice devoid of all emotion.

As a man, I have two options, I can be nice to Missy, since she's a loyal customer, and explain to Celeste that sometimes bitches are just crazy. She might be understanding or she might get upset and take off. I'll have to grovel for a couple days, but eventually she'll get over it. Or I can cut ties with Missy right here and now and end the night deep inside my woman. It's been four days and nights since I've felt the inside of Celeste's warm cunt. Which option do you think I'm going with?

Damn right.

"Missy, you gotta go," I say, getting straight to the point.

"But…but…" she stutters, while Celeste grins my way.

"One, you don't call my woman names, and two, you know damn well I've made it clear nothing will happen between us. Now you're going to have to find another shop to get your work done at." Taking Celeste's hand in mine, I walk over to the door, unlock it, and open it for Missy. "Bye," I tell her, leaving no room for discussion.

When she's gone, I close the door and pull Celeste into my arms, planting a kiss to her soft, plump lips that I've missed like hell.

"How much of that did you hear?" Celeste mumbles against my mouth.

"Enough to know better than to ever give you a reason to be jealous." I kiss her harder this time, pushing my tongue into her mouth so I can taste her. Fuck, I've missed this. Missed her.

"What are you doing here?" I ask once the kiss ends.

"I've been here since five o'clock," she admits sheepishly.

"What? Why didn't you let me know?"

"I didn't want to bug you while you were working." She shrugs. "I've been answering the phones and scheduling appointments. I met Willow and Gage. They're really nice. Oh! And I put ads in the classifieds to hopefully find you a permanent receptionist." I stare at Celeste for several seconds, absorbing everything she just told me. I texted her that I was too swamped to get dinner, so she showed up here and spent her evening answering phones and scheduling clients. A woman who pays other people to assist her, sat here all night and helped me.

When I don't say anything, too in awe of the woman I'm falling for all over again, she says, "I should probably get going. I have an early morning meeting tomorrow and you're scheduled to come in at nine for a touch up."

"We don't even open that early," I say, finally finding my voice. "We don't open until noon during the week. Ten on the weekends."

"Oh." Celeste frowns. "I didn't know that. My office opens at nine, most do, so I just assumed you guys opened at nine as well...I can call him to reschedule," she says, stepping out of my arms.

Needing to feel her, I pull her back to me. "No, it's okay. I'll be here at nine. Thank you for everything."

"Are you sure?" she asks. "Because I can—"

With a quick shake of my head, I slant my mouth over hers. Her fingers tangle in my hair as my hands grab her ass, picking her up and pressing her back against the glass door. We kiss for several minutes, until Jax clears his throat, reminding us we aren't alone.

"Come home with me," I say once we break the kiss.

"I don't want to take you away from Skyla. You said she isn't feeling well." My heart swells at her statement. She may think she doesn't have it in her to be a good mom, but she has no idea just how selfless and caring she really is.

"She started her period," I tell her. "I was thinking we could pick up some chocolate and rent a movie to watch with her. Then once she's in bed, I can spend the rest of the night relearning every inch of your body. Four days without being inside you is too long."

"You're such a good dad." Celeste smiles softly. "And that sounds perfect."

After stopping by the store to pick up Skyla's favorite chocolate—as well as tampons, pads, bubble bath, and a bunch of other shit Celeste insisted my daughter might need to make her feel more comfortable—we swing by the deli to pick up dinner, then we head home. Skyla is ecstatic to see Celeste walk through the door with me. We spend the rest of the evening eating, watching movies, and Skyla even puts on a fashion show for us when Celeste asks to see the new clothes Skyla bought recently. When it's well after midnight, Skyla says goodnight and heads to bed. Quinn went home a couple hours ago. That leaves just Celeste and me sitting on the couch together in the living room.

"I should probably head home," she says, pulling out her cell phone to call for a car. I pluck it out of her hand and place it on the table. Picking her up bridal style, she squeals in shock, and I kiss her lips to muffle the sound.

"The only place you should head to is my room," I tell her, carrying her upstairs. Once we're inside, I shut and lock the door and then drop her onto my bed.

I climb up her body, my legs on either side of hers. "Stay the night," I say. "I wasn't kidding when I said I missed you like crazy. I need to be inside you ASAP." Dropping my head down to hers, I give her a kiss. "Please."

"Only on one condition," she says. "You make sure I'm up and gone before Sky wakes up."

When I give her a confused look, she adds, "She deserves more than a woman who her dad is screwing, coming and going out of her home."

My eyes trace over Celeste's features: her beautiful onyx eyes. They're so dark, you could get lost in them. Her button nose that has just a small spatter of freckles that stay hidden with her makeup, but at night, when she wipes it all off, I get to see and kiss. Her plump, fleshy lips that have me addicted to not only her kisses but the words that come out of her mouth. Celeste is the entire package. Sexy and classy, independent and mature. And she's caring and thoughtful. Tonight, when I thanked her for buying all that stuff for my daughter because she started her period, she just shrugged it off like it was no big deal. And here, right now, in my room, her only concern is that Skyla doesn't get hurt or confused by whatever is happening between us. Celeste doesn't see it, but I do. She doesn't see the selfless, nurturing person she is. I want to explain all this to her, but I know she would fight it. She would come up with excuses or tell me I'm wrong.

So instead, I agree to make sure she's gone before Skyla wakes up, and then I spend the rest of the night trying to show her through my actions how appreciative I am of the way she puts Skyla first, and hope like hell that one day Celeste will see herself the way I see her.

Sixteen

CELESTE

"Brenna, it's been too long." I give Brenna Myers, the VP of Elite Modeling, an air kiss to each cheek. With the Global Fashion Extravaganza happening this week, everyone who is a part of the fashion world is in town.

"It has." She grins. "I saw the preview of your fall line. It's absolutely stunning. I imagine you will have more than your fair share of buyers knocking at your door after your show."

"Thank you." I can't help the grin that appears. Brenna was the first person to take a chance on me in this industry when I was eighteen. And when I won America's Elite Model and told her my goals, she didn't laugh. Instead she said, "If you want it bad enough, you will make it happen." Almost eleven years later, and I made it happen.

"Brenna! There you are!" Randy cuts in. "I'm so sorry.

Celeste, how are you, dear?" He gives me a quick air kiss. Randy is the new VP for Calvin Klein, focusing on the children's and teen lines, and hasn't learned how to breathe yet. Fashion shows can be very stressful when you're just starting out. I remember my first one. Everything that could go wrong, did. But over time, I created a team of people I can trust, and now everything runs smoothly—for the most part.

"Randy, everything is set," Brenna tells him slowly. "Breathe, darling." She laughs.

"We had several of the children and teenagers come down with the flu," he tells me. "It's like one of them got it and it spread like wildfire. Never create a children or teen line, trust me," he whispers. "It's more trouble than it's worth." I know he's only saying that because he's freaking out. I've looked at the numbers for a potential children's and teen line, and the profit would be well worth the trouble. You would be surprised at how much parents spend to make their kid's look good. And unlike adults, kid's grow, which means constantly having to purchase larger sizes, new lines. My thoughts go to Skyla and how adorable she dresses. When I hung out with her and Jase, she showed me all of her clothes, putting on a fashion show. She knows every designer and all the latest trends. She reminds me so much of me at her age, only I didn't have the money to actually purchase the clothes. Instead, I would buy a new fashion magazine every month and cut out all of the outfits and glue them into a book I made.

"And I told you I would handle it," Brenna tells Randy, and an idea pops into my head.

"Hey Brenna, do you by any chance have room in any of the lineups for one more teen?"

Brenna gives me a curious look. "A friend of mine has a daughter who wants to be a model…"

Her eyebrows go up. I'm sure she's heard this line a million times. It's part of being in this business. Everyone who has a kid thinks he or she is model worthy, everyone who likes fashion is a potential designer. And of course everyone with a camera thinks they have what it takes to be a photographer. But when I watched Skyla put on that mini fashion show for me, I knew instantly, she definitely has what it takes.

"I know, I know," I say with a laugh. "But I've seen her walk and she's got it. She's not part of this world, but it would make her life, and maybe it could get her foot in the door." When she doesn't say anything, I add, "It would be a personal favor to me."

Brenna nods. I've never asked for a favor. I've learned over the years, you don't want to owe anyone in this industry because they will collect. But Skyla is worth it. Plus, it really would be great exposure for her.

"Okay," she agrees. "She can walk for Randy." Randy opens his mouth to argue. "He is desperate." He closes his mouth. "On one condition."

I wait for her to tell me.

"If she's worthy of the runway, you have her sign with me."

"Deal." There's nobody I would trust more than Brenna.

Excited to share the news with Skyla, I finish up the

details for tonight and head out. Margie is shocked when I tell her I'm leaving, but I know she can handle it.

"Celeste!" Skyla yells when she spots me walking inside Forbidden Ink. She sets the pool stick against the wall and comes over. I can't help the way my thighs clench at the memory of Jase eating me out on the pool table only a couple days ago.

"I wiped it down," Jase whispers, as if he knows exactly what I was just thinking.

I jump at his words. "I didn't see you there," I admit.

"I can see that." He's about to pull me in for a kiss when we both remember Skyla is standing here. While we've been spending a lot of time together lately, we haven't really discussed what to say to her. That would mean labeling us. After my freak out last week over Skyla finding us in bed together, I told Jase the other night, I didn't want to be there when Skyla woke up. I tested the water by saying that I didn't want her to see some woman he's sleeping with coming in and out of the house. I held my breath, hoping he would correct me, but he didn't. Instead, he agreed. I know that's for the best. I'm not stepmom material. But I can still admit—not out loud—somewhere deep in me, I was hoping Jase would tell me I was. But he didn't.

"You guys can kiss," Skyla states with a silly smirk on her face. "I know you're dating." She giggles. "I have had boyfriends…"

Jase growls at her last statement. "What boyfriends?"

"Chill, Dad," Skyla says with an eyeroll.

Jase glares at his daughter, but decides to let it go. "So, to what do we owe the pleasure of you coming all the way down to the East Village?" he says, shifting his focus to me.

"Up," I clarify.

"Huh?"

"I came up because I was in Tribeca at Spring Studio."

"For GFE!" Skyla screeches, excitedly.

"Yep, and I have some news." I waggle my eyebrows at Skyla.

"You got me a ticket?"

"Nope." I frown.

"Oh." Her mouth curls down into a pout.

"I didn't get you a ticket because models don't need one." It takes her a second to understand what I'm saying, but once she does, she screams so loud, I'm pretty sure the entire block heard her.

"Are you serious?" She runs over and throws her arms around me, then looks up. "Please don't let this be a joke. It would be a very mean joke."

"It's not a joke. You're going to be walking for Ralph Lauren's teen line."

"Oh my god!" she screams again. Then she looks up at me again, this time with tears in her eyes, and says, "Thank you," and my heart feels like it's just been removed from my chest and handed to her. How could those two words and that look make me feel like this?

"You're welcome, pretty girl." I don't even realize the words are out of my mouth until I've said them. I've just called her the nickname my mom always called me. The one name that made me feel like I was more than just Celeste, the trailer trash on the wrong side of the tracks.

"When is it?" she asks.

"It's actually tonight. I was thinking we could spend the day together. Get manis and pedis. Get your hair done…"

"Really?" Skyla smiles. "Can I, Dad?"

She looks over at her dad, who is currently staring at me with a slight frown marring his features. Why is he upset? And then it hits me. Skyla is asking her dad for permission. Because he's her dad. And she needs permission. Oh my God! I'm so stupid.

"Oh, no," I say out loud. Jase's frown deepens and his brows furrow together.

"Sky, go get all your stuff together," Jase says, and she takes off down the hall.

"I messed up, didn't I?" I ask. "I should've asked you first. I'm so sorry."

"Whoa, calm down." Jase's lips form into a soft, comforting smile. "Sure, you probably should've asked me first, but you didn't mess up." He grabs my hips and pulls me toward him until our bodies are flush against one another and then kisses me. The kiss is slow and gentle and has me melting into a pile of mush.

"Then why did you look upset?" I ask him once we separate.

"I'm not upset."

"You were frowning."

"I guess I was a bit confused that you went from freaking out the other day over being in Skyla's life to wanting to spend the day alone with her. You seemed like you were okay the other night hanging out with all of us, but I just want to make sure *you're* okay with all of this. With spending the day with Sky on your own." I bite down on the

231

inside of my cheek while I contemplate what he just said. He's right. I have been hot and cold. It's no wonder he didn't jump at correcting me or putting a label on us the other night.

"I guess I have been all over the place lately," I admit sheepishly. "I was just so excited to share my love of fashion with someone else who loves it, I didn't even think about it." And it's not like I'm parenting her or anything. She has Jase for that. What harm can I do in one day? Plus, she'll be busy getting ready for tonight.

"I'm ready!" Skyla comes running out with her purse slung over her shoulder.

"You sure you're okay with this?" Jase murmurs low enough that Skyla can't hear.

"Yeah, it will be fun." I give him a kiss on his cheek.

"Can my dad come?" Skyla asks.

"Of course. I'll send you some tickets in case your brother and sister want to go as well."

"I'll just be a minute!" I yell across my condo to Skyla. Spending the day with her has been nothing short of amazing. She's so mature for her age, and we've had a great time. It's everything I always wanted with my mom but never got to experience. We got manis and pedis at the spa, then went to my favorite Bistro for lunch. I took her to get her hair done, even though once we arrive at the show, they will do it how they want. We were on our way there when Margie called and asked me for the designer credit files for tonight. Apparently she can't find the electronic copy on the cloud, but luckily I keep all files on my home computer as well.

"Can I look at your jewelry?" Skyla asks.

"Go for it!" I find the files, send them to Margie, and then head into my bathroom so I can freshen up before we go. My outfit for tonight is at the studio.

"See anything you like?" I ask when I come out and find Skyla combing through my jewelry box.

"This." She holds up the dandelion necklace Jase gave me years ago. I almost threw it away the day I thought he slept with Amaya, but something stopped me. Instead, I put it in my jewelry box and never looked at it again.

"It's just like the one at my dad's shop…like the one on the bracelets you made for my career day."

I remember she mentioned that before—that Jase has a painting of a dandelion at the shop, but I didn't see it when I was there. "I haven't seen it."

"It's in his room where he tattoos people," she says. *Hmm…looks like I'm going to have to make it a point to check out Jase's room at the shop.*

"He also has a tattoo of one on his ribcage," she adds, eyeing the necklace with a soft smile. *Interesting… guess I'll also have to make it a point to check out his body more thoroughly as well.*

"Your dad gave me that necklace," I admit. "A long time ago, when we were… friends."

"You mean boyfriend and girlfriend?" she asks, a hand moving up to her hip. "I'm not a baby, you know. I'm thirteen. I hate that my family acts like I'm still little." I stifle my laugh because to her thirteen is old, but to someone who is about to be thirty, thirteen is still in fact a baby. But I won't tell her that.

"Anyway," I say with a smile. "He gave me this necklace and told me to follow my dreams."

"It's beautiful," Skyla murmurs.

"Why don't you wear it tonight? You can't wear it on the runway since it's not Ralph Lauren, but you can wear it before and after."

"Wow, okay, thanks." She nods and lifts up her hair, so I can put it on her.

"Hey Celeste," Skyla says when I finish clasping the lock on.

"Yeah?"

"Thank you." She turns around and gives me a hug, and the way she holds me tight makes me think she might be thanking me for more than just allowing her to wear my necklace. But I can't go there...

"You're welcome, pretty girl."

We arrive at Springs Studio and Skyla stays with me through the afternoon. Just like Fashion Week, GFE is running all week, at several venues, and all day, well into the evening. My fall line is being showcased today and then Skyla will be walking this evening. She stays with me the entire time, asking questions and commenting on the line. Several times Margie gives me an impressed look at how much Skyla knows about the industry at only thirteen years old.

Once the show is wrapped up, we head over to where Skyla will be getting ready, so I can introduce her to everyone she needs to know. Most girls would be nervous, but not Skyla. She's bubbly and outgoing and excited. She's polite to everyone she meets. Jase texts me when he, Quinn, and Jax have arrived and are seated. I couldn't get them in the front since that's only for the press, designers, and the who's who of fashion, but they do have decent seats. Skyla is taken from hair and makeup to wardrobe, and then is walked through what she'll be doing. I stay with her the entire time, not letting her out of my sight. Her dad is trusting me to take care of her, and I don't take that responsibility lightly.

When Ralph Lauren gets announced, all the kids and teens line up. Skyla has made a few friends, so I give her some space and tell her I'll be here when she's done. There are months and months of prep that go into getting everything ready for these shows, and oftentimes I'm too busy to actually enjoy what's happening around me, but today, with Skyla a part of it, I'm actually stopping and taking the time to watch and enjoy the show.

Skyla—dressed in an adorable tile-print mini-skirt with a matching top, leggings, and black, leather boots—walks out onto the runway doing exactly as she was told and practiced. The cameras flash as she hits the end and then turns around to walk back. I look out and find Jase watching his daughter, a large grin splayed upon his face. He looks every bit the proud father. And my heart has never felt so full.

"I want her," Brenna murmurs into my ear. "She's going to be the next you."

I laugh softly. "No, she's going to be so much more." And then I turn to find Skyla. She's stepping back behind the scenes and her eyes lock with mine. Her smile is so wide, so pure, I want to bottle it up and save it.

"That was…amazing!" She squeals. "Thank you!"

"You were amazing," I tell her. "And being here, watching you has inspired me to consider creating my own children's and teen lines."

"Can I help you?" She clasps her hands together.

"Of course!"

Jase: Hey gorgeous…

Jase: I have a big favor to ask of you

Jase: Like huge

Jase: Gigantic

Jase: A word bigger than gigantic

Jase: I'll make it worth your while ;)

I've just finished holding a meeting with my team—to go over the details of the buyers who have contacted Leblanc after seeing the show—and have found two seconds to look at my phone. This week has been insanely crazy in an amazing way. There is nothing more magical, or exhausting, than putting on a fashion show. It's been a couple years since I've stopped modeling and have attended the shows strictly as a designer, but the butterflies still appear with every show, and I hope they never go away. They remind me that my dreams have come true. That everything I've worked hard for is finally in my hands. But as I stare at Jase's texts, and my heart speeds up, I'm reminded that there's more to life than career goals. It's why I broke things off with Chad. Because I want more. I haven't seen Jase since Skyla's big debut into the modeling world, but we've talked every night on the phone, even if it's at four in the morning when I finally collapse into bed. For the first time, I'm looking forward to the craziness dying down. In the past, I lived for every fashion show, for the long days and even longer nights, but now it feels like it's only keeping me away from where I really want to be, which is with Jase and Skyla.

Me: anything

I've only just hit send when my phone rings. "Hello?"

"I was worried I scared you off with my hundred text messages," Jase says with a strained laugh.

"Sorry, it's been insane around here."

"Everything okay?"

"Oh yeah, great actually. We've already surpassed the number of buyers for the fall line than predicted."

"That's amazing! Congratulations," Jase exclaims.

"Thank you." Then I remember the point of this call. "Is everything okay on your end? I saw all your texts."

"Yes, actually everything is great here as well. Have you ever heard of Max Harper?"

"The rapper?" I ask, confused.

"Yeah. I guess he has some reality show, and the producer called and said Max wants to come in for a tattoo.

Apparently Killian recommended me at some event."

"Wow! That's awesome. Are they going to film it?"

"Yeah, it will be incredible publicity for the shop."

"What do you need from me? Want me to dress you?" I joke. "I think I have a nice suit that would look rather dapper on you."

Jase laughs. "Nah, I got my wardrobe covered."

"So you're going with your usual jeans and a white T-shirt?"

He laughs again. "Am I that predictable?"

"Yeah, but I think we got off subject. What's the huge, gigantic favor you need from me so badly that you're willing to make it worth my while?"

"Right. Quinn is attending some last minute function with her boyfriend and she was supposed to keep an eye on Sky. The producer said they don't want a kid on the show, and even if they did allow her to be on it, I don't really want her here at the shop. I imagine guys will be cursing and talking about things I don't want my thirteen year old daughter to hear. So, I was wondering if you could watch her." I smile inside at how good of a dad Jase is. The guy is going to be on television and his biggest concern is making sure his daughter is taken care of and isn't exposed to anything that might affect her in a negative way.

"Of course, I can. When?"

Jase is silent for a second before he says, "Now?"

"Ahhh…" I laugh, now understanding why this is such a huge favor. "Where is she?"

"At home. Quinn had to leave to get ready. She's okay being left alone. I'm just not sure how long I'm going to be…Quinn offered to bring Sky to the charity gala, but I don't want to put her out. She's not even sure if she could get her a seat and—"

"Jase, breathe." I laugh. "I'll head over there now."

He releases a soft breath. "Thank you."

"You're welcome."

Seventeen

JASE

"Look, man, you don't need to thank me. That's what friends are for. Besides, your work speaks for itself," Killian says. I'm on my way home from the shop. The episode has been recorded, and Max Harper has been permanently tattooed with a custom piece, designed and inked by me. It's crazy. He posted one image, tagging the shop on Instagram, and we all spent hours making appointments—including the new receptionist, Evan, that Celeste found for me. The guy will be apprenticing with us at the shop while working in the front. It works out perfect.

Shocked over the fact that all of us are now booked well into September and the episode hasn't even aired yet, I called Killian, wanting to thank him again for recommending Forbidden Ink.

"Did everything go okay?" he asks.

"Everything went smoothly. Luckily, the tattoo he wanted wasn't too bad." I laugh. "I've seen some ugly as hell tattoos shown on those shows. The episode will be airing next month and this will without a doubt be a game changer for the shop. You can't pay for this type of advertisement."

Killian laughs. "Yeah, I've seen some, and not even the best artist can make them look good. I'm glad it all worked out."

"It did, so thanks."

Killian chuckles into the phone. "No problem. What are you up to tonight?"

"I actually just pulled up to my house," I say, putting my car in park and stepping out. "Celeste watched Skyla for me."

"Celeste, huh?" Killian laughs. "Giselle told me all about your past. I never would've guessed you and Celeste would've had a past...or a present." I know he doesn't mean it as a dig, it's just merely an observation, but his words remind me once again how different Celeste and I are.

"Yeah, I guess she doesn't usually date guys like me," I say, leaning against the side of the car.

"Nah, I didn't mean it like that," Killian says, trying to backpedal. "She just usually...shit, okay, it's exactly what I meant." We both laugh.

"I get it," I tell him. "We're complete opposites. I know it doesn't make any sense. But trust me when I tell you there's so much more to her than what she lets people see."

"Yeah," he agrees. "That's what Nick has always said, and my wife is good friends with her...I guess I don't really know her all that well. But if there's one thing I've learned this past year, it's not to judge a book by its cover."

After talking for a few more minutes, we end the call with Killian telling me he's found a new piece he wants tatted, and that he'll be calling me tomorrow to schedule.

When I unlock the door and step inside my house, I hear the sound of laughter coming from the kitchen. I throw my keys into the key bowl and head that way to check it out. I was going to pick up dinner, but when I texted Celeste, she told me she and Skyla were taking care of it.

"I'm home," I say as I step around the corner.

"Jase!" Celeste laughs.

"Dad!" Skyla giggles.

I glance around at the destroyed kitchen, confused as to what the hell happened in here. There is what looks like flour everywhere. On the counters. All over the floor. It looks like it snowed. Celeste's hair is tinted white, and so are Skyla's clothes. They're both standing on opposite sides of the kitchen and holding balls of something gooey in their hands.

"What happened?" I ask.

Celeste laughs again then steps toward me. "Try this. Tell me what you think." She holds her fingers up, which are holding what looks like cookie dough, and brings them to my lips. "Open," she says playfully, so I do. She places a small bite of dough into my mouth, and Skyla's giggles get louder.

"Is it good?" Celeste asks. I chew the bite and swallow. It's a tad bit salty.

"Delicious," I say, and she grins.

"Ha!" She looks at Skyla.

"Try mine, Dad." Skyla hands me a piece of dough. I chew and swallow.

"How does mine taste?" It tastes like there's way too much vanilla.

"Delicious," I tell her.

"So, whose is better?" Skyla asks. Oh, shit… I didn't see that coming.

"They're both delicious."

Celeste cackles devilishly. "I think he needs to try some more," she tells Skyla, who grins mischievously.

"I agree," Skyla adds. "I think he needs to *experience* the dough to make a decision."

"Agree," Celeste says.

I watch as both of them walk over to where they were standing when I came in, unsure what they mean by *experiencing* the dough. But less than a minute later, I find out exactly what they mean, when Skyla balls up a piece of the dough and throws it at me. The sticky dough smacks me in the face, and the girls crack up laughing.

"Hey!" I yell. "That's not cool."

"Oh no!" Celeste says, feigning concern. "Did the dough stick to you?" She cackles, and it sounds scary as fuck. "It's probably because it doesn't have enough flour. Here, let me help you." She takes a handful of flour and walks toward me. Then, before I can stop her, she dumps it over my head.

Now the mess in the kitchen makes perfect sense. Skyla laughs so hard, she snorts.

"So, it's like that, huh?" I ask no one in particular. "All right…" I walk over to where the dough is sitting in the bowl, and grab it. "Game on!"

Celeste's eyes go wide, and she ducks, thinking I'm going to throw the dough at her. But instead, I take a large dollop in my hand, bridge the gap between us, and smoosh it all over her mouth.

Skyla is now laughing so hard, she's bent over, holding onto her stomach. But when she sees me eye her, she stops and grabs a handful of dough. "Don't come any closer or I will be forced to use this on you." She raises her fist, and I laugh. And then I cut across the kitchen, and grabbing her by the waist, throw her over my shoulder.

"Dad!" she squeals. "Put me down." Taking some flour in my hand, I turn her right-side up and dump it over her head, at the same time Celeste dumps more over mine.

We spend the next however long throwing dough and flour at each other. I don't even want to think about the mess I'm going to have to clean up.

When the doorbell chimes, Celeste raises her hands in surrender. "I'm waving the white flag!" She laughs. "That's dinner."

"You ordered?"

"Well…" She traps her bottom lip between her teeth, nervously, then releases it. "I tried to cook."

"But it burnt," Skyla adds with a shrug.

"Yeah," Celeste agrees.

"You two go get cleaned up, and I'll pay for the food," I tell them.

"I can get it," Celeste insists. "It's my fault that dinner got ruined."

"I got it, babe," I tell her with a kiss, forgetting my daughter is in the room.

"I knew you two were a couple!" Skyla yells as she runs up the stairs. "Friends my butt!"

After we finish eating dinner and clean up the mess in the kitchen—though, flour will probably be found in every nook and cranny for the foreseeable future—Skyla asks if we can all watch a movie together. I look to Celeste, unsure if she has anywhere she needs to be, and she says she would love to.

Skyla and Celeste pick out the movie, while I make the popcorn, and then the three of us pile onto the couch to watch the movie. Jax comes home halfway through it, but says he's heading back out and not to wait up. When the movie ends, both Skyla and Celeste are passed out. I lift them off me then carry Skyla to bed. It's not often I get to carry my daughter to bed, and her body dangles over my arms, so I try to engrave the moment into my memory, for the times when she's rebelling against me and telling me she wants nothing to do with me.

Once she's tucked in, I head back down for Celeste. I should probably wake her up and ask if she wants to go home or stay, but she's out. So instead, I carry her up to my room and lay her down in my bed. Apparently burning food and having food fights is exhausting. I laugh as I recall the look of embarrassment on her face as she explained how she misread the directions for the roast, and then when she and Skyla tried to make cookies, they ended up spilling and eating more than actually got placed onto the cookie sheet.

In Celeste's eyes, she failed. There was no roast for dinner or cookies for dessert. The kitchen was a mess that we had to clean up. She apologized several times.

But in my eyes, she succeeded, and I told her just that.

She made my daughter smile and laugh. She bonded with her—created memories that will last a lifetime. When I told her that, she just blushed and shrugged like I knew she would, and then apologized again, confirming just how guarded Celeste really is. With her fancy makeup and designer clothes, she appears strong from up in her high-rise expensive condo. As if she's on top of the world. But hidden behind her makeup and clothes, behind the walls she's built up to protect herself, is a vulnerable, insecure woman who just wants to be loved. And that's exactly what I'm going to do. I'm going to love her.

"Damn, I can't believe how busy we are, " Jax says, falling onto the couch next to me in the breakroom we have set up in the back of the shop. It has a couple of couches, a fridge, a sink, and a bathroom. Nothing fancy, but somewhere we can go between clients. It also has a door that leads out to the back alley, where those who smoke, can, since I don't like anyone smoking in the front. "Thank God for Celeste finding us Evan." He drops his head back against the wall and sighs in exhaustion.

"I know," I tell him. "We would've been screwed." My cell phone rings, and like the nosy-ass he is, Jax looks over to see who's calling me.

"Tell Celeste I said hello," he says as I stand and walk away to speak to her without an audience.

"Hey, Dimples, how's it going?"

"Not good, Jase."

"What's wrong?" I close my office door behind me. With all four of us working today, there's several different songs going at once along with everyone bullshitting over the music.

"A couple years ago, when I first launched my fashion line, I joined up with a couple other designers to start a charity called I Heart the Arts. It raises money to help the art programs in schools and clubs. This year we're going to be showcasing several models using body art to help raise money."

"That sounds like a good cause," I tell her, surprised and proud of this new fact I've just learned about Celeste.

"Yeah, it is. But the artists we hired for the show just canceled on us, so now I have twenty models with no art, and a show that's supposed to start in eight hours."

"What do you need from me?"

"Artists. I was wondering if maybe you knew anyone…well a few someones. Like maybe there's some network all artists are a part of. I know you're a tattoo artist, but maybe you all run in the same circles. I don't know." She sighs. "It's a paid job."

"I'm in, and I'm sure Jax and Gage and Willow will be too. And I can bring Evan. He's still apprenticing but he can draw well."

"Oh," she says, breathlessly. "I didn't mean you…"

"Am I not good enough?" I laugh. "I am an artist."

"No! I know you are. But you're super busy. You were just saying you're booked until like next year. I can't ask you to shut down for me."

"You're not asking. Text me the location and we'll be there soon."

"Yeah?" she asks with hope in her voice.

"Yeah."

"Thank you, Jase! I love you." The phone goes silent, and I pull it from my ear to see if Celeste is still there, or if she hung up. "What I meant is…" she starts to say, but she can't think of a way to justify, or fix, what she just said, which means she meant the words.

"What you mean is you love me," I tell her boldly, praying I don't spook her, but needing to tell her how I feel, "and I love you too."

There's another bout of silence and then Celeste whispers, "You do?"

"I do. See you soon, Dimples."

We hang up, and with the biggest fucking grin on my face, I call everyone into the office to ask them if they're willing to help. Of course they say they are. After telling everyone waiting that we have an emergency and need to close up shop, we start calling all of our clients who were supposed to come in today and reschedule them. After locking up the shop, we head over to Spring Studios where the show is being held. On the way, I call Quinn to let her know I'm not sure what time I'll be home, and she lets me know Rick has gone out of town for business, so she can keep an eye on Skyla without issue.

From the moment we arrive, everyone is in a frenzy. I wasn't sure what was needed to be done, but luckily Celeste has all of the supplies. All she needs from us is our talent. We spend the next several hours painting body art on each of the models. They are completely naked, but with the art painted on, it looks as if they are fully clothed. Celeste has specific outfits that need to be drawn on, and several designers, who are part of the show, oversee everything we're doing. Some of the names even have my eyes going wide. These aren't lowly up-and-coming designers. These are bigtime. And it hits me that the woman I'm dating is bigtime. She's a famous supermodel who has taken the fashion world by storm. I can still remember the teenage Celeste, who laid in my bed and shared her dreams with me. I didn't know it at the time, all that was against her—that the hand she'd been dealt was even shittier than mine. She might've been Nick's best friend, but she wasn't raised with a silver spoon in her mouth like he was. She's fought for everything she has.

As I finish up the last model and stand to stretch my legs, the show begins. I hear Celeste's voice come over the microphone, and without getting in anyone's way, I peek out of the curtain. She's standing at the end of the catwalk speaking to the hundreds of people who are surrounding the stage about the charity and how all the proceeds will be spent. She's dressed in some sexy-as-fuck crème-colored tight dress that shows off her pert ass. Her sky-high fuck-me heels make her toned legs look like perfection. When she thanks everyone and turns around to walk back, our gazes clash. As she walks toward me, with her chin up and eyes bright with pride, she gives me a gorgeous smile that, I'm man enough to admit, takes my fucking breath away. And it's in this moment, I know that while our worlds may not fit perfectly, I will do whatever it takes to make sure they orbit close enough to keep her near me. Even if it means I have to jump into hers.

Eighteen

CELESTE

"I can't believe you did this!" Olivia throws her arms around my neck for a hug, her pregnant belly hitting my front. "I...I...just thank you." She sobs.

Patting her on the back, I say, "You're welcome," while I search for Nick in hope of him saving me. When she finally releases me, her tears have dried up. But then she looks around, taking in her surroundings, and starts to cry again.

We're standing under an air-conditioned white tent I rented that overlooks the East River. It's Fourth of July, so there will be fireworks later, which is why I picked this particular park, but it's also a party to celebrate Nick's graduation and Giselle and Olivia's upcoming births. There are several tents set up throughout the area. A couple for people to sit and relax under, one where food is being catered, another where there's a bar set up, and one more for desserts and presents. Since Olivia and Giselle are both having girls, pink streamers, balloons, and other decorations are strung up all over the area.

"Celeste," Nick says, walking up, "this is too much." He gives me a hug and a kiss on the cheek. Reed, their eighteen month old son, toddles over with a balloon in his hand, and Skyla running behind him.

"Ba-oon," he squeals. "Ba-oon! Da-da, ba-oon." Nick laughs and picks his son up.

"He let go of two of them," Skyla says with a laugh, "so I tied that one to his wrist."

"Good thinking," I tell her with a wink as Killian, Giselle, and Giselle's mom, Sarah, walk up to join us.

"Celeste!" Giselle squeals. "This is all amazing! When you told me you were throwing Nick a party, you didn't tell me it was also a baby shower." She points to the tent that's holding the three-tier Disney Princess cake. "That cake is amazing! Have you seen it, Livi?"

"No, not yet, we just got here," Olivia says.

"Come here, I have to show you." Giselle gives me a hug. "Thank you."

"You're welcome," I say. "If you're hungry, there's food over there." I point to one of the tents. "And there's a full bar set up in that one."

Giselle, Olivia, and Sarah head over to the tent to see the cake as Jase comes walking up with Jax, Quinn, and her boyfriend, Rick, who is staring down at his phone.

"Hey, Dimples," Jase says, giving me a soft kiss to my lips. "Everything turned out great." Jase and Skyla came here early this morning to help me set up, then left to take showers and get ready. Since I needed to go to my place to get ready, which is in the opposite direction, we agreed to meet back here.

"Thank you," I tell him. "There's tons of food and drinks. Please help yourself," I say to everyone.

"I'm starved," Quinn says to Rick. "Join me?"

"Sure," Rick says with a small smile, but doesn't look up from his phone. He reminds me a lot of the men I used to date. I try to think about all the times I've hung out with Jase. Maybe it's because his job isn't as demanding, but I can't think of a single time where he's been with me and didn't give me one hundred percent of his attention.

Gripping the curves of my hips, Jase pulls me in front of him and wraps his arms around my front, nuzzling his face into my neck. His two-day stubble tickles my skin, and I laugh, pushing him away. "You need to shave!" I joke.

"No, I don't," he growls into my ear. "I know you like my beard." He's not wrong. I love running my hands up and down his stubble.

"Hey, Dad, I'm going to get something to eat. Wanna go with me?" Skyla asks Jase.

"Sure, sweetie, let's go," he says, then turns to me. "You hungry?"

"I'll meet you guys over there in a minute. I just want to make sure the bounce house gets set up." The vender I ordered from was running late and is finishing up now. There aren't a lot of kids here, but Skyla thought it would be fun for Reed to play in, so I ordered one.

"All right." He gives me a kiss on my cheek then heads

over to the food tent with Skyla. Since Reed has become her shadow, he follows, and Nick follows him—leaving Killian, Jax, and me standing here.

Killian steps closer to me. "You did good," he says. "Thank you."

"You're welcome."

"So, you and Jase, huh?" he asks.

"Yeah." I nod slowly.

"That's good. I'm happy for you guys."

"Thank you?" I squeak out, unsure of how to respond to Killian's overload of niceness, and a bit stunned that we've somehow apparently moved on to discuss my love life.

He laughs, and Jax joins in. "Ah, man, just be glad you don't have to live with Jase." He shakes his head. "It's disgusting to watch on a daily basis how in love they are."

"Oh, shut up!" I smack Jax's arm playfully, and he chuckles.

"Who would've thought, little miss 'I'm marrying a fortune 500 guy' would fall in love with a tattooist from Piermont." Killian laughs, hip bumping me. Had he said that a few months ago, I would've taken it the wrong way and gotten pissed, but I can see it in his face, he's just playing around—and he's not all wrong. When we were younger, that's exactly what I planned to do.

"So, what's next?" Killian asks. "A wedding? Babies?" He laughs harder, thinking he's so hilarious, and of course, Jax laughs right along with him. "I can see it now… Little Celestes and Jases dressed in Gap and Nike, running around with fake tattoos all over their arms."

"My kids wouldn't be dressed in Gap or Nike." I scrunch my nose up in mock disgust. "More like Dior and Dolce & Gabbana." Killian and Jax both cackle.

"I'm just messing with you," Killian says. "You gotta admit, though. It's crazy how far we've come from the teenagers we once were, hanging out in the dorm room, refusing to fall in love while Nick ragged on us."

I laugh, remembering exactly what he means. Nick was the only one out of the three of us I ever imagined falling in love. Hell, when I was younger, I didn't even believe in love. Or maybe I did, but was too scared to admit it…"Yeah, sometimes it feels like it was another lifetime."

"Agreed." He nods once. "I better go check on my baby mama," Killian says with a smile, excusing himself. As I watch him walk away, my mind swirls with everything that was just said. I know he was only joking, but at the same time, what he said has truth to it. When two people are in a relationship, marriage and babies are what comes next, right? Does Jase want to have more kids? I just assumed since he already has a teenager, he wouldn't want to start all over again. What if I was wrong, though, and he wants to have more children? Give Skyla a brother or sister…

"You okay?" Jax asks. "You look like you've seen a ghost or something."

"Yeah…No…I'm okay," I choke out. "I'm going to go make sure everything is taken care of for the bounce house," I say as an excuse to escape for a moment before I have a panic attack.

"All right," Jax says, looking concerned.

After I make sure the party rental company is paid and

let them know when to pick up the bounce house, I take a walk along the river, trying to calm my nerves over what Killian said. Everything with Jase and me feels like it's all happening so fast, yet slow, at the same time. I think a lot of the reason for that is because of what we had all those years ago—it was so easy to slip back into where we left off. I think back to the day Jase and I discussed me not wanting to become a mom. I never asked him what he wanted.

"Hey," a baritone voice calls out from behind me. When I turn around, Jase is walking up to me. "Jax mentioned you seemed off. Everything all right?"

He stops a few feet in front of me, and I stare at him for a few seconds, taking him in. His black hair that's usually neatly gelled is messy, as if he was running his fingers through it, his perfect lips turned up into a slight nervous smile, and his signature white T-shirt stretched taut across his chest with his hands stuffed into his pockets. I should ask him right here and now if he wants more kids, but I can't bring myself to do it. Because if he says he does, I know I will have to break things off with him. And if he says he doesn't, I will always wonder if he's lying, putting my needs first.

Instead, I take the couple feet toward him and wrap my arms around his neck. His arms encircle my waist as I run my tongue across his lower lip, then his top one, teasing him. He groans, pulls me closer to him, and kisses me hard. His tongue massages mine, and I lift up his shirt, sliding my palms over his abs. His skin is hot and I crave his warmth. His hands glide down my back, landing on my ass. He lifts me into his arms, then carefully brings us both down to the grass. Hovering above me, with both his arms on either side of my head, Jase and I make out like teenagers, his body grinding against mine, until we hear Skyla calling out our names. Quickly rolling off me, Jase stays lying down, his arm propping himself up, while I sit up and adjust my clothes.

"I've been looking everywhere for you guys," Skyla says. "Can we do cake and presents?"

"Sorry," I say, giving her a smile, while praying she didn't see her dad practically dry humping me in the grass. Jase stands first, and reaches down to help me up. "Yeah, we can do cake and presents." I stand and wipe the grass off my backside.

"Cool! You can go back to making out now." She winks and runs back over to where everyone is. With my hand in Jase's, we follow behind her. I think maybe Jase forgot about what he asked me when he walked over, until he leans in and whispers, "I know you were upset about something, and while that distraction was nice, I will ask you again later, and you will answer me."

The rest of the evening runs smoothly, and luckily, we're so busy with our friends and family that Jase doesn't find the time to ask me again what's wrong. We do cake, watch while Olivia and Giselle open their baby gifts, and Nick announces that he's been signed by a publishing company for the romance novel he wrote, based on Olivia and his love story. Then, at nine o'clock we all make our way down by the river to watch the fireworks. Jase holds me in his arms while the bright colors shoot off, creating beautiful designs. And while

I should be enjoying this moment, a small piece of me is wondering if every memory we're creating is only another weight being added to the reality that's going to drop right on top of us and knock us out of this fantasy we're currently living in.

Nineteen

CELESTE

"It's so beautiful out here!" I spread my arms out wide so I can feel the cool breeze against the front of my body. I'm currently standing on the front deck of a seventy-five foot luxury yacht as we enter the Atlantic Ocean. Killian and Giselle, Nick and Olivia, and Jax and some woman—Kirsten—he met at a bar the other night are all on board as well. I'm not sure where everyone else is, but what I do know is that Jase is currently standing directly behind me, with his arms wrapped around my naked torso and his chin resting on my shoulder. I can feel his bulge pressing into my ass, and it has me wanting to find one of the empty rooms on this boat and put it to good use.

"Not as beautiful as you are," Jase murmurs into my ear, and I can't help the giggle that escapes my lips, remembering the last time he spouted a cheesy-ass line to me, ended with me losing my virginity to him.

"Smooth," I say through my laughter.

"It's the truth," he says. "The second you took off your bathing suit cover and turned around, my dick went hard." His hands glide down my sides and land on my nearly bare ass. "Please tell me you only wear this tiny fucking bikini in private," he says, squeezing a handful of each cheek. "Your sexy ass is hanging out for all the world to see."

"It's the style," I say by way of explanation. "They're called Brazilian bottoms."

"Well, I'm not sure I like everyone getting to see what's mine," he growls, and the sound of his voice has my thighs clenching.

"Okay, caveman," I say with a grin plastered on my face. I've never had a guy get jealous or possessive before, and it's definitely a turn on. Schooling my features, I turn around so my back is pressed against the railing and my chest is pressed against Jase's. "Next, are you going to tell me you want me to quit my job and spend my days barefoot and pregnant in the kitchen?" When Jase's eyes light up, clearly more than okay with that image, I laugh nervously at my slip up. It's a typical cliché joke that everyone makes, but my making it can lead to a conversation about babies, and that's the last thing I want to discuss with Jase. It's been almost two weeks since the Fourth of July. I told myself if he brought up me being upset, I would be honest, but luckily, he hasn't, so I'm pretty sure I'm in the clear.

"Down boy!" I say to hide my uneasiness. Then, standing on my tiptoes, I pull him in for a kiss, knowing if the talk of babies is on his mind now, it will distract him.

"Get a room," Nick yells just as the kiss is getting more heated, which has us pulling apart, both of us breathing hard with want.

"I think we should listen," I say in a whisper, and Jase's eyes go wide in shock that I would say such a thing. Before he can argue, I walk around him and head toward the stairs which lead down to the rooms. "I need to use the restroom," I announce without making eye contact with anyone. I've only just stepped off the stairs and into the cabin when I feel Jase's hands on my body. He shoves me into an open door and slams it shut behind us.

"That bathing suit is a fucking tease, woman," he growls as he lifts me onto what looks like a table of some sort and shoves my legs apart. He removes my bottoms and kneels down, set on eating me out. My back and head hit the wall with a thump as he spreads my lips and suckles my clit with his talented mouth. My hands go to my breasts, and I pull at the hardened peaks, losing myself to the pleasure.

When I've come so hard I about see stars, Jase lifts me off the table and turns me around so my back is to him. With my ass in the air, and my breasts mashed against the hardwood surface, Jase enters me in one fluid motion. Gripping my hair, he pulls my head back so he can suck on the side of my neck. His lips trail down and kisses my shoulder as he continues to fuck me, hard and deep. It doesn't take long until my legs are shaking and I'm screaming his name as we both come completely undone.

When he stills, his hard-length still deep inside me, he places another kiss to my shoulder and murmurs, "One day I'm going to tattoo this flawless body." I let out a content sigh. "I'm going to mark you permanently," he growls. "Make you mine." His voice is so matter-of-fact, it sends heat through my whole body.

He pulls out of me, and I miss the contact immediately. Turning around, I wrap my arms around him, not wanting our connection to end. He lifts me, and with my legs wrapped around him, carries me to the bathroom to get cleaned up. With me sitting on the luxurious marble countertop, Jase gently opens my legs and cleans me up—and my heart picks up speed at how sweet he is.

My thoughts go back to what he said earlier: *make you mine*. I've never wanted to be anybody's before. I've wanted to be wealthy and successful, have a nice home, a comfortable life. And I wanted to find a man who would help ensure that I would have all of that. But until Jase, I never wanted to actually *be* somebody's. Belong to them. Be their everything. Now I can't imagine anything I want more. And with that thought, I say a prayer that one day, when we have the conversation we need to have, our futures align.

After spending the rest of the day on the yacht, hanging out and relaxing with everyone else, we head back to Jase's place. He said he's cooking Skyla's favorite—Chicken Fettucine Alfredo—and asked me to join them for dinner. Jax says he'll be home right after he drops Kirsten off. It was obvious she wanted to be invited back, but Jax either didn't catch on, or didn't care, because he made it clear he was dropping her off first.

When we arrive at Jase's house, we're greeted by a very excited Skyla and a glaring Quinn. I'm not sure why Quinn still has such an issue with me, but at some point we should probably discuss it.

"Dad! Celeste!" Skyla hugs her father and then me. "Did you guys have fun?"

"We did," Jase says, giving his daughter a kiss on her forehead before excusing himself to go start dinner.

"Aunt Quinn showed me a picture of a yacht. I wanted to go today, but Dad said no," Skyla says as we walk into the living room. "It's so beautiful!"

"They are," I agree. "Today was just for adults," I tell her, sitting down on the couch, "but we can go on one if you want."

Skyla sits next to me, her eyes as wide as saucers. "Really?" She pulls out her phone and shows me the image of a yacht a little smaller than the one we went on today. "One like this?"

"Sure." I smile at her. "You can invite some of your friends if you want, too. And we can even have the captain anchor, so we can go swimming."

"That would be so much fun," Skyla exclaims. "Aunt Quinn, do you want to go?" She turns her attention over to Quinn, who is leaning against the wall, like she's not sure if she wants to join us—well, more like join me—and is shooting daggers my way.

"Sky, why don't you go wash your hands, so you can help your father start dinner?" she says, not answering the question.

"Okay." Skyla shrugs and then takes off upstairs.

Once she's out of ear sight, Quinn says, "You aren't her parent. You shouldn't make plans with Skyla without asking Jase." I frown at her words. She's right, I'm not Skyla's parent, but I didn't think it would be an issue.

"You're right. I'll ask Jase in the future."

"And what about the fact that renting a yacht will cost thousands of dollars?" Quinn continues. "You don't think that's a bit excessive? She's thirteen years old and needs to learn that she can't just have whatever she wants."

"Maybe." I raise a shoulder, not understanding why my wanting to make Skyla happy is such an issue. Her grandparents spoil her with materialistic possessions. "But if it's what will make her happy, then who cares?"

My phone rings with an incoming call, so I pull it out of the pocket of my bathing suit coverup and click the side button to silence it since it's my mom. Not having had spoken to her in a while, I'm about to excuse myself to call her back, when Quinn says, "You might be some rich and famous model or whatever"—she flicks her hand in the air— "and Sky may look up to you, but Jase wants more for his daughter."

Ouch! Okay, then. "What's your problem, Quinn?" I stand and walk toward her.

"You," she says simply.

"Well, that much is obvious." I roll my eyes. "But what about me is exactly your problem?" Other than a few times of hanging out during the week Jase and I spent together all those years ago, we barely know each other.

"For starters, my brother cares a lot about you, yet you were able to walk away from him without so much as a goodbye." I open my mouth to argue why I did just that, but she continues, "And how about the fact that you only date wealthy, white-collar businessmen." Her brows raise, daring me to argue.

"Isn't your boyfriend wealthy?" Rick Thompson owns several investment firms all over the world.

"Yes, but unlike you, I don't have a type, and my brother definitely isn't your type. So what are you doing with him? Getting your fix of the 'bad boy.'" She actually uses air quotes. "And once you've had enough, you'll what…leave him again?"

"For your information"—I step closer to Quinn, so I don't have to raise my voice—"Jase knows why I left. Not that I have to justify myself to you, but it was a horrible misunderstanding. I regret that I didn't speak to him before I left, but I can't take it back now. And while, yes, the wealthy, white-collar businessman was my go-to type, it was only because I wasn't looking for love."

"And now you are?" she volleys.

"Yes," I say with a nod, "I am, and I love your brother."

"And I love you, too," Jase says, pulling me into his side. I don't even know when he joined us. "Quinn, I know you mean well, but please give Celeste another chance. What happened back then was a shitty misunderstanding, and Celeste and I have both moved forward. I would appreciate if you would do the same."

"Fine," Quinn says, "but do you really think it's wise that Celeste is offering to take Sky on yachts? She's going to think that's normal."

"And her wearing Burberry boots and Coach glasses is?" Jase says, defending me and pointing out exactly what I was just thinking. "Not everything is black and white, sis."

"That's different," she argues. "You don't have a choice. It's the only way Amaya's parents will leave you alone."

"We always have a choice," he says, "and you're right, it is different. My thirteen year old walks around in outfits that sometimes cost as much as the mortgage on this house." He chuckles softly with a shake of his head. "And it's because her grandparents choose money over love. They're doing the same thing to my daughter that they did to theirs. They're trying to buy her love. But as her dad, it's my job to teach her the difference. And I don't, for a second, think Celeste offered to take Skyla out on a yacht as a way to buy her love." My heart swoons at Jase's words. He didn't even hear our conversation yet he's giving me the benefit of the doubt.

"And," he adds with a sexy smirk, "I would like nothing more than for Sky to end up just like Celeste." Oh! He did hear our conversation. "Yes, she's rich, but that's only because she's strong and determined and motivated." Hot tears well up in my eyes at his words as he continues. "There are a million models out there, *almost* as gorgeous as Celeste." He winks at me playfully. "But not all of them are as successful. Not all of them work as hard to pave their own future. Celeste isn't just some model. She's a smart and savvy businesswoman, and I fully support my daughter looking up to her."

Unable to take another second of hearing Jase talk about me, I pull his face down to mine and kiss him hard, hoping to convey every emotion I feel right now. When our kiss ends, I say in a whisper, "I love you. Thank you."

"Just speaking the truth, Dimples."

My phone begins to ring again. I pull it out and see it's Victoria this time, and my stomach knots. What if something is wrong with my mom? "I need to take this," I tell him. Then to Quinn I say, "I really do care about your brother and Skyla. I hope you can give me a chance." She nods once but doesn't say anything, so I press answer on my phone and walk outside to take the call.

"Victoria, how are you?" I say politely.

"I'm calling because of your mother," she says, getting straight to the point.

"Is everything okay?"

"No, she's been admitted into the hospital for alcohol poisoning. Someone found her passed out in front of the diner."

"The one that shut down?" Victoria had told me my mom was still going there daily in case Snake showed up, but I didn't know she was drinking while there. This has gotten out of hand. I need to give my mom answers once and for all. I should've done it sooner, but Adam was right. I was too scared. I'm not sure what would be worse: to find out he's alive and living his life, which would mean he just didn't want us, or to find out he's dead and all this time my mom has been waiting on a man that will never show up.

"Yes," she says, "I think you need to come back. She needs help, Celeste, and she won't let me help her."

"Okay," I tell her, "I'll be there as soon as I can." We hang up and I go inside. The aroma from the dinner Jase is cooking wafts into my nose and my stomach rumbles.

"Smells delicious," I tell him when I enter the kitchen. "Can I do anything to help?"

"Nope." He gives me a kiss on the tip of my nose. "Sky is setting the table and the fettucine is almost ready."

"Okay, I'll get the drinks," I offer.

Once the table is set and the drinks are poured, Jase spoons heaps of pasta and chicken onto all of our plates, just as Jax walks through the door and joins us at the table.

"Rick will be gone all week," Quinn says to Jase as we eat our food. "So, if you need any help with Sky this week, I'll be available."

"Jase mentioned you have a photography business," I say, trying to make an effort.

"I do, but it's slow-building," she admits. "I started it about five years ago, but it's hard to get my name out there."

"What kind of photos do you take?" I ask.

"Mostly family portraits. I don't have an office. I shoot on location, like at Central or Bryant Park." I remember that earlier when Giselle, Olivia, and I were talking, Olivia mentioned she wanted to get professional pregnancy photos done. Giselle said she did too.

"My friends, Giselle and Olivia, want to get pregnancy photos done. Is that something you do?"

"Yeah." Quinn nods. "But you don't have to—"

"Don't do that," I tell her. "You're running a business. When someone offers to bring you in business, even if you think it's out of pity, you take it." I shoot her a wink, and she laughs.

"Actually," Jase says slowly, "Sky and I are going to be

flying down to North Carolina to visit her mom."

"Oh, yay!" Skyla exclaims. "I can bring her the signed paper Celeste gave me."

"I was wondering if maybe…if you don't have too much going on…if you would want to join us," Jase says softly.

"I was actually planning to fly down myself," I say. "My mom isn't doing so well, and I need to go check on her."

"Oh, what's wrong with her?" Jase asks with a look of concern.

Not wanting to get into it with Skyla at the table, I simply say, "She's just not feeling well, and I haven't seen her in a while." I don't mention that I actually haven't seen her in over ten years—since I left. I refused to return, and she refused to leave.

"All right, then how about we look at flights when we're done eating?" Jase suggests. "We can book a room, and while you're visiting your mom, we can visit Amaya."

"Sounds good," I tell him, taking a bite of my food. "And can we just make it official that you're the cook in this relationship? This is so delicious!"

Twenty

CELESTE

"Sky, please hurry up!" Jase yells across the hotel suite to his daughter. We arrived in Piermont late last night. After checking in, we were all so exhausted from flying, we crashed into our beds the second after we changed our clothes.

Now it's morning, and Jase is taking Skyla to go see Amaya while I go visit my mom. She's already been discharged from the hospital and is back home. While I haven't spoken to her, knowing she would just downplay it or lie to me, I spoke to the doctor at the hospital to make sure she was okay. I also put a call in to Duncan, my PI, hoping he might have some answers for me, but I haven't heard back yet.

"Coming," Skyla yells back. A few seconds later, she steps out of the bathroom looking so adorable and fashionable. She's wearing pigtail french braids I did in her hair earlier, and is dressed in a cute jean skirt and a flowery flowy top. To complete her outfit, she's sporting silver glitter Kate Spade high-tops. Every time I see her dressed, the desire to create a children's and teen's fashion line increases. Skyla and I have been working on several designs together, and I'm getting excited. I spoke with my partners and they're completely onboard.

"I'm going to head out too," I tell Jase.

"You're not going with us?" Skyla frowns.

"You knew Celeste was going to see her mom," Jase tells her.

"I know, but I thought you could go with us first and then go see your mom," she says with the saddest look on her face. "Please."

Powerless to say no to her, I nod. "Okay, yeah, I can do that."

"No, you can't," Jase argues. "Sky, we'll see Celeste later. She needs to go see her mom." He wraps his arms around my waist and kisses my cheek. "It's okay to tell her no," he whispers.

"I know," I tell him, "but I don't like to see her sad, and it really is okay. I can go...unless... you don't want me to." I didn't even consider he might not want me there.

"Of course I do," he states seriously. "I just don't want you to feel obligated."

"Well, I don't mind." I give him a quick kiss. "I can go see my mom afterward."

"We can go with you...if you want," Jase offers, but I shake my head.

"I appreciate that, but I have no idea the condition she'll

be in, and I don't want to chance exposing Skyla to whatever state she may be in."

"When's the last time you saw your mom?" Jase asks.

I swallow thickly. "Eleven years," I whisper. My eyes dart to the picture on the wall, not wanting to look Jase in the eyes.

"Celeste, look at me," he says. "You never returned? Not once?" His tone is one hundred percent full of concern and curiosity, not an ounce of judgment in words, but that doesn't stop me from feeling shame. What daughter doesn't visit her mom once in eleven years?

"No," I admit softly, "and she wouldn't visit me. I-I pay all her bills, but I haven't seen her since I left when I was eighteen."

Jase nods once. "Monica and Phil asked if they can take Skyla to dinner. I'll tell them they can take her, and then I'll go with you. You're not doing this on your own."

"You don't have to do that…"

"I can see it in your eyes, Dimples. You're scared. I'm here. You don't have to do this alone."

We arrive at the long-term care facility, and after signing in, head up to the third floor where Amaya is. When we get to the room number the receptionist said she's in, Jase stops and folds slightly at the waist so he's at Skyla's level. "Remember what I told you. Because your mom is still in a coma, there's a good chance she's not going to look like the same person you've seen in the pictures Grandma and Grandpa have shown you."

"I know," she says with a nod. "I remember from last time." Jase sighs like he wants to say something more, or maybe take her away from here, but instead he simply nods back.

Not wanting to interfere in this moment, I attempt to stay back while Jase opens the door and walks inside with Skyla, but she notices, and taking my hand in hers, says, "Can you please come with me? I want you to meet her."

"Sure," I say, then walk inside with her. The room is a harsh white and smells like a mixture of bleach and antiseptic. There's a single bed in the middle of the room and only the sound of the monitors fill the silence. It takes everything in me to stifle my gasp when my eyes land on Amaya laying still in the bed. She looks nothing like the woman I met all those years ago. Her face is pale and gaunt. There's no meat on her, which you would think would be the opposite since she's unable to exercise. Her hair is down and straight, as if it was recently brushed, but it's greasy looking, like it rarely gets washed.

Skyla's steps falter and the grip she has on my hand tightens. She's scared, and I don't blame her. Amaya doesn't look scary per se; she looks sick. Knowing Skyla wants me to meet her mom, I step forward, guiding us to the side of her mom's bed. We stand together in silence for a few minutes, and when I'm sure Skyla and Jase aren't going to speak, I do.

"Hey, Amaya," I begin. Skyla's hand squeezes mine. "I'm not sure if you remember me. We only met once."

"You met my mom?" Skyla asks. I look down at her, confused. Then I play back what I just said. Shit!

"I did once," I admit. "When we were really young. She was hanging out with your dad when I went over to his place to visit him." I'm not sure if I've said the right thing, but it's too late now.

Skyla nods once, but doesn't say anything. "Why don't you show her what you brought her?" I suggest.

"She looks so different from what I remember," Skyla says, assessing her mom.

"It's probably because you're getting older," I tell her. "When we're little, we don't see things the same way we do once we're older."

"Do you think she can hear me?" she asks, sounding way younger than her thirteen years. "The nurses said before that she can, but now I'm not sure if they're right."

I have no clue if Amaya can hear or not, and I can't lie to her. "I'm not sure," I say, "but a lot of people believe that when someone is in a coma they can hear what their friends and family say to them, so it's worth a shot." I did hear that once on a show.

"Okay," she says, then steps forward and begins to tell her mom about me—who I am, what I do for a living, how we met, etcetera. My eyes find Jase's and our gazes lock. He mouths a 'thank you' to me.

We spend the next half-hour talking to Amaya—until her parents show up. They walk in and greet us, introducing themselves to me, but not once acknowledging their daughter. Skyla says bye to Amaya, leaving the signed paper on the nightstand next to her bed, and we all leave. Monica

274

and Phil tell Jase they're going to take Skyla to eat and do some shopping, and will call him when they're done so he can pick her up.

After giving Skyla a hug goodbye, we get back into our rental car and head toward my childhood home. Jase is driving, so I have to guide the way. When we cross over the train tracks, my heart plummets into my stomach, weighing down on my insides like a lead weight. I'm holding Jase's hand, but I let go, feeling my palm getting sweaty. My heart gallops in my chest, and it gets harder to breathe.

"Hey," Jase says, darting his eyes to me. "It's going to be okay. I'm here with you. We'll get through it together."

"I know," I tell him. "Turn here." I point to the upcoming stop sign, and Jase follows my directions.

"What you did for Sky," he says, "the way you took charge and made her less afraid. Thank you."

"Why has she been in a coma for so long?" I ask. "Is there a chance of her waking up?"

Jase exhales a harsh breath. "Is there a chance? Yeah, but it's small. So damn small." He shakes his head. "Six months after Amaya was found, the doctors told her parents they had the option to pull the plug, but they were so riddled with guilt, feeling like they failed her, they refused. I think in some weird way, they think they're finally being good parents by keeping her alive."

"Wow, that's so sad," I tell him. "Turn here." I point to the stop sign. "It's the fourth trailer on the left."

"It is sad," he agrees as he turns onto the street I grew up on. "Unfortunately, since they're her parents, they get to make that call. Once the doctors said there's only a fifteen percent chance she'll ever wake up, they had to move her to the long-term facility. I don't even think they ever visit her. It's just the idea that she's alive and they're taking care of her that makes them feel less like failures."

"I can't imagine having to make that decision," I say truthfully. "Having to decide whether someone lives or dies."

"This one?" Jase asks, pointing to my childhood home, if you can even call it that. *A home.* The trailer itself isn't bad looking. While it's older, it doesn't look as such. I pay a window cleaner to come out every six months to clean the windows and pressure clean the exterior, a lawn service to mow the lawn, and a housecleaner—despite my mother's protest—to clean the inside once a week. But no amount of cleaning can make this place *feel* like home.

"Yeah," I whisper. He parks in the driveway behind my mother's newer Audi that I bought for her a couple years ago. She, of course, argued, but eventually gave in since her car needed to be fixed and I refused to pay for it. Allowing me to purchase her a car was the only way she could get to work and home every day since the bus service stops before her shift at the diner ends—or I guess did end, since the diner is now shut down.

We get out of the car and head up the sidewalk. Unsure of the condition my mother is in, I stop Jase and say, "Would you mind waiting out here?" I point to the table and chairs. "I just don't want to make her feel uncomfortable if she's not dressed," I add.

Jase nods his understanding. "Sure, I'll be right here."

"Thank you." I give him a chaste kiss, then step up the

three small steps and take a deep breath, nervous of what I'll find in there. The door is unlocked, like always, so I walk right in. Everything is the way it was when I left eleven years ago. From the shit-colored brown couch, to the cheap pressboard cabinets my mother painted an ugly mustard yellow. She purchased this trailer when she found out she was pregnant with me. Snake helped her find the place and even paid for it. It's why she won't leave. She's afraid if she moves, he won't be able to find her.

"Mom," I call out to let her know I'm here.

"In my room," she croaks out. I enter her room and find her lying in bed with her sheets pulled up to her chin. The room is pitch black, save for a tiny sliver of light seeping in through the slats of the blinds. I can't assess her features. It's too dark. Flipping the switch, a soft yellow glow lights up the room, but my mom doesn't open her eyes. Her hair is still the same color, but now there's gray mixed in. Her face is free of all makeup, and tiny crow's feet have been added to the corners of her eyes and mouth. But, despite all that—and the years she's spent smoking and drinking—my mom is still beautiful.

"Mom," I say again, and this time her eyes open.

"Celeste," she whispers. "You're here." She sits up and smiles sadly. I'm not sure what to do or say, until she opens her arms wide, and then I cut across the tiny room and fill them. I hug her tight, ignoring the smell of cigarettes that bleeds from her pores. "Oh, pretty girl," she murmurs, "I've missed you so much." I'm too choked up to speak, so I just nod my head into her hair in agreement.

We hug for I don't know how long, and only separate

when the sound of my phone ringing breaks through the silence. I pull it out of my purse. It's Duncan. Not wanting to answer the call in front of my mom, I press the button on the side to silence the call, then drop it back into my purse.

"I'm so sorry I stayed away for so long," I tell her. "I should've come home and visited."

"No, don't you dare apologize," she says. "You did it. You became everything I knew you would be." Tears fill her eyes, and when she blinks, they fall. "Please don't tell me Victoria called you."

"She did, and of course I came, Mom. Alcohol poisoning, dehydration." I don't bother to mention the fact that she's spending her days at the diner. It's pointless. If after almost thirty years she's still refusing to give up waiting for Snake, she's not going to now. I need to find out what the PI found out first.

"It's the anniversary of the day he told me he loved me." She sniffles. "The day he left."

"Oh, Mom." I pull her into my arms again. "I'm so sorry." I almost tell her I'm going to have answers soon, but stop myself.

There's a soft knock on the front door, and I remember Jase is waiting outside. He's probably worried I haven't come back out to get him yet. "My boyfriend came with me," I tell my mom. "If you're not up for company, we can leave. We're in town for a few days. Maybe we can go to dinner or something."

My mom smiles. "I would love to meet him. Chad, right?"

I clear my throat. "Actually, Chad and I broke up. His

278

name is Jase."

"How about tomorrow? We can do lunch," she suggests. "It will give me time to get myself together."

"Okay," I tell her. "I'll call you and let you know the name of the place. Do you need anything? I can run to the store for you…"

"No, pretty girl, I'm okay. I'll see you tomorrow." She leans over and kisses my cheek. "I love you, Celeste."

"I love you too, Mom."

When I walk outside, Jase is standing by the door. "Everything okay?" he asks. "I didn't want to bug you guys, but I wanted to make sure she's all right."

"She's…okay," I say. "We're going to meet for lunch tomorrow. She wants to meet you, but doesn't want you to see her like that."

"That's understandable," he says. "Skyla will be with her grandparents for a few more hours. What do you say we head back to the hotel and spend the rest of the day with me inside you?" He waggles his eyebrows, and I throw my head back with a laugh.

"You're so crude."

"And you love it."

Twenty-One

CELESTE

"Isn't it so pretty?" Skyla flips her sketchpad over so I can see the dress she's drawing.

"It's beautiful," I tell her honestly.

While Jase watches a baseball game downstairs at the bar, Skyla and I are sitting outside on the balcony of our suite—I'm drinking a glass of wine, and she's drawing in her sketchpad. She returned from dinner with her grandparents a little while ago and put on a fashion show with all of her new clothes. The girl has exquisite taste, that's for sure. Afterward, Jase asked if I minded if he met up with a few of his friends downstairs at the bar to watch the game. It's been a while since he's seen them, so they all wanted to catch up. He invited Skyla and me to join, but neither of us wanted to go—plus, none of the other guys were bringing their significant others. So I told him Skyla and I would hang out up here and insisted he go.

"We should make a swimwear line too," Skyla says while drawing the beginning lines of a swimsuit. Her tongue sticks out just a bit, her teeth biting down on it, something she always does when she's concentrating. "When I went shopping today there were so many ugly bathing suits." She scrunches her nose up in disgust. "So many ruffles and hearts." She mock-shivers.

"There's nothing wrong with ruffles or hearts," I tell her. "You just have to know where to put them, and always remember less is more." I shoot her a wink and she giggles. "Speaking of bathing suits…" I glance down at the lit up pool. "Why don't we go swimming?"

"Really?" She stops drawing to look up at me, her adorable face lighting up in excitement. "I've never been swimming in the dark!"

"Yes, really, and it's called night swimming. Let's go put our suits on and we can go down for a little while."

There are a few people at the pool, but because it's already almost ten o'clock at night, they're all adults and keep to themselves. One couple is making out in the corner of the deep end and look like they're halfway to going all the way. So I suggest we check out the shallow end, which luckily, since the pool is shaped like a kidney, is around the corner. The last thing I want to do tonight is have the sex talk with Skyla.

We spend the next hour or so swimming laps and talking about fashion. She tells me about a boy who she likes and is looking forward to seeing when school starts up again. When the jacuzzi empties, we turn it on and relax in the bubbles for a little while. I can tell when Skyla is getting tired because she yawns several times and rubs her eyes. She may act like she's older a lot of the time, but she's still barely a teenager.

After we rinse off and change into our pajamas, she asks if we can watch an episode of Elite Model on her iPad. Snuggling into her bed with her, I pull it up on YouTube. Not even ten minutes into it, her eyes are fluttering closed. I click pause on the show and her eyes open a little at the silence before closing again.

Climbing out of her bed, I stand and lean over to kiss her forehead. "Good night, pretty girl," I say softly. I turn to walk out, when Skyla murmurs sleepily, "G'night, Mom, love you."

My heart stills then picks up speed. She didn't mean to say that, I tell myself. She saw her mom this morning and the word just slipped out. But as I walk to my room, I can't get the three letter `word out of my head. Maybe she didn't mean to say it, but what if she did? And if she didn't mean to, who's to say that one day she won't say it on purpose? Every girl deserves to have a mother. One who loves and protects her. Skyla was cheated out of having a mom, and she deserves better than to have me as a poor substitute. I'm just learning how to love Jase. I can't be responsible for both of their hearts. I can't fail them both.

What was I thinking? That's the problem…I wasn't! My heart and body have been dictating my decisions. My thoughts go back to the conversation I had with Killian. *"What's next? Marriage? Babies?"* I should've pulled the brakes on all of this the minute I found out Jase was a dad. We never should've even begun. Instead I chose to live in denial, refusing to give thought to what our future would look like. How could I be so irresponsible? I run a multi-million dollar cooperation for God's sake! I make huge decisions every day, yet I went into this thing this Jase without even giving it a second thought. I can't be someone's mom. I can't be responsible for the welfare of another person. My heart cracks at the thought of letting Skyla down in anyway. And that's what will eventually happen. I will let her down. And with that sobering thought, I know what I need to do. Sure, we'll all be hurt on some level, but it won't be nearly as bad as it will be if I stay. With every day that goes by, we all get in deeper, and the deeper we get, the more it will eventually hurt.

Climbing into bed, I face the wall and pull the covers up to my chin. My eyes burn with unshed tears, but I refuse to allow them to fall. I'm doing this to myself. I'm making the right decision. I don't deserve to cry.

I hear when Jase gets back. When he joins me in bed, he tries to pull me close. I can smell the alcohol on his breath. I can feel his erection pressing against my butt. But I don't move. I pretend like I'm asleep, and a few minutes later, he's snoring softly.

Carefully, I roll away from Jase and off the bed, so as not to wake him up, and then quietly pack my luggage. I don't bother getting dressed. I don't want to risk waking anyone up. I'm about to exit the room, when the guilt of leaving yet again without a goodbye hits me. I find a pen and paper in the desk drawer and scribble out a note.

Jase,

I couldn't leave without saying goodbye. It's better to break our hearts now than later. I'm sorry. Please don't call or text me. It will only make this harder.

xo Celeste

"Not that I'm not happy to see you, but I thought we were meeting for lunch." My mom is standing over me with her hands on her hips, her head tilted to the side in confusion.

"I broke up with Jase."

"Oh, no, why?" Mom joins me on the couch and pushes my messy hair out of my eyes, just like she used to do when I was little, during the rare moments she was nurturing.

"Because Skyla called me Mom when I was kissing her goodnight," I tell her honestly.

"And who is Skyla?"

"Jase's daughter."

"And her calling you Mom is a bad thing, why?" She gives me a perplexed look, needing me to explain the issue. But how do I explain to her that my issue of not wanting to be a mom stems from my own mother. Before I can come up with a way to say what I'm feeling, my phone vibrates.

Picking it up from the coffee table, I see it's Duncan again.

"I need to take this," I tell my mom, pulling the sheet she must have covered me with off of me, and standing. "Hello," I say as I step outside.

"Celeste, it's Duncan, how are you?"

"I'm…okay. I saw you called yesterday, but I wasn't able to answer." Still in my pajamas, I walk a little ways down the sidewalk to make sure my mom can't overhear.

"That's okay. I didn't want to leave a message. I found your guy." My steps falter. Duncan continues, "Snake aka Fredrick Leblanc was killed in a motorcycle accident on July eighteenth, nineteen eighty-nine on State Road seventeen." I gasp as I recall what the date is today. July twentieth…which means July eighteenth was two days ago. He died the day he left my mom. "He was hit by a semi who had been driving for too long and fell asleep at the wheel. His mother was his emergency contact and she identified his body. The funeral was held three days later at Holy Cross Cemetery in Atlanta, Georgia where he was born and raised."

"He died the day he left," I murmur mostly to myself. All these years of her wishing and hoping and dreaming, and the entire time there was no hope.

"I have some more information that I was able to find, but I know you wanted to know what happened. I'll email it all to you, and if you have any questions, please call me."

"Thank you," I say before I hang up.

When I get back inside, my mom is walking out of the bathroom in her robe with her hair wrapped in a towel. "I was thinking we could still go to…" She sees the tears falling down my cheeks and her words trail off. "What's wrong?"

I cover my mouth with my hand as my tears turn into a loud sob. I'm not mourning the loss of the father I've never known, but the loss of the mother I never had. The mother who spent my entire life waiting for a man who was dead within hours of driving away. I should've looked him up sooner. I might not have been able to afford it at first, but the last several years I could've.

"Celeste, talk to me." She pulls me down onto the couch. "You're scaring me."

"I found him," I choke out through a loud sob. "I found my father." My mother's eyes widen and her teeth bite down nervously on her bottom lip. "He died, Mom." More tears glide down my cheeks. "I'm so sorry."

"When?" she asks, her voice wobbly.

"The day he left here. He was hit by a semi who fell asleep at the wheel."

She nods a few times slowly, the rims around her eyes turning red. "You found him," she says.

"I hired a PI," I admit. "I should've done it sooner. I'm so sorry."

"Oh, Celeste," she murmurs, "I knew there was a chance something happened to him. I could've asked you to find him. I think I was just too afraid of what I might find." Her fears mirrored mine.

"I was too," I tell her truthfully.

"I only had him for a couple of months," she says softly. "Only a couple short months. But I loved him with almost all of my heart." She looks at me, her eyes assessing my features like she's just now seeing me for the first time. "Oh, Celeste." She weeps. "I was so focused on wishing he would return to spend our life together, I forgot to live *my* life. I'm so sorry." Her hands come up to her mouth, and she shakes her head, gut-wrenching sobs wracking her entire body as she stares at me.

She stands and walks toward the kitchen. She stops and twirls in a circle. Her eyes find mine. "What did I do?" she whispers. "What have I done?" She spreads her arms out. "This shitty trailer. My shitty job." She sniffles. "All I had from my love with Snake was you, and instead of taking care of you, I abandoned you."

I want to argue, tell her that's not true, but we both know it is. She may have been here every day in body, but in mind, in heart, she was gone.

"It's not too late," I tell her. "You can still start your life over…"

A fresh flood of tears gush down her cheeks, and she walks back over to me. She kneels in front of me and cups my face with her hands. "Start over?" She cries. "I missed it all! We were living under the same roof, but I missed everything. Every milestone in your life. I was here yet never present. Now you're thirty years old. I don't want to start over, Celeste. I want to go back in time." Her lips tremble as she cries. "You must hate me."

"No, Mom." I reach up, and removing her hands from my cheeks, entwine our fingers. "I don't hate you."

"It's why you never came back," she mumbles. "I didn't give you a home worth coming back to."

"Mom…" I choke on the word, unsure of what to say. She's right, but I'm not about to kick her while she's down. She might've been a shitty mom, but I still love her.

"How do I fix this?" she pleads. "Tell me it's not too late."

"Move to New York with me," I blurt out. "Move into my condo with me and we can get to know each other. I can help you start over…please."

More tears fall down her face as she nods. "Okay, on one condition," she tells me. I nod once, and she continues. "You stop running from love, and you don't use me to hide from it anymore." Her tone is pleading. "I messed up…bad. But I can't sit by and watch you miss out on love and life because of what I did to you. You deserve it all, pretty girl."

"I-I'm not…"

"Yes, you are." She looks me dead in the eyes. "The scariest part of finally getting what you want is the fear of losing it. When you have nothing, there's nothing to lose, but once you do, once you've gotten what you dreamed of, you now have everything to lose."

"I don't think I could handle losing them, Mom," I admit.

"I would give anything to have more time with Snake. Don't you dare waste a second being without the people you love because you're scared. I might've failed you while you were growing up, but I still know you. The last ten years, I've watched you from afar, work your way up the fashion ladder. And I know damn well, you didn't get to where you are by being afraid. It's time to be brave, pretty girl. It's time for you to live and love."

Twenty-Two

JASE

Three days ago I woke up and reached for Celeste, only to find the sheets cold and empty. I don't know how, but I knew she was gone before I even got out of bed. Before I saw her luggage and clothes and toiletries were gone. Before I found her note. It was as if she left and took a piece of me with her. My heart no longer whole. Ignoring her request not to call or text, I did both. Several times. Until her phone went straight to voicemail, indicating it had been turned off.

Then Skyla woke up and asked where Celeste was, and I lied. I told her there was an issue with work and she had to fly back. Maybe it was my refusing to admit we were over, or maybe it was that I wanted to prolong my daughter's heart being shattered into a million pieces the way mine was.

We spent most of the day with me showing her around my old stomping ground and then the rest of it at the pool.

The next morning we packed up our stuff, had breakfast, and then headed to the airport to go home. As I was pressing the button to turn my phone off before we entered airport security, my phone lit up with a call from Monica, Amaya's mom.

"She passed away early this morning," she said. "She developed an infection and they couldn't stop it. The funeral will be held the day after tomorrow."

Without explaining anything to Skyla, I went back to the rental car company and rented the car again. Then, on the way back to the hotel, I called them and booked the room for three more nights. Once we were in our new room, I went out onto the balcony and called my brother and Quinn. They both wanted to fly out immediately, but when Jax checked the flights, there wasn't one available for a couple days, so they decided it would be best to drive down.

A couple hours after we hung up, Jax called back to let me know he spoke with Killian, who was in the shop with a teammate, who was getting some work done. After speaking to his coach, Stephen Harper, Olivia's dad, he offered to fly them here on their team's plane. I asked him to thank Killian for me, and told him I would see them when they arrived.

About an hour later, Jax called again to ask why Nick wanted to know if Celeste was flying down with them—you know, because she was back in New York, but everyone in my family thought she was with me. I had to tell him she broke things off and left, which made it feel real and made me realize I needed to tell Skyla, right after I told her that her mother died. I made it through telling her that Amaya passed away, but she was so upset and confused about her feelings,

I didn't have the heart to tell her Celeste and I are over as well.

Now, it's the day of the funeral. I'm dressed in a black suit I had to purchase at the mall, and Skyla is dressed in a black dress her grandmother brought over. Skyla has asked for Celeste too many times to count. She doesn't understand why she isn't here. When you love someone, you're there for them. Quinn and Rick are sitting in the main room of my hotel room while my brother finishes getting ready in his room. Quinn is doing Skyla's hair for her. I know she wants to say something about Celeste leaving, but she's at least considerate enough to wait until after the funeral.

"All right, your hair is done," Quinn tells Skyla, who gives her a small smile.

"Thank you, Aunt Quinn," she says softly. Skyla mentioned last night that she feels bad she hasn't cried over her mom. I told her that's completely normal. Everyone handles their grief in different ways.

There's a knock on the door, and for a split second I wish it were Celeste on the other side, and that thought makes me realize how easily I would be willing to forgive her. I know she's just scared. I don't know why or what happened, but I know she didn't run because she doesn't love me or Sky. The problem is, it's not just me this time around. Now it's my daughter too, and I have to protect her from being hurt, even if that means letting Celeste go.

I open the door and it's Jax, dressed in his suit. "Ready to go?" he asks.

"Yep." We all pile into the SUV they rented when they got here and head to the funeral.

The first part of the service is at Saint Catherine's Church where Amaya's family are members. The priest will speak and then we'll drive over to their family plot for the burial. Because of Skyla being family, we sit in the front row for the service, next to Monica and Phil. My family sits behind us. It isn't until the service ends, and we're asked to stand and make our way to the burial, that I see *her*. She's standing, like everyone else, in the back, and next to her is her mother. I never saw her that day we went to check on her, but today, standing next to Celeste, she looks good. Like a slightly older version of her daughter. Both with auburn wavy hair, olive skin, and slim yet toned bodies. They're both wearing black dresses. Celeste's eyes meet mine and her lips curl slightly into a nervous smile.

Of course, my daughter spots her and insists on going to her. Celeste's eyes widen when she realizes Skyla is heading her way, telling me, while she wanted to be here for us, she wasn't sure if she was going to make her presence known. "Celeste, you're here," she says softly.

"I am. I'm so sorry for your loss." Celeste points to her mom, who is standing next to her with a sympathetic smile on her lips. "This is my mom, Beatrice. Mom, this is Skyla and her dad, Jase."

"Nice to meet you," I say politely.

"How are you?" Celeste asks Skyla. I feel my siblings come up behind us, and without even looking to confirm, I can feel the anger radiating off Quinn as she glares at Celeste.

"Quinn, chill," I murmur, not wanting a scene to be made right here in the church.

"I'm okay," Skyla says to Celeste. "But…my mom died,

and…I haven't cried." Skyla looks down in shame.

"Oh, hey," Celeste murmurs, pulling my daughter into her arms. "It's okay. Not everyone cries when they're sad."

"Do you?" Skyla asks.

"Sometimes, but other times I just get quiet, or I work a lot. Some of my best work was done while I was sad. And sometimes when I'm really sad, I feel like I can't cry. My throat burns and my stomach hurts but the tears just won't come."

"That's how I feel," Skyla says. "My stomach hurts." My heart hurts for my daughter. No kid her age should ever have to bury their mother, but Skyla's situation is even worse because the only Amaya she's ever known has been the one laying in a coma in a hospital. She has no good memories, no photos of the two of them smiling. She's trying to mourn for a woman she never really knew.

"We better get going," I tell Skyla. "Everyone has already left for the cemetery."

"Okay," she says, then gives Celeste a hug. "Will you come with me?"

"Umm…well…" Celeste bites down on her bottom lip, unsure of what to say. If she's waiting for me to tell her to join us, she'll be waiting forever.

"The burial is really just for family," I tell Skyla. Then, without giving Celeste a second glance, I take my daughter's hand and walk out of the church.

Twenty-Three

CELESTE

"Are you okay?" my mom asks once we get into our car. The entire flight I was quiet, using my laptop as a shield to keep my mom from asking me any questions. It worked, because even she gave me a couple sympathetic glances, she didn't press me to talk. Now, though, the laptop is gone, my shield removed, and she's ready to talk.

"I made a mistake," I blurt out, then close my eyes. I don't want to discuss this with my mom. She's too fragile, too delicate. Having this conversation would mean telling her that in a lot of ways I blame my childhood for the way I am, and I don't want to make her feel bad.

"Going to the funeral was not a mistake," she says, misunderstanding what I meant.

"No, running away," I tell her honestly.

We're both silent for the rest of the ride. When we pull

up, Mr. Walters, the concierge in my building, helps us with our bags and to the elevator. The silence continues until we're inside. I'm about to head to my room to get settled when my mom's hand lands on my wrist to stop me.

"We never finished our conversation the other day, Celeste. When you showed up at the trailer and told me you ran because Skyla called you Mom."

Taking a deep breath, I shrug, unsure what to say. The last thing I want to do is hurt my mom's feelings. She guides me over to the couch and sits down, patting the cushion for me to join.

"When I found out I was pregnant with you, I was beyond ecstatic." I try to school my features not to look shocked, but I must do a shitty job because she laughs humorlessly and says, "I know, you would never know it."

"No, Mom…it's not that."

"Don't you dare make excuses for me." She gives me a pointed look. "The entire time I was pregnant, after Snake left, I stayed positive. I focused on making the trailer a home. I decorated the nursery with pink." She shakes her head like she's remembering that time in her life. "When you were born, reality hit," she says with a frown. "The money Snake left me ran out and I had to keep working at the diner. I was running on empty with a broken heart. Month after month the chance of him returning, dwindled. Back then there wasn't the internet like there is today. It was harder to find someone, especially since I only knew so much. Victoria helped me out by allowing you to hang out with Nick and his nanny, but I felt like I was drowning. My heart shattered more and more every day, and instead of holding onto the one person in the world who loved me, I pushed you away. I saw the black of his eyes in yours, the straightness of your hair. Your button nose was identical to his."

Mom swipes away a falling tear. "I'm not making excuses, only trying to explain how it all got so out of control. Every day you went to Nick's home, you saw the wealth and luxurious lifestyle."

"They're far from perfect," I tell her. It took a long time for me to learn and understand that, but once I did, I knew I didn't want to be anything like Nick's parents.

"I know, but if I would've been giving you the love and attention you needed, you wouldn't have grasped onto thinking what they had was the way to live…to love. I felt it, Celeste. I felt love so deep in my bones, it had the ability to rock me to the core. And when I lost it, I was so wrapped up in my heartbreak, so afraid to love again, I didn't open myself up to let you in. You needed me and I failed you. The truth is, had I shown you what love was, it wouldn't have mattered if we had electric or water. It wouldn't have mattered that I drove a shitty car, or that we lived in a rust-filled shitty trailer. Because real love is so overpowering and all-consuming it knows no bounds and overrides any hardships."

The tears that were burning my lids, fall. I know exactly what she means because it's the way I feel about Jase and about Skyla.

"I love you." My mom pulls me into her arms, and my head rests on her shoulder. "You don't see it, but you would make an amazing mom, because for your entire life, you've taken care of me. Even when you ran away, you never stopped caring for me. I gave up on life and love and lost myself, but you never once gave up on me."

"I should've visited," I tell her through my tears. "I should've came and got you sooner."

"No." She shakes her head. "You had to find yourself first, and you have through the love you found in Jase and Skyla. Go get your family back, pretty girl."

My first thought was to go see Jase first. I have a lot I need to say to him. But then after I thought about it, I decided I needed to see Skyla first. She will always come first and that starts with talking to her before I go to see Jase.

Knowing that Jase is at work—I called earlier—I call Quinn to see if Skyla is with her.

"I don't think it's a good idea for you to see her," Quinn says. "She's been through a lot."

"I understand, but I would just like to speak to her. You were upset that I left all those years ago without a goodbye, but now I'm here and trying to talk to her. Please."

"You're saying goodbye?" she questions.

"No, I'm not." Even if Jase and I don't end up together, I'm going to make sure Skyla and I continue our relationship, if she'll forgive me.

"Fine, but just so you know, she doesn't know you ran. Jase told her you had a work emergency." Oh my heart. Of course he did. Because even when I'm failing at life, he's right there to save me.

"Okay. Can I come over now?"

"We're at my place. I'll text you the address."

I arrive at Quinn's condo, which is in the Upper Eastside. After security lets me through, I take the elevator to the penthouse. When I step off, I notice it's the only door on the floor. I knock once and Quinn opens the door.

"She's in the guestroom, drawing."

"Did you…tell Jase?"

"No, you can tell him yourself."

"Thank you."

The bedroom door is open, but I still knock once. Skyla turns in her chair and smiles big. "Celeste!" She runs over to give me a hug. I take a second to breathe in her scent, to lose myself for just a moment in her love. This girl is literally the best part of Jase, and if I'm honest, the best part of me. I might not be her mother, but I want her to be mine in every way that matters. We separate and she sits down on the edge of the bed.

"Dad said you've been busy with work." She looks at me for confirmation, and I know I can't lie to her. She deserves the truth.

"Actually, that's what I wanted to talk to you about." I sit next to her. "I left that day at the hotel because I was scared."

Skyla's brows furrow. "Of what?"

"Of how much I love you and your dad."

She gives me a look of confusion. "Did I do something wrong? Did Dad?"

"No, pretty girl," I tell her, pressing my palm against the side of her cheek. "You did everything perfect. I was scared that I wouldn't love you the right way. That I would let you down. Hurt you. I know I'm not your mom, but I want to be in your life. I want to love you and be your friend."

Skyla nods once, and I hope she understands what I'm trying to say. I've never tried to have an adult type of conversation with a thirteen year old. But then she says, "What if I wanted you to be my mom? Would you...maybe want to?"

I want to tell her yes, that I would love nothing more, but I haven't spoken to Jase yet. Sure, he's texted me every day that he loves me, but I don't want to assume that means he'll forgive me and we'll end up together.

"I messed up with your dad," I tell her honestly. "I hurt his heart when I left."

"I knew he was sad, but I didn't know why."

"I plan to apologize to him, and if we end up together, I would love nothing more than for you to be my daughter. And even if your dad and I don't end up together, I want you to know I'm always going to be here for you. Even if it's only as a friend. I love you so much, Skyla. I already see you like family and that's never going to change."

"Dad will forgive you," she says with a smile. "He loves you."

I smile back, but don't say anything. I hope she's right. I would give anything to be thirteen again and view the world and love with such innocence.

"When you guys get married, can I help design your dress?" she asks, and I laugh.

"I wouldn't have it any other way."

After hanging out with Skyla for a little while, drawing and sketching more items for the fashion line we're planning to create, I say goodbye to her with the promise that I'll see her again soon. Then I put a call into Forbidden Ink to make an appointment so I can see Jase.

Evan tells me he'll have to move some clients around, but promises me he'll make sure it's taken care of. After going home to check on my mom—who tells me she spent the afternoon finding a place where she can attend AA meetings and looking at colleges, since she wants to go to school—she's thinking about studying to be a nurse—I get changed and then head over to East Village. When the cab pulls up, the place is dark. The shop is closed, but Evan convinced Jase to stay late. He also assured me that nobody would be there but Jase—he would make sure of it.

Opening the door that Evan told me would be unlocked, I step inside and lock the door behind me. The bell chimes and Jase walks out. When he sees it's me, he says, "We're closed."

"The door was unlocked," I say, walking toward him.

"I have a late appointment."

Walking past him, I head back to his room.

"Did you not hear me?" he asks, walking behind me. "We're closed. I'm only here for an—"

"An appointment," I say, finishing his sentence. "I know. I'm your appointment."

Jase's eyes go wide, but he quickly covers it up. "Great, then I can head home. My daughter is waiting for me."

"Did you not hear me?" I ask, pulling out my phone and pulling up an image. "I have an appointment." I turn the phone around so he can see the image. "I want this."

Jase stares at the picture for several seconds, not saying a word. When he does, his voice is gravelly. "You still have it."

"I sent it to every email I've ever owned, put it in the cloud and every other online storage, to make sure I would never lose it."

"Why?"

"Because even thinking you slept with Amaya, I still loved you. I was young and immature, and I'm not even sure I knew what it meant to be in love back then, but still, in my own eighteen year old way, I knew I loved you. I loved who I was with you. And every day when I woke up I would look at this image and remind myself what you said to me: Never stop wishing and dreaming."

I step toward Jase, but he steps back. It's his turn to be scared, and I need to understand that. "I love you, Jase. I love you and your daughter, and I love what we have together. You're the only person I've ever loved. You see me, beneath the makeup and the clothes and the fake smiles. You see the real me."

"You ran."

"I did," I admit, owning up to what I did. "Skyla called me Mom and I got scared. I was so afraid of screwing up, of failing her and you. I didn't think I was capable of loving Skyla like she deserved."

"And now?"

"Now, I see that I'm the perfect person to love her, because I know what it feels like to not be loved like she deserves."

"A tattoo is permanent," he says, nodding to the image on my screen.

"Everything about us is," I tell him matter-of-factly. "We wasted so many years apart. I don't want to waste another second. Love me, Jase," I plead, "and let me love you and Skyla."

Wordlessly, Jase cuts across the room and picks me up. The phone almost falls out of my hand, but he catches it and tosses it onto the counter before dropping me onto the chair where his clients lay down to get inked. He slants his mouth over mine and captures my lips. He sucks on my tongue, then licks the seam of my lips before working his way down my neck and over my collarbone. My shirt is lifted over my head and my bra is unclasped. Then he's lifting my ass up so he can push the skirt and thong I'm wearing down my legs.

While kissing all over my body, he slides his fingers into me, just enough to gather my juices, then slides them back out, circling his fingers over my clit. When I let out a needy moan, he chuckles softly—the vibration hitting my throat and sending chills down my spine—then he does it again, slowly building me up but never letting me come down.

"I can't take it anymore." I groan when he dips his fingers into me once again. "I need you. Now. Right fucking now. Please." Jase chuckles at my craziness, but I'm too high-strung to care. All I want is for him to grant me my release.

"Soon," he murmurs as he pulls a nipple into his mouth

and sucks on it, his fingers still teasing and taunting. And it hits me that he's punishing me. I ran away, left him hurting. I didn't answer my texts or calls. I left him hanging. And now he's trying to punish me by leaving me hanging as well.

"No, now." I pull his face back and look him dead in the eyes. "Either you make me come, preferably on your cock, or I'm going to do it myself." I push his chest back so I can touch myself. I know it won't take much, just a couple flicks to my clit and I'll be soaring.

Jase releases a loud growl, grabs my legs, pushes them apart, and then pushes into me. It's been over a week since we've been together, and at first, the fit is tight. But holy hell, does it feel good. His mouth finds mine and he kisses me hard, rough. He nips my bottom lip, then bites down on my earlobe. His fingers are digging into the insides of my thighs as he fucks me like a crazed man who can't get enough.

I'm so close to coming, I can feel it, but it's not enough. I need to touch myself, but I'm afraid of what he'll do, that he might stop fucking me. As if he can hear my thoughts, he grunts into my ear, "Go ahead, Dimples, touch yourself. Make yourself come all over my cock." And with his permission, I do just that, with Jase finding his release right behind me.

Twenty-Four

JASE

*She came back…*Unlike eleven years ago, she actually came back. She might've run scared, afraid of how strong our love and connection is, but this time, she turned her ass around and came back to face her fears. I could've pushed her away, made her prove herself. But that's not what you do when you love someone. You open your arms and heart and love the person, cracks and all. Every day I woke up and forced myself not to chase her. I texted her once a day, telling her I loved her, but ultimately I knew she needed to find her own way back. I didn't know the reason she ran, but now knowing that it was because Skyla called her Mom, I can understand where she's coming from. Being a parent isn't something to be taken lightly, and Celeste's upbringing was as flawed as it comes. But the moment she told me she was the perfect person to love my daughter, I knew she was ready. Because for the first time, Celeste let her guard down. She allowed me to see who she really is. She's always shown me who she was, but until today, she's never done it on purpose. Until today, she's never made the conscience decision to show what's beneath the surface: her heart.

"Are you sure you want to do this?" I pull on my gloves and open the different colored inks I'm going to need.

"Yes," she says, her voice sounding raspy. I glance over at her and see she's staring at me. My shirt is still off, so I reach down to pick it up, but she leans over and puts her hand on mine. "Can you leave it off?" She blushes a beautiful shade of pink. "It will give me something to focus on."

I chuckle. "It's being done on the back of your hip. You won't see me."

"Fine, hold on." She sits up and snaps a picture of me with her phone camera. "I'll just stare at this. "

I laugh and nod. "Okay, Dimples." I prep the area I'll be tattooing, then lower the seat some more so she's more comfortable. It's not a big tattoo, so I'll get it done in one sitting if she isn't in too much pain…which reminds me. I grab a packet of Tylenol from my drawer and hand them to her with a bottle of water.

"Take these to help with the pain." She swallows them without questioning me then lays back down. "You're not going to be able to lay on your back for a few days," I tell her.

"We'll just have to have sex doggy-style," she says with a laugh.

"Woman, don't talk about sex right now. I need to focus." I grab the gun and turn it on. I dip the tip into the black ink and am about to begin when Celeste moves to look at me.

"Don't you have to draw it first? It's been like eleven years since you drew it."

"One, you can't move while I'm tattooing." I give her a serious look. "And two, it's my design. One I looked at many times over the years." Her brows rise at my admission. "Do you trust me?"

"I do."

And from the chaos of her soul flowed beauty

CELESTE

Four Years later

I wake up to the feeling of something tickling along my back, and without even opening my eyes, I know my husband is drawing on me. It's been three years since we got married and he, for the second time, inked my body—a small piece of his wedding vows that he recited to me at the alter: *you are every one of my dreams and wishes come true.* After we returned from our month long honeymoon, where I got to show Jase and Skyla my world—literally and figuratively— including all of the clothing shops I've opened in Milan, Paris, and Italy, I made an appointment. He tattooed it along my right shoulder blade freehanded.

"Good morning," I say, my voice raspy from sleep. I got in late last night and it feels like I've only slept for a couple hours. "Can I turn over?"

"Not…yet…" he says back. He's quiet for several seconds, and then I feel the tickling stop and the camera on his phone click. "Okay," he says, "roll over and spread those sexy thighs, Dimples."

I can't help the giggle that escapes me as I do what he says, noticing it's already almost seven in the morning. "You better make it quick," I tell him as he pulls my panties down and climbs up my body. His mouth presses against mine, and I can taste the mint on his breath. "How long have you been up?" I murmur against his lips, running my fingers through his messy hair.

"Long enough to brush my teeth and draw your next tattoo." With one hand above my head, he glides his other hand downward, his fingers landing on my sensitive nub. He nips at my bottom lip at the same time his fingers massage my clit, and I squirm slightly, letting out a soft moan. It's been too many days since I felt his hands on me.

"Well, if my calculations are correct"—I kiss the side of Jase's neck—"we have about twelve minutes before our door will get trampled through." Reaching down, I wrap my hand around his cock and stroke it up and down, getting it rock hard. I love the cold feel of his cock piercing under my touch. I shiver slightly at the thought of it inside me, stroking my insides. Taking his face in my hands, I pull him up, so his dick rubs against my clit as he pushes into me, filling me completely.

"Fuck," he grunts, slowly thrusting in and out of me at a leisurely pace, like we don't have three kids under our roof that can wake up and interrupt us at any time. Bringing my hand down, I take over massaging my clit, working myself up. Time is of the essence.

"Don't fucking touch yourself," Jase growls, knocking my hand away. "That's my fucking job."

"Jase…time," I murmur breathlessly as he thrusts deeper into me.

"We have all the time in the world, baby," he murmurs, placing open-mouthed kisses along my jaw and neck.

"Did you give away the kids?" I joke.

"Dimples, no talking about the kids while I'm fucking you," he hisses. Lifting my thigh, he wraps it over his forearm to go deeper, hitting the special spot in me that's going to have me exploding in no time.

"Okay." I exhale a soft moan, focusing on my impending orgasm building higher and higher and not on the door, that if unlocked, is going to fly open any minute.

"Come on, baby." Jase growls, his thrusts getting rougher and harder. His mouth crashes down on mine, and my body comes undone with Jase following right behind, spilling his warm seed into me. I try not to think about whether this will be the time we make a baby. I don't want to get my hopes up.

He's barely rolled off me and onto his back, when I sit up and run to our bathroom to get cleaned up. I can hear him chuckling from our bed. His laughter gets closer as I pull my night shirt off my body and turn the hot water to the shower on.

"What's so funny?" I ask, stepping into the shower. The door is barely closed before Jase pulls it back open to join me. "Jase!" I shriek. "Have you forgotten about our kids?" I laugh.

He grabs the soap and begins to wash me down. "Relax, woman," he chides. "I locked them in their rooms."

I know he's only joking, but I still gasp. "That's not funny! Do you have any idea the mess we're going to walk out to? I doubt Skyla is awake yet. She's immune to them."

Jase laughs harder. "But it was so worth it to have morning sex with my wife." With his hands holding my cheeks, he kisses me hard before he lets go, so he can squirt shampoo into his hands. "I missed you," he murmurs.

"I missed you more," I say, turning around, knowing he's going to wash my hair. When he's done, we rinse off and then get out.

"I need to do my hair and makeup," I tell him. "The caterers, party planner, and setup crew will be here soon. Can you show them to the back, please, if I'm not out yet?"

"Sure thing, babe." Jase gives my butt a playful smack and then walks out.

As I get ready, I think about how excited I am for the party today. I visualize where all the tents will go. Where everyone will sit. Where all the kids will play. Three months after Jase and I got married, I found out I was pregnant, and we started looking for a bigger house, one where we can grow our family. Jax decided to stay in the townhouse, moving his girlfriend, Willow, in with him, and my mom is still living in my condo. The second I saw this house with its massive backyard and pool, I knew it was the one. I could see the kids running around and playing on a swing set. I could picture Skyla swimming in the pool during summer, hanging out with her friends here. I always told myself there was no point of living in the suburbs when living in New York, but the minute I heard my babies' heartbeats, I knew I wanted a place they would feel at home. A few weeks later, we moved in, and I can't imagine ever living anywhere else. At the time, Jase thought a six bedroom, seven bath house was excessive, now he's grateful for all the rooms.

Once I've finished getting ready, I head out of our room and down the hall, praying the place isn't too much of a disaster. You would never imagine the amount of destruction two two-year olds can cause in such a short amount of time. When I see all the rooms are empty, I head downstairs, thinking to myself that it's way too quiet. *Where is everyone?*

When I get to the kitchen, I see Skyla sitting at the breakfast nook eating homemade waffles while looking at her cell phone. I walk up behind her and give her a kiss on her cheek. "Happy eighteenth Birthday, pretty girl," I tell her.

She looks up and sets her phone down, giving me a huge smile. "Thanks, Mom." That word will never get old coming from her mouth.

"I would've made you breakfast." I point to her food.

"That's okay. Grandma made them." She waggles her eyebrows. Turns out my mother is an amazing cook—who knew. And instead of going to nursing school, she ended up going to culinary school, and now runs a very popular restaurant near Hell's Kitchen. I've offered to give her the money to open her own restaurant, but she insists she loves it there.

"My mom's here?" I look around.

"She's outside with the hellions." She laughs.

"Must you call them that?" I try to say sternly, but end

up laughing as well. Because she isn't wrong. She just gives me a knowing look.

"How was the show?" I ask, changing the subject. I place a K-cup into my Keurig and press start.

"So good. I can't believe I walked for Versace and in freaking Milan."

"I wish I could've been there," I tell her. Never wanting her to turn out like most of the teen models, I make it a point to accompany her everywhere she goes. Unfortunately, I couldn't be in two places at once and couldn't be there. But thankfully, Margie and Adam were both there and hovered over her like mama hens.

"I know," she says, taking a bite of her food. "Oh! Did you see the shoot proofs for the upcoming line?"

"Umm…yeah." I give her a *duh* look. "You were gorgeous," I say, grabbing a mug from the cabinet, while inhaling the blessed scent of the coffee percolating. "Are you excited for your party?" I can't believe she's officially eighteen and in a couple months will be graduating from high school. While her modeling career had the potential to blow up, her father and I made the decision to keep her in school. We wanted her to stay young for as long as possible. We're hoping she will make the decision to go to college, but she's mentioned wanting to model fulltime once she graduates. I was hoping, on the other hand, she might want to come to work with me one day. Leblanc's children's and teen clothing lines took off, and because a lot of the designs came from Skyla, I had my attorney create a contract and trust for her, where she receives a percentage of all the profits the two lines bring in. We haven't discussed it yet, but between her earnings through Leblanc and as a model, Skyla is already a very wealthy girl.

"Yes," she says, cutting me from my thoughts. "And today is doubly amazing because I have the best news!" she exclaims.

"What is it?" I ask.

"I want to tell you and dad at the same time." The corners of her mouth curl into a huge grin.

"Tell me first, and I'll decide if he should know," I joke. "The last time you said that, you introduced us to your college-aged boyfriend and your dad almost had a heart attack."

Skyla giggles devilishly. "That was funny."

"No, it really wasn't," I say, trying to hide my laughter at the memory of Jase growling and threatening the kid's life when he walked through our door, covered in piercings and tattoos. Jase told him he looked like he belonged in an orange jumpsuit, and I about died laughing—especially since the kid looked so much like Jase, it was scary. Luckily, her relationship with that kid was short-lived, and a week later she moved on to someone closer to her age and with less metal in his face.

"Well, this news won't give him a heart attack, I promise," she says, standing and bringing her plate to the sink. I add some cream and sugar to my coffee while she rinses her dish, then we walk together outside to go find everyone.

When we step outside, I notice Angela, the party planner is here, giving orders. The tents are being set up just like I pictured, and the caterers are getting everything prepared. Skyla and I continue, past the pool and jacuzzi, to the backyard.

I spot them before they see me, and I take a moment to watch the beautiful scene in front of me—my entire world. Jase is holding onto Melina, our two-year-old daughter's hand, while she slides down the slide of the massive treehouse-slash-swing set Jase had custom designed and built, while he holds our other two-year-old daughter, Mariah, on his hip. My mom is waiting at the bottom of the slide and catches Melina when she reaches the bottom, dramatically dropping to the ground on her back and lifting her in the air. When Melina spots me, she squeals and wiggles to get down.

"Momma! Momma!" she yells. Setting my mug down on the table, I drop to my knees and pull my little hellion—as Skyla likes to call them—into my arms.

"Good morning, sweet girl," I murmur, giving the top of her head a kiss. I inhale her sweet scent, a smell I will miss like crazy when she gets older and no longer smells like a baby. I know I have baby fever like crazy, but I can't help it. Jase and I have been trying to conceive again for the last year with no such luck, and I'm starting to get worried it won't happen.

Melina hears her sister and comes running over to join us. "I missed you, Momma!" she squeals.

"I missed you two more," I whisper through my happy tears.

Since I gave birth to our twin daughters, I've made it a point to only travel when necessary. I had an issue at one of the stores in Miami and have been gone for three days. Even with Facetiming them every day and night, it was too much. I cried to Jase every night and told him the next time I go, I'm taking them with me. He laughed and told me I was crazy.

"Before people start arriving, there's something I need to tell you both," Skyla says.

"If you're dating another guy like—" Jase begins, but I cut him off.

"Tell us," I say nervously. While Skyla knows I would love for her to join me at Leblanc, Inc. I told myself I wouldn't push. I mentioned it once and never again. I want her to follow her own dreams, wherever they may take her. Sure, if she chooses to model fulltime, I'm going to miss her like crazy, but it's all part of kids growing up.

"I was accepted into Columbia, and I have decided to go. While I love modeling, I want to major in business and intern at Leblanc." Skyla traps her bottom lip between her teeth. "So, what do you think?" She holds the letter out for us to see, and I walk over and take it from her.

Skyla Leblanc-Crawford, the letter begins. I smile at her last name. The day I married Jase, I took his last name, keeping mine as well because of my company and reputation. The following month, I legally adopted Skyla and was shocked when she insisted on taking my name as well. *"Leblanc is part of you, and I'm part of you now,"* she said. I swear I cried for an hour straight. I read through her letter of acceptance into the college of her dreams, my heart swelling at how proud I am of her.

"Well, this is no longer just a birthday party," I say through my tears. "This is now a celebratory party. I am so proud of you." I pull Skyla into my arms for a hug.

"You're okay with me officially interning for you?" she asks.

"Nothing would make me happier," I tell her honestly.

"Congratulations, Sky," Jase says, yanking Skyla out of my arms and into his. "You're going to stay living at home, though, right? Columbia is expensive."

"Jase," I chide, smacking him in the arm.

"I was thinking I would live on campus." Skyla shrugs. "Do the whole college thing, if that's okay."

"Of course it is," I tell her. "We are so proud of you."

I grab my coffee from the table and take a sip. The coffee hasn't finished going down my throat when a wave of nausea hits me full force. Dropping my mug into the grass, I run toward the house to throw up, but don't make it in time. Instead I end up vomiting all over the hedges that surround our back patio.

Jase is right behind me, holding my hair back, until I finish. When I turn around, he's sporting a huge grin on his face. At first, I'm annoyed that my husband thinks it's funny I just threw up, but then my mind plays catch up, and I'm grinning just as hard. We don't have to say the words. I'm pregnant.

It's almost five o'clock and Skyla's party is starting to wind down. The only guests left are a few of her friends she's lounging by the pool with, as well as a couple of our friends. Jase and I are sitting at the table under the tent watching Melina and Mariah run around and chase Reed, Olivia and Nick's six-year-old son.

"If history repeats itself," Nick says, "my poor son is going to have not one, but two of your daughters following him around for years." He shoots me a playful wink, and I laugh. I'm so thankful for our friendship, but also really glad he met Olivia. Had he not, who knows if we both would've found true love.

"It's not just my daughters," I point out, watching Killian and Giselle's four year old daughter, Alice, chase him as well, up the stairs of the treehouse.

"Poor kid," Olivia says. Francesca, her four-year-old daughter, lays against her mom's chest, sleeping soundly with her thumb in her mouth. "One of us needs to have a boy to attempt to even this all out."

"Maybe we will," Jase whispers into my ear, so only I can hear.

Quinn's gaze meets mine, and she smiles softly, but it's forced and a little sad. I would like to say that over the years she and I have gotten closer, but the truth is, we haven't. Not that she hasn't gotten nicer, because she has. She's accepted me into their family with open arms. But I worry about her. She married Rick a few years ago, but I don't think they're happy. She used to talk all the time about wanting to create a family of her own, but after a couple years of them trying with no success, she stopped mentioning it. I've watched the bright light that used to surround Quinn, dim little by little. I watched her put on some weight—not that she isn't still gorgeous, because she very much is—and slowly hide more and more of her body. I feel so helpless, unsure of how to help her get that light back. When I've tried in the past to bring it up to her, she always pushes me away, so lately I've stopped bringing it up. The last thing I want is to push her completely away—she barely comes around as it is—especially when I have a feeling that one day she'll need us. No judgement. And when she's ready to talk, I'll be here.

"Did Nick tell you?" Olivia says, breaking me out of my thoughts. "He signed with the publisher on his third romance novel." She beams proudly.

"Congratulations!" I tell Nick. "Look out Nicholas Sparks, there's a new Nick in town." Everyone laughs.

"I've decided to retire," Killian says. "Giselle and I are expecting again, and I would like to be home more with this baby." Everyone congratulates them, and Jase gives me a look. There's a good chance Giselle and I will be having our babies close to the same time. I don't want to get my hopes up, but I've been feeling queasy all day.

"Oh my god!" Olivia exclaims. "You didn't tell me you were pregnant."

"We just hit twelve weeks. We were waiting."

"You know I don't count!" She laughs. "We're expecting too! I'm eight weeks."

Giselle laughs with her. "And you're giving me crap? You didn't tell me either!"

As everyone is congratulating them, I notice Quinn sneak away. Concerned, I tell Jase I'll be right back. Jax, who's been sitting off to the side with Willow snuggled in his lap, watching the kids play, notices her leave as well. He looks like he's about to lift Willow off him to get up and check on his sister, so I give him a small nod to let him know I'm going.

On my way inside, Skyla calls out my name. "Yeah?"

She gets up and comes running over to me. Her arms wrap around my neck and she hugs me tightly. "Thank you for everything," she murmurs into my ear.

"I'm glad you had a good time," I tell her.

"I did, but not just for the party. For loving me and being here for me. Growing up, I never thought I would have a mom. Mine was… well, you know…and my dad was always enough. But…" She backs up slightly and her eyes are glossed over. "I'm just so thankful to have you," she says through a sob.

"You never have to thank me, pretty girl." I tell her. "You're my daughter, my world."

After we hug once more, I head inside to find Quinn. She's sitting on the edge of the tub in my bathroom. "You okay?" I ask, noticing her cheeks are stained pink from her tears.

"I think I'm pregnant," she whispers.

"And that's a bad thing…" I tread carefully, afraid if I'm too forceful, she'll feel backed into a corner and attack like a defensive feline. I need her to know I'm here for her.

She just shrugs, and I can see it in her face, in her posture, she's broken, defeated…maybe even scared.

"Well, there's only one way to find out." I pull out the box from under the sink and hand her a test.

"You keep tests on hand?" she asks.

"We've been trying for the last year," I tell her. "We

thought it would be as easy as it was last time, but it hasn't been."

"I'm sorry, Celeste. Here I am, unsure if I'm happy or sad that I'm most likely pregnant, and you're wishing for a baby."

"Everyone has their own stories," I tell her. "Take it, and I'll be right here with you."

I step out of the room while she pees, and once she lets me know she's done, I go back in. A few minutes later, the word **pregnant** lights up the screen, and I give her a hug. "Jase and I will be here for you," I tell her, "no matter what."

"Thank you, Celeste." She kisses my cheek. "I think I'm going to head home."

I want to beg her to talk to me, tell me what's going on. Is Rick hurting her? Is he emotionally abusive? What has happened that she's only a shell of the woman she used to be? But I don't. Instead I give her a small and say, "Okay. If you need anything, call me." And I pray that she will. I also decide it's time to talk to Jase about his sister. I should've done it sooner.

Quinn leaves, and I'm left alone in the bathroom. I eye the test, wanting to do one but afraid of the disappointment I'll feel if it says I'm not.

"Celeste," Jase says, making himself known. He sees Quinn's test and his face lights up. "You're pregnant?"

"No." I quickly shake my head. "I mean, I might be, but that test was Quinn's."

"Oh," he says flatly. It's no secret that Quinn's brothers are not a fan of her husband. "Is she okay?"

"Truthfully," I tell him. "I don't think she is. I think

maybe we need to get her alone and speak to her."

"You think that fucker's hurting her?"

"I don't know…but she never comes around anymore."

"I know," he says, choking up. Jase and Jax both love their sister so much. "She doesn't even visit the shop anymore."

"It's time we speak to Jax and figure this out. I have a feeling Quinn's going to need us."

Jase pulls me into his arms and kisses my forehead. "We'll talk to Jax tomorrow. I love you."

"Love you more."

"Want to take a test?" he asks, nodding toward the box with two more tests inside.

"I'm scared," I admit. "I shouldn't be. I have three amazing, healthy kids. I have a husband who loves me. A career I love. My mom is my best friend. I am so blessed. I shouldn't want more."

Jase looks down at me. "First of all, you never have to be scared, Dimples. I'm right here." He kisses the tip of my nose. "Second of all, there's nothing wrong with wanting more."

"What if us not being able to get pregnant is fate's way of saying fuck you to me?"

Jase chuckles softly.

"I'm serious," I say, "I never wanted to have kids and now that I want a house full of them, we can't get pregnant."

"I'm pretty sure me knocking you up with twins shows fate isn't out to get you."

"I think if I'm not pregnant this time, we should stop trying," I say.

"If that's what you want, then that's what we'll do." He hands me a pregnancy stick.

After I go pee and dip the test into the urine, I set it on the sink then walk away. Three minutes later, Jase stands and looks at it. He turns to face me, his features giving nothing away.

"Well?" I ask. "Tell me."

"It's a good thing you insisted we buy this ridiculously huge house because in nine months, we're going to be needing another one of the rooms."

I jump into Jase's arms, and he holds me tight, kissing me like I'm his entire world. "Thank you, Jase," I whispers against his lips.

"For what?"

"For seeing what's below the surface. For seeing the beauty in my chaos. For seeing *me*."

THE END!

Other Books by Nikki Ash

The Fighting Series
Fighting for a Second Chance
Fighting with Faith
Fighting for Your Touch
Fighting for Your Love
Fighting 'round the Christmas Tree

Fighting Love novels
Tapping Out
Clinched
Takedown

Imperfect Love series
The Pickup
Going Deep
On The Surface

Stand-alone Novels
Bordello
Knocked Down
Unbroken Promises
Heath

Acknowledgements

First and foremost, I want to thank my children. There's not a single book I've written that they haven't supported me in their own way. My daughter spent hours helping me plot this book. I love you two more than life itself. To the bloggers who spend their time promoting and reading and reviewing my books. Thank you! To my readers, I only get to continue to do what I love because of your support. Thank you! To all of the member of The Fight Club. You all have become more than readers; you have become my friends. Thank you! To Ena and Amanda with Enticing Journey, thank you for keeping me sane. To my beta readers, editor, proofreaders, talented cover designer, and my amazing teaser-maker, I don't know what I would do without you guys. You are the heart and soul of this book: Brittany, Andrea, Krysten, Ashley, Nicole, Stacy, Juliana, Rachel, Thank you! Kristi, you have nothing to do with this book, yet everything to do with my sanity. I am so thankful for your friendship. Bret, thank you for sitting and listening to me talk for hours upon hours of every plot and idea with a smile on your face. And last but not least, thank you to everyone who has given me a chance in some way or another. It's because of you On the Surface is my fifteenth published novel.

About the Author

Nikki Ash resides in South Florida where she is an English teacher and writer by day and a writer by night. When she's not writing, you can find her with a book in her hand. From the Boxcar Children to Wuthering Heights to latest single parent romance, she has lived and breathed every type of book. While reading and writing are her passions, her two children are her entire world. You can probably find them at a Disney park before you would find them at home on the weekends!

Reading is like breathing in, writing is like breathing out.–
Pam Allyn

To stay in touch, join The Fight Club:
www.facebook.com/groups/BooksByNikkiAsh

Printed in Great Britain
by Amazon

79847390R00190